BERLIN

BERLIN

A NOVEL

Michael Mirolla

Leapfrog Press
Teaticket, Massachusetts

Published in 2009 in the United States by
Leapfrog Press LLC
PO Box 2110
Teaticket, MA 02536
www.leapfrogpress.com

Distributed in the United States by
Consortium Book Sales and Distribution
St. Paul, Minnesota 55114
www.cbsd.com

Printed in the United States

First Edition

Library of Congress Cataloging-in-Publication Data

Mirolla, Michael, 1948-
  Berlin : a novel / by Michael Mirolla.
     p. cm.
  ISBN 978-0-9815148-1-9
  1. Berlin (Germany)–Social life and customs–Fiction. I. Title.
  PR9199.3.M4938B49 2009
  813'.54–dc22
                                                          2008014721

BERLIN

POSTSCRIPT I

Giulio Chiavetta (ex-stationary engineer by trade and self-styled freelance circus mime by inclination) became visibly agitated after unfolding the newspaper that had been placed on his lawn chair. This was the chair—"Prop. of G.A. Chiavetta" scratched with a rusty nail across its back—on which he liked to sun himself every chance he got. Even when there was no sun. Even in the most impenetrable fog. Even after the first permanent snow had arrived and he had to huddle beneath several blankets just to keep from shivering to death.

Normally, he would peruse the day's news without allowing it to cause the slightest blip in his behavioural patterns. No telltale raising of an eyebrow or sneerish curling of a lip. And definitely no angry diatribes at the sorry state of world affairs or on the local hockey team's inability to score. In fact, it was impossible to ascertain if he actually read the paper or only stared for hours on end at the inkblot patterns formed by the headlines, articles, photos, photo captions and advertising come-ons. And then turned the pages only when some mysterious internal clock gave the signal.

But, on this particular afternoon in late October, he barely looked at the front section before he tossed the paper aside, stood up abruptly from the chair (so abruptly, in fact, it tipped over sideways) and headed with a stiff gait towards the Victorian-style building where he'd been a reclusive resident for the past two years.

A few moments after entering the building, he re-emerged with a key clutched tightly in his left hand and began to walk across the expanse of recently mowed grass. He walked as if on a tightrope, placing one foot directly in front of the other. He walked past his upside-down chair and the newspaper slapping against its leg in the wind. Past the white-vested players on the cricket pitch practicing their overhead tosses and batsmanship. Past the handyman in the flowerbed turning the earth for one last time in preparation for spring planting. Past several Sisters of Charity coming up the road for their daily round of volunteer work.

He walked until he bounced against the barbed-wire fence, installed more to keep pesky kids, nosy neighbours and angry ex-residents out than any of the patients in. He bounced once . . . twice . . . a third time. And then, ignoring the ever-increasing shouts and instructions from those behind him, he proceeded to attempt to scale the eight-foot obstruction. Even for a self-described freelance circus performer, this proved difficult as he could only use his right hand (the key being clutched in his left). As well, he was barefoot and the fence cut into the soft soles of his feet.

Nevertheless, Chiavetta would have made it over (feeling no pain) if his loose hospital robe hadn't become badly entangled on the barbed wire strung across the top. Because of this, he was left dangling and flapping his arms while school children below him snickered at the fact he had no underwear on and adults crossed to the other side of the street just to put more distance between them and him. The staff had to position several ladders against the fence to hold him steady while the handyman cut the snagged cloth away with her gardening shears.

But that wasn't the end of it. The moment he'd been lowered back on solid ground, Chiavetta, robe now in tatters, resumed his straight-ahead walking. Tick tock. This made him resemble very much one of those windup toys that can be deterred, deflected and derailed but not completely defeated until the spring . . . the battery . . . the locomotive force . . . has wound down to zero.

When Doctor Wilhelm ("Billy") Ryle, the psychiatrist who'd been treating Chiavetta during his stay at the clinic, came alongside and asked him where he planned on going, Chiavetta answered without hesitation: "I have to get back. It's important I get back. Now!"

Ryle, after having recovered from the shock of hearing him utter a clear and complete sentence for the first time in two years, then inquired exactly where it was he had to get back to. Chiavetta answered, with a hint of impatience: "Berlin, of course! Where else is there?"

And he continued to walk away. To bang once more into the fence. To attempt to scrabble up the obstacle—even if his fingers were scraped and bleeding. At this point, Ryle decided that, much as he hated to dispense them on principle, the only short-term solution was to inject Chiavetta with a mild tranquillizer.

After several orderlies and nurses—the same ones who'd held him down for the injection—had carried the semiconscious Chiavetta to the hospital infirmary, Ryle paid a visit to his room. He hoped to uncover clues to what had caused this sudden deviation from almost two years of placidity, hibernation and utter silence.

He knew already about the front-page newspaper article announcing the imminent union of the two Germanys and the pictures of students smashing holes in the Berlin Wall. But that, in itself, might only explain the trigger, not the cause. And Ryle was a firm believer in cause and effect—even on a psychological level. *Especially* on a psychological level. Explanations of this sort were very important to him. In fact, he held them to be the glue that prevented the world from coming apart at the seams. If psychological cause and effect could be unraveled, then everything else fell into place.

Chiavetta's room was the same as all the others in the hospital—with the largest objects being a small cot in one corner and a desk beneath the shatterproof window. The only difference was the computer on Chiavetta's desk which had been part of the patient's personal effects. Some of the administrators had questioned the allowing of this privilege but Ryle had overruled them, saying he could see no harm in it. In fact, he felt it might speed up Chiavetta's recovery if he kept himself intellectually active—or even if all he did was play computer games day in and day out.

Chiavetta had installed himself in front of its amber screen every day for the two years he'd been there. Those looking in could see him hunched over with arms spread across the face of the monitor, as if jealously protecting what he was doing from the outside world. And no one, to date, had been able to even catch a glimpse of that work, let alone examine it with any notion of trying to make sense of it.

But, in keeping with his belief in cause and effect, that's precisely what Ryle was now determined to do. Thus, in deliberate imitation, he sat down in front of the computer himself and switched it on. He quickly found the word processing software but, to his surprise, there were no document files. That's not possible, he said to himself. Chiavetta had hammered away at this computer keyboard practically 365 days of the year for two years straight. Surely there had to be something there to show for it. Some tangible result. But, search as he might, he could find nothing. Aha, hidden files! Of course, Chiavetta must have known how to create hidden files, the kind only he could access through some special code or password.

Ryle put in a call to another of his patients, the facility's resident computer whiz. The whiz had been invited to spend some time at the hospital after insisting that his programming was all wrong and that he needed new wiring (which he tried to install himself by plugging into the nearest electrical socket). The word was that if he couldn't decode a computer program or get a machine to work properly then you'd better go directly to the maker himself (the Prime Digitalizer, that is).

After half an hour, the whiz leaned back and declared: "There's nothin' in here. No hidden files, that's for sure. My guess is that, if there was anything here in the first place, your friend erased it all." "What!" Ryle exclaimed. "Shit! Now, why would he go and do that?" The whiz was about to say something else when Ryle waved his hand: "Never mind. It was a rhetorical question."

But the whiz had no intention of answering that particular rhetorical question. What he wanted to say was that there still might be a chance of getting back what Chiavetta had so maliciously killed—as long as no new files had been processed on the computer since that act. The whiz explained it as some sort of afterimage, the files remaining in the hard disk's various addresses—or clusters—until some more recent information was stored there.

That's more like it! Ryle said. If deleting is the last thing he did, then they're still in there. Now, how do we get them out? No problemo, the whiz said, pulling a diskette out of his back pocket. With my "UnErase" utilities program. It's like bringing back the dead—only a little bit easier. If you know how. Ryle smiled and rubbed his hands together. Let's do it then. And to himself: I might find the key to a cure for this guy after all. Hey, I might even be able to write him up in the *Psychiatric Digest*. And wouldn't that be a feather in my cap. Might even lead to a promotion out of this place. A job at one of those private clinics where the patients are only genteelly mad.

In the infirmary, Chiavetta, still clutching that key in his left hand, stirred from a restless half sleep. He dreamt badly every time they gave him tranquillizers—which fortunately hadn't happened very often. In fact, the only other time had been the day they'd brought him to the hospital—when he'd reacted poorly to the threat of having his recently bought computer confiscated.

As on that previous occasion, the dream disturbing his sleep was one of very large family gatherings, unending parties down unending tables, loud banquets verging on orgies, of drinking, singing and dancing under white-blossomed apple trees and bursting grape trellises. And a murky vision of Chiavetta somehow floating above it all. Or perhaps hiding in the branches of the nearest tree, afraid to partake fully. To "lower himself to that level," as it were.

The odd thing about all this was that Chiavetta couldn't recollect any such feasts in his own family history. All he could remember was being an only child. Spoiled and doted upon but nevertheless alone. As for relatives, they were kept at a respectable distance, to be visited on certain holidays more as an obligation than out of any pleasure. Everything prim and proper. Everything in its place. Nothing done on the spur of the moment. In that way, the Chiavetta family had always seemed more upper-class British than peasant Italian.

Well then, it's obviously your subconscious speaking out, Ryle would have said if he'd known about the dreams. Trying to compensate for an impoverished childhood. Or a genetic memory of sunny afternoons along Mediterranean seascapes, balancing on a cliffside as the waves crashed below. In any case, the dream always ended in a sudden fall from the tree and served to wake Chiavetta up.

He looked around and realized it was early evening—

and he was in the rundown infirmary in a rundown psychiatric hospital in a rundown Montreal suburb. Which was strange in itself because, since being admitted to the hospital, he hadn't understood his surroundings in those terms. Only as certain blockages and colours, certain angles of sunlight and shade, certain limitations to his movements. And voices. Voices that spit out portions of something that may have been sensible at some other time and place. But not at that particular time and place.

Immediately, he arose and, once again, tried to head out of the building, following a green line painted on the floor so that patients wouldn't lose their way. But the doors to the outside were locked and the key in his hands wouldn't work. Normally, he would have simply continued trying the key again and again until one of the orderlies spotted him and led him gently—or not so gently—back to his room. But not this time. This time he whirled suddenly, stood for a moment scratching his head, and then descended on tiptoe into the ramshackle basement.

Why the basement? From somewhere came the knowledge there was a way out from the basement that no one else knew about, that no one would have thought to lock or bolt. This was an old coal chute from the time when the furnace still had to be fed by hand. How did Chiavetta know that? Perhaps 20 years as a stationary engineer and automaton tours of the grounds might help explain it. Or he might have simply sensed as much as he groped around in the dark, fearful that switching on a light might attract a bat-like flock of orderlies.

A few moments later, a figure pushed open a trap door, looked from side to side and then emerged cautiously from the defoliated, pre-winter shrubs at the edge of the building. One had to strain to see him, covered as he was in ancient coal dust and recently descended darkness. And even straining brought only a dim outline into focus. But who else could it be save Chiavetta, making his trapeze-artist, high-stepping way across the lawn? There were more surprises to come. Suddenly, out of the blue, he remembered a small rip in the fence where he'd seen boys wiggle onto the grounds to retrieve their street hockey balls—and to poke fun at the patients spread out on the lawn for their daily constitutional. So, this time, he didn't impale himself or further tear his hospital clothing as he slipped easily out of the compound and onto the street.

The whiz had managed to pull back and put into readable files a good portion of Chiavetta's work by the time an orderly discovered he was missing and rushed to inform Ryle. But that's not possible, Ryle exclaimed. Everything was locked up? That's right, the orderly said—and it's still locked up. He'd double-checked. No doors forced; no windows broken. No way out. Yet Chiavetta was nowhere to be found. What about the grounds? Yes, it was possible he was hiding somewhere on the grounds. But it would be hard to check those until morning.

Ryle didn't think Chiavetta had the ability to understand the mechanism of escape but, in light of what had happened earlier in the day, he told the orderly he'd better give Chiavetta's description to the police right away. "My poor Chiavetta has never posed a threat to anyone but himself," Ryle said, thinking out loud. "But it wouldn't do to have someone like him roaming the streets. Now would it? The good citizens might do him some harm."

After the orderly had left and the whiz was led back to his own socket-free room, Ryle sat down and, with quite a bit of nervous anticipation, opened Friday.doc, the first of the recovered files, under a sub-directory labeled Berlin. nov.

The opening screen of the document was titled: *Berlin:*

Berlin

A Novel in Three Parts, by Giulio A. Chiavetta, Freelance Circus Performer. Ryle began to scroll the document, reading as he went along.

1: FILE—FRIDAY.DOC

Antonio G. Serratura: "When my father died, among the things the family found in the basement hideaway, where—as the end approached—he'd spent more and more of his time, was a crude wooden box with a sloped, hinged top. It was painted in the dull brown varnish that was my father's favourite finish and was slapped on everything from bathroom doors to bedroom closets to picture frames. An eye-and-hook latch, of the type used to keep gates and screens in place, held it shut. The box, about two feet long, a foot wide and half a foot in height, had obviously been homemade and of the same species as the outsized wooden spoons he liked to give out in lieu of Christmas presents.

"Inside this box were assorted mementos—an expired Italian passport with the photo excised, a ticket stamped 'S.S. Cristoforo Colombo: Greek United Steamship Lines—Pre-Pade Rome to Montreal, 05/03/55'; a '*Croce al Merito di Guerra* (*Soldato di sanita*, n. 4202)' medal and ribbon dated more than 20 years after the end of the Second World War; honourable discharge papers from the Italian army; smudged, yellowed pictures of several young men in uniform, arm in arm, standing cockily before a military motorcycle and smiling into the camera; and, right at the bottom, a thin four-by-eight-inch soft-covered and pebbled black book containing some 20 pages in all.

"Judging from the alphabetical tabs still attached to its sides, it had originally been intended for phone numbers or addresses. Addresses, most likely, as there wouldn't have been too many phones in the Southern Apennine mountain

16

village where my father had been born and had lived the first 20 years of his life—excluding, of course, the five spent as a soldier. The pages, each line and column squared off into individual compartments like graph paper, had been worn bare and dog-eared. A good number were bent in half, a now permanent crease that had lasted almost 50 years, and some were missing altogether (tabs 'A' and 'B,' for example, as well as 'Q').

"However, instead of the names and addresses of friends, let alone phone numbers, the book was filled with my father's self-learned script, a fine Italianate hand that combined block lettering and stylish calligraphy and gave the lie to his barely completed third-grade education. Much of the writing had faded away and there were whole sections where the pages had stuck together due to sweat or perhaps the effect of moisture. But some of it was still legible, in particular a sizable stretch near the beginning (labeled 'C' to 'F' for convenience) and the final few pages ('X,' 'Y' and 'Z').

"I took this book home with me after the funeral (actually a little before for fear it would vanish in the turmoil and heat of partition). But, once it was in my possession, I immediately put it away and, several years later, I hadn't yet summoned up the courage to make an attempt at deciphering it. At first, I used a heavy study load, work on a doctoral thesis and deplorable Italian as an excuse. Then the fact that my father's memory was still too fresh for objective prying. Finally my own approaching wedding and preparations for the start of a career as a lecturer in the philosophy department of the local university—with the hope of a full professorship and tenure-track security when the opportunity arose.

"Now, all that had come to pass and I was both married and permanently ensconced at the university, with in fact a minor following in the insular world of logical theory. But somehow, even though I'd never completely forgotten about it and kept it at the top of my papers (or rather it seemed to float occasionally to the surface as if of its own accord), the deciphering had been left benevolently undone. Should it have been kept that way for all these years? Who am I to say? For the longest time, I considered myself merely the carrier of the message, the Platonic form perhaps. Whatever that message would eventually turn out to be could be left for others to uncover."

The fact that Serratura chose that very moment—as the plane wheeled for its final descent into West Berlin's Tegel Airport (aha! Ryle could be heard exclaiming back in the hospital, now, it's beginning to make some sense)—to bring his father's address booklet to mind was, much as he would've preferred it to be, no serendipity. Nor, despite the destination, was there anything subconscious or Judaeo-Freud-Germanic about it.

The truth of the matter was that he'd deliberately slipped the book into his jacket pocket before leaving Montreal—in the hope that he might have some time, between seminars, conferences and lectures at the Wittgenstein World Symposium on the Realism/Anti-Realism Debate in Contemporary Philosophy, to unravel its mystery. The word "mystery," too, is a bit of an overstatement. Serratura knew the general import without having had to look at the actual text. The book was a diary of the period his father had spent in a German prisoner-of-war camp from Mussolini's fall in 1943 to the time of the American liberation.

Why he felt this might be a good occasion to begin a line-by-line translation, he couldn't rightly say. Not with any certainty. He didn't think it was the obvious reason—Berlin and all that such a city might have brought to mind at the time. Perhaps he was counting on it having some literary merit, something that would allow him to boast: "Well, well, look at that. The old man might have passed himself off as a peasant gardener and amateur wine-maker who worked nights in a foam factory. But deep down he was an embryonic intellectual. He had the makings of a writer. His emotional stoicism, bordering at times on cold-heartedness towards his family and a stony reticence when it came to anything that smacked of sentiment, was a result of deeply held secrets and the knowledge that comes from having to dig your own grave—day after day—and not knowing when you'll be dumped into it."

And perhaps that might have lent legitimacy to Serratura's own nascent claims, his own belief in manifest destiny and the call to scholastic greatness. After all, hadn't he been chosen to read a paper at a prestigious conference, while his colleagues at the university—many with much more seniority and, to tell the truth, expertise than he had—stewed in the juices of their own jealousy?

Anyway, for whatever motives, Serratura had the diary safely in his breast pocket and it gave him a warm feeling to know it was there, a little pebble-embossed black book, a little subversive black book ready to point its smudged, impolitic fingers: the *je t'accuse* of the common man caught up in uncommon times. See, he already had a title for it. *Je T'Accuse*. All he needed now was a suitable target. Or sharp hook on which to hang it.

Serratura leaned back in his seat and slipped on the Walkman earphones, starting up, at the same time, the travel tape he'd picked up prior to departure at a Mirabel Airport gift shop. A woman with a mellifluous, almost hypnotic, voice was intoning a brief history of the city coming up quickly below:

"Isn't it a crying shame about poor old Berlin? Split in

two. Isolated. Schizophrenic. Surrounded by hostile forces that can't be reconciled. Caught in a vicious tug-of-war between the two snapping, snarling superpowers. In short, a paradigm of all that's wrong and hellish in this Cold War world. Well, weep no more. The trumpets are blowing; the wall is coming down. It's long past time to bury that popular—and probably wishful thinking—image. Simply put, Berlin—at least on the western side—is one of the most vibrant and hotly alive cities in Europe, a city as paradoxical as the Wall—*die Mauer*—that runs down its middle, itself a hideous reminder of the disease that threatens to toss all of us over the brink into annihilation. The city's not only a symbol of what can be achieved under the most strained circumstances, but living proof that adversity can open up new avenues for those with the luck, strength and flexibility to survive. And Berliners are, above all, adept at surviving. Witness the fact the city is celebrating its 750th birthday this year with a broad spectrum of cultural activities and exchange programs from world-famous operas in 'Berlin Hosts the World' to Japanese fireworks at Tempelhof airport to walking tours of the city's historic Bohemian Village. For those with an interest in the early history of the area, one of the most interesting displays is the Citizens, Farmers, Noblemen exhibit at Spandau Citadel which runs all summer long. . . ."

The sweet, syrupy prose of the ad man, Serratura said to himself, to be taken in small doses. He stopped the tape to look out the window, hoping for a symbolic breath of fresh air—if not the actual headwind of reality. They'd broken, at last, through the cloud cover that had dogged them across Europe, giving Serratura the impression they were floating in a world of their own that was completely removed from the supposedly solid one below. But, as the plane banked and prepared for its final descent, he could see to one side the famed Broadcasting Tower (from which Radio Free Berlin sent out its messages on behalf of democracy and unfettered entrepreneurship); then a tight group of white sails turning as if in formation on a glinting lake; and finally the slender hexagonal shapes of street-front apartment blocks lining broad boulevards. From the air they reminded him of strait-laced and well-educated old ladies who put up their most conservative fronts to hide the riot of passion and emotion still bubbling and seething within them.

Serratura was busy trying to figure out where the image had popped up from—(the grandmother in *The Tin Drum* perhaps, a movie he'd recently seen?)—when the balding, middle-aged man in the seat beside him suddenly tapped his arm and said something in German. Serratura was surprised as the man, boarding at Frankfurt, hadn't spoken a word till then, preoccupied as he seemed to be with bills of lading and balance sheets.

"Sorry, I don't understand." Serratura struggled with his bit of German, the few words he'd learned from travel brochures and the very antithesis of understanding: "*Bitte, ich verstehe nicht.*"

"My apologies," the man beside him said smiling and with only the slightest trace of an accent, one which Serratura couldn't immediately place. Brooklyn? "I was just asking if this is your first time coming to West Berlin."

"Yes, yes," Serratura said as he glanced out the window. "It's definitely the first time. Never had the opportunity before. And you?"

"Me? Oh no, I practically live here. Or it seems that way sometimes. Fly in every month or so from the States on business. Restaurant supplies: grills and deep fryers are my specialty. I think you'll like Berlin."

"I hope so. It certainly isn't anything like I expected—at least not so far. A lot more . . . normal."

The man nodded and looked at Serratura, then past him to the window. Below them, the golden Victory Column swung into view at the intersection of five massive highways. Serratura could make out long lines of buses down the tree-bordered boulevard where both Frederick the Great and Hitler staged their military reviews and triumphal marches. Surrounding it was what looked like a portable barbed-wire barrier. It ran along the countryside in a semicircle and finished up against the Wall on either side of the Brandenberg Gates.

"Yes, that is the usual reaction," the man said finally, removing his bifocals and rubbing his eyes. "One of my American business associates says there's too much light—and green space. Too much commercial activity and general busy-ness. Not enough of that sense of being trapped, of being surrounded by the relentless pincers of the enemy, the grasshopper's spurt of brown in the grasp of the praying mantis. He feels that it's shameful in a way. Sometimes, he almost wishes that the fires and bomb craters would suddenly spring up again—eternal punishment, as it were. Some sort of grim reminder. Or at least a perennial memorial, a ghost city dedicated to the millions of dead, undulating as the methane gas seeps to the surface from the bodies—and souls—rotting below."

"Well, I can understand his point but I wouldn't go that far," Serratura said, laughing uneasily as the word "palimpsest" popped unbidden into his mind. The thought of some ferocious memory remover stripping away the protective layers to reveal the raw images beneath it. Mental Varsol. Inquisitorial flaying of brain cells. But what if there weren't any images beneath? What if all was nothing but energy and flux? Eternal change for the sake of change? Heraclitus revisited. He laughed again.

"Did I say something funny?" The man cocked a thick eyebrow in Serratura's direction.

"Oh no. Not at all. Just following an amusing train of thought to its conclusion." He rubbed his hands together. Sweaty. And slightly cool. "A curious habit of mine."

The plane's "Fasten Seat Belt" lights blinked on; the landing gear clicked into place with a whine.

"Almost there," the man said, struggling with the straps. "My colleague thinks I'm crazy for coming here so often. He says it's like returning to the heart of the evil kingdom itself. Me, I say forgive and forget. That's the only way to live. In the present, you know. Don't you agree?"

"I don't know." Serratura settled back. "Yes and no. Sometimes, it's necessary to forget and sometimes it's just as important to remember, don't you think? To have events before you and to keep the past alive in some form or other."

"To keep the past alive?" The man shut his eyes and leaned back in his seat. "Do you really believe that?"

"I hope so. It's all part of the historical process, is it not? A way to structure the past so that it can be analyzed — if not made sense of?"

"I gather you're an historian, yes? You certainly speak like one."

"No. Not at all. Although I do dabble in it occasionally." Serratura couldn't hold back. He wanted to tell people. To let the world know of his semi-notoriety. "Actually, I'm a philosopher. I've been invited to Berlin to read a paper at a conference."

"A philosopher!" the man exclaimed, momentarily placing a hand on Serratura's knee. "That's fantastic! I've always wanted to meet a philosopher. A seeker after the truth, eh? Socrates and Aristotle and all those highbrow fellows with their thinking caps screwed permanently on, questioning, doubting, standing on principle. Right?"

"Umm. I suppose that's one way of putting it."

"When I was an undergraduate student, I took a philosophy course once," he continued. "Let's see. We did Boethius and his *Consolation*. That's right. I even remember a few lines from it: 'My hair untimely white upon my head/ And I a worn out bone-bag hung with flesh.' It was a pleasant break from the steady diet of economics classes. Later, I dabbled a bit in what you would probably call murky waters—mysticism and that sort of thing. But you must have gone much beyond that and done it much more systematically, didn't you?" He leaned over, almost conspiratorially. "Tell me, in your experience, which philosopher do you recommend? Which one can a layman trust most not to confuse him? Or lead him astray?"

"Sorry. I'm not really what you'd call a philosopher's philosopher," Serratura said. "I'm a logician. As for seeking after the truth, well, both 'seeking' and 'the truth' are a bit nebulous and hard to define. The attempt to get a solid grasp on either makes for some tough sledding."

"But you think about things, right?" He leaned even closer to bring his face right up to Serratura's. Serratura could smell his aftershave. It wasn't unpleasant.

"Yes," Serratura said, "that's a valid point—if a somewhat general one."

"And you make up theories—about the past, for example. And historical processes, as you called them."

"Some of us do, I suppose." Serratura hesitated, trying to figure out where it was all leading. He always felt uncomfortable when he didn't know exactly where some line of argument was headed. "Philosophers of history perhaps make up theories—when it comes to the past."

"And do you think that it's logical to do such a thing, to reach back there, as it were, and stir things up—like a stick in a hornet's nest?"

"Depends on what you mean by logical." If Serratura was

about to engage in a discussion, he'd make sure to steer the man towards his own field of expertise. "There are many ways of approaching that word."

"I'm sure there are." The man pulled back and smiled. "What I mean is: Does it make any sense to you?"

"As a logician, I'm—"

"No, no!" He gripped Serratura's arm this time—and squeezed ever so gently. "Never mind as this or as that. Just tell me what you think—as a human being if you have to be anything."

"About the past?" The man nodded. Serratura prepared to cover himself, to make sure there were no chinks in his intellectual armour. "What I think—and this is strictly a nonprofessional, off-the-cuff opinion subject to immediate revision and backtracking—"

"Of course, of course," the man said, at last showing a hint of impatience. "No lawyers here."

"I haven't thought about it very much but my ideas are pretty conventional, I guess." Serratura stared at the head of the passenger in front of him, at the swirls of hair spiraling out from a central comb line. "The past has to be kept alive in some form or other." He looked out the window, searching for the right words. "There has to be a wholeness to the universe, a place for rectification where things are patched up when they go wrong. That's part of what I believe. Or, at least, what I can come up with on the spur of the moment."

"Yes, I find that interesting: a place for utopias to be created—or worked on until we get them right."

"Something like that. Take this city, for example." Serratura felt himself warming up to the subject. "Anyone who didn't know its history would have no idea why some people—your business associate, for example—can hardly bear to think of it complete again and thriving with barely a scar in sight. Not to mention the danger of repeating the mistakes, the horrible errors that cost so many useless lives."

"Oh yes, I see—instead of learning from those mistakes like good human beings should. Conventional wisdom, as you say: He who ignores the past is condemned to relive it. Over and over again. Like a series of burps from eating too many dill pickles. Correct?"

"Well," Serratura said, thinking how he hated dill pickles, "I wouldn't put it quite so literally but—"

The plane bounced once and taxied down the runway. After a few moments, the brakes caught with a jerk and the plane slowly made its way to the terminal entrance.

"Ah, look," the man said. "We've landed. That's always a wonderful feeling, isn't it? To come down from the sky safe and sound—especially in this day and age." He unbuckled his seat belt and let out a sigh. "Tell me, would you say you've learned from your past mistakes?"

"Hmm. Have I learned from my mistakes? It's hard to say but, on the whole, I'd like to think so."

"Yes, we'd all like to think so, wouldn't we? You, me, this city."

He stood up and took down his stowed baggage—a beautiful sea-blue bag with Lake Como written across its side.

"Do you know what I've learned from the past? Or rather what it has taught me?"

Serratura steeled himself for a homily or some witticism, the amateur's homespun philosophizing that he detested so much. Instead, the man pulled up his shirt sleeve to reveal a tattooed number, barely visible, at the base of his wrist.

"This is the lesson. A dead weight one is forced to carry, like a flag for existence. An identity bracelet so that others know how to treat the disease—or its symptoms at least. And, for those who allow it, an excuse not to live in the present, to remain forever stuck in that slice of the past that makes them valid, stamps them as important and not just fodder for earthworms." He continued to talk as they walked off the plane and into the airport. "As for myself, I'd rather hawk restaurant equipment, thank you very much. Even though the irony of selling gas ovens is almost too delicious to entertain."

He smiled and shook Serratura's hand, his grip firm and unwavering, yet at the same time almost feminine in its softness. "I'm sure you'll find Berlin a very pleasant place and much to your liking. Enjoy your stay."

Serratura stood there, wanting to say something significant, to point out that being "flagged for existence" was a technical term in logic, meaning an attempt at matching up an existential quantifier with every object in the universe. Or perhaps he could simply apologize. But for what? Instead, he just thanked him—and felt foolish about it afterwards.

"Oh yes," the man said and took out a business card— Singer's Restaurant Supplies: We Cater To The World—to give Serratura. "Here's the number where I stay when I'm in Berlin. In case you become bored or just wish to talk, you might like to give me a ring. Meet some of my friends. If nothing else, I would very much be interested in knowing how the age-old search for truth goes—and then maybe show you a side of the town you mightn't otherwise see. Would you be interested in losing yourself for a while in our company?"

"I certainly would be," Serratura exclaimed, a bit too enthusiastically as if making up for a faux pas only he had detected in the first place. "And I'll call you up. I'll definitely call you."

Following the instructions of the conference's organizers and a helpful lady at the airport information counter, Serratura made his way to the Kurfurstendamm area, a hotel and shopping district near the centre of town where a room had been found for him at a small *pension*. Normally, he'd have been put up at the Freie Universität campus where most of the action was to take place. But the dorms were all booked up by the time he'd made his application and paper submission.

Serratura didn't mind, however, as he felt this would give him the opportunity to see things from a different perspective, to be in a "real" environment, as it were, rather than the artificial one of a university campus. As well, it might spare his having to small talk his way through breakfast with the other participants who would, no doubt, want to know if his affiliations were with the neo-Marxist critical school faction, the anti-revisionary laissez-faire fringe or—what was then rapidly becoming the orthodoxy—the hermeneutics radicals (already split into the ordinary language and scientific analysis camps).

And, while he was more than looking forward to locking horns with his colleagues during the seminars and conferences scheduled, breakfast had always been a sanctified period for him—to be savoured in utter silence and peace. Even at home, he preferred breakfast alone rather than in the company of his wife and child. Besides, the morning was not his best time. It always felt as if a fog were just on the verge of lifting, as if one could reach in for ideas but only haphazardly and at one's own risk in a world not yet properly compartmentalized, not yet "tagged for existence."

So, the *Pension Aryana* could turn out to be a veritable blessing in disguise. At least, that's what he thought when he first spotted the modest sign on a quiet side street just off the Ku'Damm, as Berliners fondly call the area (a bit of tourist info gleaned from the syrupy tape). Like most buildings in Berlin, this one was situated around a central courtyard and housed a number of different establishments. These included a high-class dress shop and a computer firm whose ghostly green monitors, lined up across the front window, shimmered and flashed indecipherable data.

Serratura rang the outside doorbell that corresponded to the *pension* number and was answered a few seconds later by the buzzer. The feeling of peace—almost like a disembodied yet tangible quality hanging in the thick air—continued inside the covered hallway that led to the actual rooming house. But, as he was about to knock on the *pension* door, several screams came from within, followed by what sounded like a slap and a young woman bursting into tears.

"*Scheisse!*" a male voice shouted. Then there was a harsh string of words even Serratura with his little German gathered weren't compliments. The whole outburst was topped off in English with: "Fucking bitch! Do your work or else! It is easy for me to put you back on the road where you belong."

There was another slap and more tear-bursting. Serratura waited for the furor to die down before rapping on the lion-face knocker. The door flew open, almost as if the person had been waiting behind it all along, as if the screams, shouts and slaps had all been for Serratura's edification. The man at the door had a thickset, extremely robust upper body which dwindled badly by the time it got down to the hips, thighs and lower extremities. On his head was a well-worn New York Yankees baseball cap tilted towards the back so that the peak pointed at the ceiling. His attitude was aggressive—almost belligerent—as he stood with hands on hips and chest thrust forward.

"*Ja?*" he said, looking Serratura up and down ferociously, as if ready to start a punch-up. "*Was willst du?*"

"I'm sorry. I don't speak German. Do you speak English?"

"*Ja.* Of course, I do. Speaking for myself, I am a man of civilization—at the least."

Serratura felt himself reddening. He'd often used the "dripping with scorn" approach on others—especially students—but had seldom been on the receiving end.

"I'm looking for the *Pension Aryana*," he said, looking down at his notepad to make sure he got the name right.

"This is she," the man said with little enthusiasm. "What is it you want? You must know we have no rooms available. The time it is very busy."

"My name is Serratura," he said as the man was about to shut the door on him. "Anthony G. Serratura. I believe a reservation has been made for me at the *Pension Aryana*."

"Serraruta?" the man said, pushing his cap back even further and scratching the front of his head.

"No, Serratura." He spelled out his name. "I'm with the philosophy conference at the university."

"Ah so. Der Professor, *ja*? I am Karl—but you will please to call me Fritz. It is to be preferred."

"Hello, Fritz," Serratura said, holding out his hand. "Glad to meet you."

"You will not stand at the door, ja," Fritz said, not bothering to shake and instead stuffing his hands into his pockets.

Suits me fine, Serratura said to himself as he lifted his suitcase and prepared to step in.

"But first," Fritz said, blocking his path, "clean your shoes, *bitte*? The floors are newly scrubbed."

"Yes, of course."

Serratura wiped his shoes and entered a very dark, very sombre room lit only by a small desk lamp at the far end. Everything was low-keyed, almost to the point of vanishing. He could make out just barely several sofas covered in purplish velvet, a stack of brochures beside a phone, a massive painting—all shade and pitch-black hues of a battle scene from what looked like The Hundred Years' War—

framed in gold. In one corner, blurred black-and-white images flashed across a TV set with the sound off. They were scenes of people marching and waving flags, buildings going up in flames, security police in riot gear chasing black-masked and hooded youths with "*Direkt Aktion*" scrawled in paint—or maybe blood—across their chests. Welcome to living history, Serratura thought. This is where they take their politics very seriously.

"Indeed. You have come at a strange time," Fritz said when he noticed Serratura watching the screen.

"A strange time? How so?"

"Ah, as you can very well see, the city is in revolt. Chaos, *ja*. Yesterday down the Ku'Damm, thousands of students marched to protest the cowboy's visit."

"The cowboy's visit? I don't understand. Is there going to be a Wild West show?"

"Wild West show!" Fritz burst into laughter. "You are a very funny man, *ja*." Then he looked at Serratura and realized he was genuinely puzzled. "But you are American, are you not?"

"Sorry. Canadian."

"Ah, so you do not know the great President Reagan is coming to visit Berlin tomorrow? He is coming to give a speech at the Wall, near to the Brandenberg Gates. Just like the great John Kennedy, is that not so?"

"That's right. Of course. I had read it somewhere but I guess it slipped my mind."

Fritz looked at him again as if he were an idiotic child—how could anyone forget such an important event?—and then shrugged.

"The students have done in all the windows of the automobile dealers," he said. "All down the Ku'Damm. *Kaputt*. Then, they have set off the bank alarms and chased the whores away." He laughed. "For a little while anyway. Tomorrow morning, there will be another march no doubt. They will protest the Americans in Central America and the remainder of the windows will be damaged. They protest others and damage us. That is always the way it is, no? You—are you for or against the Yankees in Central America?"

Serratura started to say he was definitely against U.S. involvement when he realized the question was loaded—especially in a city surrounded on all sides by the "enemy."

"I'm neither for nor against it," he finally said. "And right now, I'm very tired. Could you show me to my room?"

"*Ja*, of course. Your room."

Fritz shouted and clapped his hands. There was the echo of footsteps down a long corridor. A red-faced, thick-armed young woman wearing a kerchief on her head came skidding around the corner, like a silent film comedy character. She wiped her hands on a blood-stained apron. When she saw Serratura, she giggled and quickly lowered her eyes.

"You must clean this gentleman's room, *bitte*," Fritz said. She nodded frantically, then once again dashed down the hallway, making a ninety-degree turn at the corridor.

"Oh," Serratura said, "I hope I haven't arrived too early."

"Yes, in terms of fact, you have. Will your stay be long with us?"

"I believe I should be booked for three days. And I'll be leaving first thing Monday morning."

"You must pay in advance, *bitte*. Three days with breakfast. You will take breakfast, *ja?*" Serratura nodded. "And you must be out by noontime sharp or we will charge an extra day to you." He leaned back, took the cap off and then replaced it. "You should know we do not take credit."

For what? Serratura thought. Certainly not politeness. Or diplomacy.

The young woman came rushing back. She seemed to be out of breath and had to lean against one of the velvet-backed chairs. But she quickly jerked to attention as Fritz turned towards her.

"Ah *güt*," he said, with the kind of smile that Serratura sensed promised unpleasant things later on. "Frieda, lift the gentleman's bag."

"No, no. That's alright," Serratura said, pulling the bag a bit closer. "It's not very heavy. I can carry it myself."

But Frieda reached for the handle and the two tugged back and forth until she tore it forcibly out of his grasp. Then she stood there with a satisfied grin on her face.

"My sister," Fritz said, making a gesture with his fingers against the side of her head. "She is not—how do you say it?—not quite there all of her. Cuckoo. Nutty as a bread-fruit."

"Fruitcake," Serratura corrected without thinking—and immediately regretted saying it.

"Fruitcake, *ja*. An accident from her childhood. Fell down a flock—*nein*, a flight of stairs."

"I'm sorry to hear that."

"But why? Intelligence in a woman like her would be too much a waste. It would be like giving the brain to a . . . a chimpanzee. She is very strong and very *güt* at housework, at room-fixing. That is most important for a woman. Especially when our guests make their arrivals so early. Is that not so?"

Serratura was starting not to like this peacock of a *pension* owner. Or front man. Or whatever he was. In fact, he even entertained the thought of turning around and looking elsewhere for a place to stay, just to let the fool know he didn't appreciate his manner. But he realized that would be inviting disaster. Especially as he wasn't at all familiar with the city and could easily find himself caught as an unwilling buffer between rabid demonstrators and equally serious riot police. Or worse still, slowly being squeezed up against the Wall with thousands of others running just ahead of the electric cattle prods. Perhaps, if things didn't work out, he could search for a place later. In the meantime. . . .

"Come," Fritz said, dangling a set of keys right up against Serratura's face. "Your room, it is ready."

It was a small space on the ground floor, not far from the *pension*'s main entrance, and dominated by an oversized double bed and a writing table. But at least it faced out onto a pleasant courtyard garden and had a floor-to-ceiling window that made it brighter than it had any right to be.

"Yes, this will do fine," Serratura said, taking the bag from Frieda and placing it on the bed.

"Please," Fritz said, looking skyward as if seeking help against these boorish barbarians from across the sea, "the sheets have been changed only now."

"Sorry."

Serratura pulled the bag off the bed and dropped it— like a hot potato—on the floor.

"So, you will pay now, *ja*," Fritz said, holding out his hand. Serratura noticed a raw, thin scar on his wrist. Certainly didn't look like the suicidal type but then you never know. "Breakfast is between the seventh and ninth hour. There is no late service." He made a motion with his hands like a baseball umpire signaling someone safe at home. "Impossible absolutely. It is my duty to inform you that once you request breakfast the charge does not alter whether you eat or do not eat. I hope that is understood clearly?" Serratura nodded. "If you will please to come with me, I will show you where the showers are to be found."

After Serratura had paid the full amount and obtained a receipt, Fritz led him down the narrow corridor with Frieda skipping like a little girl in front of them. The floor sloped noticeably here and he could see stains on the walls where water had seeped through the plaster. A series of ill-fitting doors led off the corridor at intervals of three metres or so. More rooms, he surmised. More double-sized beds and writing tables. The idea, for some reason, made him feel queasy and slightly claustrophobic. The showers were at the far end, past the kitchen and what looked like a laundry room. With one last giggle, Frieda ducked dramatically into one of the doors and vanished.

"Is it to the satisfaction?" Fritz asked, after pointing out the towels.

"Yes, I think it'll do."

"*Güt.* Here are the keys then. One is for the outside door to the Strasse; two is for the *Pension Aryana*; three is for your room. Guard them well as I must insist on a charge if they are found to be misplaced. Have a stay that is pleasant."

He handed Serratura the keys and then he too disappeared behind another of what seemed a series of never-ending doors. Serratura stood in the corridor for a moment, trying to reorient himself. He found that, if he lifted his head quickly, he could make the whole thing wobble. The effect of the alternating black and white linoleum tiles, no doubt. Someone—a woman from the sounds of it—was singing in a high clear voice while taking a shower. A door opened behind him and a young man came out, wrapped in nothing but a small towel which barely hid his corpulent midsection.

"*Guten Tag,*" he said, whistling and entering the washroom where, for a moment, Serratura was able to make out the outline of a young woman showering.

As he walked away, he heard squeals of laughter and the sound of a soap bar slithering along the bottom of the tub. Ah, young love, he said to himself. Even in dark corridors it blossoms. Even in the most foreign of places, the most mouldy of corners. And he thought of his own lovely wife and child back home, a fair-haired family portrait if there ever was one. Would they still be there when I got back? Things hadn't been going too well between them. Not too well at all. As a matter of fact, she'd threatened to leave several times, kept insisting they should separate, at least for a while. A trial separation, she'd called it. I guess after that comes the verdict, Serratura had said at the time, a comment not greatly appreciated.

He was almost certain she'd taken on a lover—one of the plumbers or other handymen who'd swarmed their house as it underwent renovation. And he couldn't blame her really. He hadn't been paying too much attention to her of late. Work, you understand. The conference, the paper to write, the students to grade, the research that kept piling up, the constant pressure to publish or perish. Somehow, she'd slipped his mind for lengthy periods at a time. He found himself wishing there were two of him, dreading the thought of ending up like his father, stunted in an emotional desert, living out his life in the basement. Serratura made a resolution to call her first chance he got, to let her know he'd arrived safely and was thinking of her. Yes, I should at least do that, he said.

The sound of a dog yapping nervously snapped him out of his reverie. He looked up to glimpse, through an open door, an old woman lying on a fancy four-poster bed with its curtains drawn open. She was dressed in a fluffy, lacy nightgown with feathers and frills—and buried beneath several layers of thick quilts. Under each arm was a tiny dog. He recognized them as Pomeranians, snub-nosed creatures whose mouths always seemed to be dripping goo of some sort. One, like its mistress, was asleep. But the other kept yapping as he hurried by the open door, not wishing to be seen as snooping.

Unfortunately, however, he soon realized, after a few more steps, that none of it looked familiar. He must have taken the wrong turn where the corridor forked—one side, this side, leading deeper into the house; the other back towards the front door where his room was situated. On tiptoe, he retraced his steps past the old lady's room. Both dogs were barking now and the old lady was stirring in the bed, fluttering her eyelids. She sat up, opened her nightgown for a second to expose a heavily powdered and sadly sagging breast and then rolled over. The dogs yapped for a few more seconds and then became quiet again.

As Serratura turned the corner leading back to the right corridor, he thought he heard a harsh, scratchy voice coming from one of the rooms. It sounded as if someone's name were being recited over and over again at an ever-increasing pitch—but he couldn't really be sure. And then there was a loud burst of martial music, followed by a steady flickering of lights at the base of the door and what seemed thousands of voices all saying the same thing in a very insistent manner. Just as quickly, it stopped: music, voices, flickering of lights. All gone.

Back in his own room, he felt a sudden wave of extreme fatigue—like he was carrying the weight of the world or something. The night on the plane and time zone difference of six hours were, no doubt, catching up to him. As well, the heating made it very stuffy, so much so he had to throw open the window that looked out into the courtyard. A good time to catch up on a bit of advertising culture, he thought. So he undressed, put on the earphones and lay down on the bed:

"Oddly enough, it's from the air that you get your one good overall view of the city's private life, built around enclosed courtyards which, at ground level, you can only glimpse enticingly through half-opened portals. Unless, of course, you're invited to partake of the greenery and a pint of Berlin's famous *Weisse mit Schuss*, a pale malt beer topped with a touch of fruit syrup. But even the little you do see from the street is enough to inform you that this is not a city of picture-book proportions and one-dimensional attractions. Or one that rolls up after the last tourist has been safely put to bed."

Safely put to bed. That's me, Serratura said. The droning voice kept on and on, dropping him into a deep and dreamless sleep. Less than an hour later, he awoke shivering, the voice still going strong:

"At the east end of the Ku'Damm is one of the few reminders of the war's devastation—the bombed-out Kaiser-Wilhelm Memorial Church. It stands in hollowed-out splendour, a jagged tooth next to the ultra-modern structure (looking like a jewelled honeycomb) that's replaced it and in stark contrast to the nearby Europa Centre, 20 stories of spic-and-span shops, offices, restaurants and casinos. This is a Berlin hot spot and the natural starting point for a visit to our fair city on the banks of the Spree."

Side A of the tape came to an end. He looked at the digital display on his watch, a tenure-track present from his wife. It was early afternoon but it somehow seemed much later because the sun was no longer penetrating the courtyard. So, after getting up to shut the window, he snuggled deeper into the quilts and tried to go back to sleep. There followed a few minutes of fitful tossing before he realized that sleep wasn't going to happen.

He decided instead to dress and do some work on his paper. He'd called it *The Use of Second-Order Logic as an Alternative To Its First-Order Cousin in The Attempt to Define The World's Ontology: Or What There Is And How to Get at It.* A little pompous, yes, he said to himself. And a little self-deprecating. Such is the nature of the philosophy business. And he *had* made a little joke there by using the words "first-order cousin." Besides, it wasn't the title that worried

Serratura. He felt the paper still had some minor flaws in it, some quirks. Nothing that a bit of polishing couldn't fix, of course. He sat down at the writing desk and opened the paper at the first page:

> At a quick glance, one would think that there would be little or no trouble making the transition from first-order predicate logic to higher—or n-order ones (with second-order logic as a case in particular). After all, it does seem but a matter of extending universal and existential quantification over objects in the first-order instance to predicates (functions and relations) in the second and sets of predicates in the third and so on up the n-ladder.

"And so on up the n-ladder." That always brought to mind—for Serratura, at least—an image of a clown on a self-supporting rope ladder, stretching endlessly in both directions. Or perhaps an identical series of clowns on an identical series of ropes. How they had got there is a mystery but it doesn't really matter. So long as they keep climbing—in unison. And what if one wants to jump off? Or simply let go? Why, that would be non-rational. He'd then give up the right to be called human, a thinking being. But perhaps it was just such a leap that had landed him there in the first place—purely by accident. And it might take him another to escape what seemed, at first glance, a hopeless situation—a trap, an evolutionary dead end brought on by an over-active brain and the inability to control a chronic glandular problem that resulted in what has been labelled self-consciousness. Or it might simply be gas, Serratura said to himself, smiling at his little bit of cynical jocularism.

Putnam uses the slackness in first-order logic's ability to 'pin down' the universe—and consequent inability to show a one-to-one relation between the symbols in a formal theory and the objects of the world—to make the interesting philosophical point that no model of the universe can claim uniqueness as the 'real' one. While some may bemoan this fact, it does serve the purpose of those who believe that no formal model (i.e. no scientific theory or way of looking at the world) can guarantee the capturing of the universe fully or in a way that leaves nothing out. That we are the famous Brains In A Vat, for example, acting as if we were actually living in a full-fledged universe when our only stimuli come from wires connected to our brains.

At that point, Serratura scratched out the reference to brains in a vat, Putnam's much-debated thought experiment. It seemed to him, on second consideration, not mathematical or rigorous enough. That was the problem he had with most of the "possible worlds" scenarios. There was no escaping their anthropomorphic thrust, their lack of objectivity and a proper outside criterion. But what does one replace that anthropomorphic thrust with? Where is that "objective" viewpoint? Remove the human and uncover the . . . the what?

For some reason, he thought of the businessman on the plane and then his own father in quick succession: what had they uncovered? The old answer would have been that you removed the human to uncover the angelic—or the devilish, the temptation to either rise above it or sink below it. And that, in a way, was supposed to make it easier, was supposed to explain things. The angels are the unquestioning mirror images of the devils who are tortured by them forever by having God's grace focused on them as if with a magnifying glass. Or for only half of forever—at which point it's their turn to pin the angels down with the urge, the unquenchable thirst for knowledge. In eternal oscillation.

But that would no longer do. Serratura knew the connection between truth and the world had long ago been severed—and, in the process, drained of blood like a sacrificial lamb. The new god is the abstract, he whispered, the pure equation, the formula of language. It states: "'Someone cuts my lawn and prunes my roses' is true if and only if someone cuts my lawn and prunes my roses." And that was supposed to make it all transparently clear. That was supposed to make everything make sense.

There was a knock on his door. Frieda slid in, almost eel-like, before he had a chance to get up and open it himself. He made a mental note to lock it from now on. She looked him quickly up and down—and let out a giggle when she saw his bare feet. No doubt amused by the sight of Serratura's small toe which rode piggy-back on the one next to it.

"Yes?" he said, shifting so that his feet were hidden beneath the desk.

"*Bitte. Das Telephon.*" In between giggles, she made dialing motions with her hands. "Dring . . . dring."

"For me?" He pointed at himself.

"*Ja. ja.*"

And off she ran, giggling, glancing furtively about as if afraid someone might catch her in some forbidden act. Serratura put on his shoes and followed her into the darkened hallway, watching her grip the wall and make a theatrical ninety-degree turn down the corridor. The young man from the washroom sat beside a young woman on the sofa—the shower lady, no doubt. He was wearing too-tight leather pants and no shirt, a large gold chain dangling down his chest and resting gently on his over-sized stomach; she was dressed in a leather mini-skirt, slit to the thigh, and a leather halter top that threatened to spill her breasts over the top. They were pushed right up against one another—like two halves of a creature that had come apart through some unfortunate accident and was now desperate to reunite. The young man smiled at Serratura and he nodded back before picking up the phone.

"Hello," he said, noticing out of the corner of his eye that the young woman had suddenly inserted her tongue into the young man's ear and flicked it several times. Serratura turned away. "Professor Serratura speaking."

"Ah, Professor Serratura. This is Doctor Bruno Zweck, your host from the Freie Universität philosophy department. I pray that you remember me?"

"Of course, Doctor Zweck. How could I forget the man who made all this possible?"

"You are too modest, Professor Serratura. It is you, with your gracious acceptance, who had the most to do with it. Did you enjoy a pleasant trip? I hope so, yes."

"Yes, it was very pleasant. Thank you very much."

Despite his attempts to avoid looking, he could now see the couple clearly groping one another on the sofa and the air was filled with the sound of squeaking, sucking, sticking leather.

"I must apologize for not putting you up at the university," Doctor Zweck said. "Rest assured we will inform you the moment an opening arises. As a matter of fact . . . yes . . . one of the graduate students may leave tomorrow. I will see then what I can do about finding you a suitable place at closer proximity to the university."

"That's okay." Giggling, the couple sank slowly onto the

sofa, until they were no longer visible. "No need to put anyone out. I'm perfectly fine here. Especially as it's only for a
couple of days."

"Are you sure it is not an inconvenience to you?"

"Not at all. Besides, I've already settled in." Sounds were
coming from the sofa, moans that could hardly be mistaken
for anything but those of a sexual buildup. Serratura felt a
wave of what could only have been jealousy. He couldn't remember the last time he'd engaged in love-making so spon-
taneously—and on a sofa while others looked on. Come to
think of it—had he ever? "No, I don't mind in the least."

"That is very good of you. Very good. A taste of the 'real'
Berlin, *ja?*"

"That's right." To divert his attention from the couple in
the midst of seriously groping each other, Serratura glanced
at the TV screen. A building, edging right up to the street,
was in the process of going up in flames while the firemen
were being prevented from responding to the alarm by a
rowdy, chanting group of demonstrators. "A taste of the
city. Warts and all."

"Yes, warts and all. I am pleased with that. It is a good
expression. English is full of juicy expressions, is it not? Tell
me, have you made plans for this evening?"

"No, Doctor Zweck. I hadn't really thought about it."

The couple had disentangled with a playful slap from
the woman and the two were once again sitting straight
up.

"Und so. Listen. Some of us were thinking of a quiet
dinner somewhere, a chance to meet on, shall we say, social
grounds." He laughed. "Before the wars start in earnest,
that is. Would you care to join us?"

"Well, I've just got in and still have plenty of work—"

"Work?" Zweck said in mock horror. "The conference,
dear sir, only begins tomorrow. It is strictly immoral to do

any work tonight. Out of the question." He laughed. "Besides, your colleagues would be most upset if they felt you were trying to gain any unfair advantage over them. You would not want that, would you?"

"That would be awful," Serratura said, getting into the spirit of things. He'd always been good at that—if not quite the spirit at least the banter part. "We can't have that."

"We certainly cannot. Do you know where the Europa Centre is? I believe it is not so very far from where you are staying. Along the Ku'Damm. You cannot miss it. It has a monstrous Mercedes-Benz symbol on its top. The pride and joy of our country."

"Yes," Serratura said, watching a car being overturned on the street and students planting an anarchist flag on it. "I think I can find it."

"Good. Then meet us at seven beneath The Clock of Flowing Time. It is in the main lobby of that building. You will identify us by the patches on our corduroy jackets and our inward-turning glances. Ha, ha. A little joke, yes. To be serious, there will probably be four of us. Or perhaps three. And we will wait beneath the clock. Have you noted that?"

"Seven. At the Europa Centre. Beneath The Clock of Flowing Time. Four of you—more or less."

"Good, good. See you then."

Serratura put down the receiver and watched a bit more of the destruction on the television. This time, gangs of youths were rampaging along the edges of the barbed wire he'd seen from the plane. Now, he could make out that it was several metres high, placed in rolled layers and practically impossible to penetrate. To make doubly sure, police on horseback patrolled the inside perimeter. The reporter on the scene was speaking from a temporary podium beneath the Brandenberg Gates. The podium and gates were eerily floodlit and, at times, it seemed as if the reporter were fading in and out, like the "Beam-me-up-Scotty" sequences on *Star Trek*.

The young woman on the sofa got up with a sigh, smoothed her skirt and switched the channel. A game show that resembled *The Price Is Right*—Serratura recognized it because his daughter enjoyed shouting along when the host yelled: "Come on, down"—was in progress, complete with contestants jumping up and down and scantily dressed, large-breasted hostesses who lounged about suggestively on the bedroom furniture.

"Ah, Der Professor," Fritz said as he materialized from the corridor as if out of nowhere. "Enjoying our TV programs, I see. Do you know what the grand prize it is this afternoon?"

"Can't say that I do," Serratura said, cringing at the thought of having to exchange pleasantries with someone he'd decided was an overbearing creep.

"A pass to hear your President Reagan speak. Is that not something? Thousands have already been victorious. They have sent in the box tops from the breakfast cereals. But now there are only a few precious ones left for the thousands more who desire them."

"You're pulling my leg."

"'Pulling my leg'? What is the meaning of that, *bitte?*"

"Making a joke."

"Making a joke?" Fritz said with a shocked look on his face. "To be sure not. One does not joke about this sort of thing in Berlin. You see, only those with the proper passes—and citizens of America, of course—will be permitted to enter the barriers."

Serratura shook his head—hoping to make it a gesture both of sadness and disbelief. Democracy in action. Cereal box politics. Best not to think about it. He excused himself and returned to his room. There, he sat down once again at the writing table. It was now quite dark and he had to switch on one of the desk lamps to continue working. It made a circle of soft light on his manuscript, brightest in the middle and fading to black at the edges. Are you trying to tell me something, he said to himself, some hint of what the Higher Court thinks of my opus? Then, giving up any further attempt at making corrections or at picking out the flaws, he simply turned the pages at random:

> Just how important is this notion of complete-
> ness and 'provable in first-order logic'? For
> someone like Quine, it is of extreme impor-
> tance, for it has to do not only with the two
> notions themselves but with what objects and
> sorts of objects we admit into the universe. . .
> . And so, the answer to the question of the vi-
> ability of second-order logic is: Yes. No. Maybe.
> It may be, after all, an extra-rational decision,
> depending on which side of the ontological
> fence one places oneself—including the pos-
> sibility of sitting squarely on the top of it.

He pushed the paper aside with his arm. "Sitting square-ly on the top of it." Serratura had a sudden, uninvited image of naked Paraguayan political prisoners being slowly lowered buttocks first onto sharpened stakes, hands tied above their heads and legs tucked up against their chests to better expose the unwilling, the puckered anus. And what, pray tell, Serratura said to an imaginary courtroom filled with shadowy, hooded figures, is their ontological status? Persona non grata, at the very least. What existential quantifier could they latch on to, could they cry out for, could they pin their salvation on, saying: 'You can't do this to me. We belong under the same general category, the universal concept of humankind'?

BERLIN

But what can I, Anthony G. Serratura, professor of the purest, sharp-edged logic, guardian of completeness and consistency, of provability and axiomatization, do about it? Nothing, of course. If it's not in the premises, it can't be in the conclusion. Or better still: If it's not on the premises, then it can't be within the grounds. Against the ground rules.

Serratura remembered an old logic professor who, while making his way dryly through a modern solution to Zeno's Paradoxes, was asked by one of the students—a trouble-maker obviously who felt that philosophy should answer questions of deep import—what he thought of "God, mo-rality and nuclear war." The professor, who was actually quite a young man and brilliant in his field, said: "I save those for when I've had a little too much to drink." Beer barrel philosophy, another logic professor had described it. Lugubrious pretensions to deep feelings and thoughts when all it comes down to is a loosening of the synaptic connections, a misfiring of the electro-chemical messages that spark across the gaps and perhaps signifying nothing so much as the need for a good bowel movement. Was that really all there was to it?

Serratura experienced another rush of claustropho-bia—a long, black-and-white room that tilted and narrowed at one end with doors flapping back and forth like birds' wings straining to fly off. He began to literally gasp for air. It was his usual reaction to this sort of questioning: Meta-physics reduced to psychosis; solid space-time to the circle of soft light; objective reality to the mind's questionable meanderings. No matter what he called it though, he des-perately needed to get out, to walk around in the midst of others—even if they were, each and every one of them, strangers. Or perhaps because of that very fact.

He hurried out of the room, past the sharp, startled

faces of two old ladies who bobbed in unison—like ostriches caught out of the sand. It was dark in the passageway but considerably brighter when he stepped outside. He took a deep gulp of air and his head sang (like an electric wire) as it cleared. That was better.

A light rain was falling, almost like a shimmery mist in the air. It was quite warm and pleasant. He turned the corner on to the Ku'Damm. Everything was so new, so stainless steel and neon it was hard to believe that practically every building on this street had been razed during the Second World War, devastated by uncounted tons of Allied bombs. Now, whatever damage Serratura could see was of more recent vintage. He'd read somewhere—perhaps in another of those tourist brochures—that there was a healthy market in plate-glass repair in Berlin with companies on 24-hour call ready to board up shattered windows and seal projectile holes.

Police in green riot gear milled about in front of the more important buildings—the Berliner Bank, the new-car showrooms, the Burger King and McDonald's franchises. They leaned on their Plexiglas shields, some smoking, others talking to friends and laughing. The thing that struck Serratura about them was that, beneath the robotic gear and high-tech visors, most were barely past their teens, had hardly started shaving. They could have easily been on the other side, easily switched roles and clothing with the demonstrators. Perhaps they, too, during their time off, took to the streets, shouting leftist slogans and hurling hand-held rockets at healthy, over-tanned businessmen who dared mock them by sipping champagne on high-rise balconies.

Even more surprising to someone not used to riots—(Serratura's only previous experience was being rounded up and held for several hours for taking part in a demonstration during the 1970 October Crisis in Quebec)—was the reaction of the pedestrians and the shopkeepers. No siege mentality here. A quick sweep of the broken glass and it was business as usual, back to rare books or designer jeans, chapatis or hand-fashioned belts.

He made his way towards Kaiser-Wilhelm Church, the bombed-out memorial from the Second World War that threatened to collapse at any moment. It really did resemble a hollow tooth, rotten at the core and lacking a live nerve. A man with two giant black hounds was seated on the steps in front of it. The hounds ran loose, high-stepping and frolicking. One of them leaned up against the church door and let loose a gush of steaming urine, which flowed down to the street.

Serratura tried to imagine the rest of the area in the same condition as the church—craters where houses had been moments before; the whine of attacking bombers like the Furies of ancient Greece; the few surviving predators in the nearby zoo desperate to escape their violated Eden, roaming the streets perhaps in sudden collaboration with those who'd captured them, who'd brought them to a strange land and fed them huge chunks of raw meat daily.

But it was a pale vision compared to the well-to-do early-evening strollers; the punks with their stickers proclaiming anarchy and the Sex Pistols; the skateboarders using flower beds as ramps; and, best of all, the Ku'Damm All-Star band halfway through a spirited electrical rendition of *The Key to the Highway*.

Serratura sat down on a bench, trying to savour the irony of having come to Berlin to hear a song from the U.S. blues tradition. A young woman flopped down beside him. She was dressed all in black: black boots, black tights, black denim mini-skirt, black turtleneck, black leather jacket. Only her face was white, the makeup caked on to give it the appearance of luminous plaster—a death mask that managed to look almost virginal. She turned towards him and smiled. Several of her front teeth were missing. Serratura could see then she wasn't more than 15 or 16.

"*Drogen?*" she asked sweetly, tilting her head.

"I'm sorry." He shook his head.

"*Zigaretten, ja?*"

"*Nein.* I don't smoke."

"*Scheisse!*" She clenched her fists. "*Das Geld?*"

Das Geld? That must mean money, he thought. He was reaching into his pocket for some spare change when she suddenly sprang up and rushed away. A moment later, two policemen sauntered by, laughing and gently tapping their nightsticks against the bench. As soon as they moved off, she was back, holding out one trembling hand which she had to steady with the other. Serratura gave whatever he'd pulled out of his pocket—a couple of deutschmarks.

"*Kapitalistisch Schwein!*" She hissed as she pocketed the money and turned away. On the back of her jacket, adorned with a skull and crossbones, was written in large letters: "*Alles ist kaputt.*"

"*Alles ist kaputt,*" Serratura repeated to himself—and, for some reason, thought of his wife and child back home. It was somewhere around noon in Montreal. He decided, on the spur of the moment, it would be a good time to call. The long-distance operator advised him, in English, on how many coins to deposit. He slipped them in, one at a time, all the while thinking about what he was going to say. Of course, he'd want to speak to Cathy, his daughter, who'd be home for lunch. And she'd ask him about what he was bringing back from Berlin for her. Then, Louise. Harried Louise, trying to juggle half-a-dozen tasks at once: Cathy, her volunteer work at the nearby nursing home, gardening, taking care of Serratura's hypochondriac mother.

The phone rang. Twice, three times. The answering machine picked up and Serratura heard his own voice, so clear it was almost as if he were calling from the university just down the street from their home, calling to say he wouldn't be able to make it for lunch after all, even though he'd promised:

"Hello, you have reached the Serratura residence. Louise and Anthony. We can't come to the phone right now— but if you leave a message at the tone, we'll get back to you as soon as possible. Thank you."

A polite message, Serratura thought. We do everything in a very polite and civilized way.

He waited for the tone and then left his own message:

"Hi, Louise. Just thought I'd let you know I didn't go down over the Atlantic so there's no insurance money for you. Just joking. Give my love to Cathy and tell her I'm bringing back a huge surprise for her. Everything's going fine at this end. Oops, gotta go now. The operator's giving me the cut-off signal. Bye, Louise. I know I don't tell you often enough—but I do love you. See you soon."

He put the phone down and looked out of the booth. It had started to rain harder and the drops obscured the view, making the world a fuzzy, malleable place. Although it was still early for the rendezvous, he dashed across the square to the Europa Centre. After walking along a tunnel lined with arcades, sex shops, slot machines and fast-food joints, he came out in a cavernous area that stretched at least six stories up. The lobby was jam-packed with people—some dining; some shopping; some just hanging around. Transparent glass escalators ran up the sides of the lobby to restaurants and shops at the various levels; loudspeakers amid hanging plants imitated perfectly the songs of myriad birds—and without the mess from the real thing; a cascade of water from the upper stories turned the Clock of Flowing Time, one tick for every second. He craned his neck, following the path of the water to the upper stories.

"Fantastic, isn't it?" a voice called out behind him. He turned. It was Singer's Restaurant Supplies, the man from the airplane. "A perfect symbol for the new Berlin."

"Why, hello," Serratura said. "Fancy meeting you again so soon."

"Despite its 1.9 million diligent, ant-like burghers, West Berlin is actually an amazingly small place," Singer said, shaking Serratura's hand. "You keep running into the same people over and over again—like one of those provincial towns with only one main street and dusty paths leading to it from all directions. Probably to do with its siege mentality. Besides, the Europa Centre is like a magnet, isn't it? I bet you were drawn here as well, pulled by the glitz and the glitter, the thought of a little unplanned excitement. Come on, admit it."

"Well, my room happens to be right around the corner—just off the Ku'Damm."

"So you decided to go for a walk?" Serratura nodded. "I thought so. A pleasant evening for walking. The rain cools it off just enough, don't you think?"

"It does, yes." Serratura looked around, suddenly having little desire to dine—and mentally spar—with his distinguished colleagues from the university. "And you, what brings you here?"

"Culture, my friend," he said, gesturing expansively. "Culture with a capital 'K.' I'm here for the Multivision Theatre. Do you know it?" Serratura shook his head. "It's a mini-history of Berlin, made for the city's 750th anniversary bash. Very high-tech, tons of computers, thousands of screens and translation in every known language. Well, English, French and Spanish, at least. Say, if you have no other plans, why not join me? The next screening is in forty-five minutes and it only runs for an hour so the boredom will be minimal. You haven't made any special plans, have you?"

"No," Serratura said, glancing about to make sure no professor-like creatures were lurking in the vicinity, ready to point him out, to expose his perfidy. "Just exploring."

"Good, good. Come on. Let's have a quick go at the one-armed bandits first. That's also a form of culture—albeit of a more universal and primitive kind."

He took Serratura by the arm and led him towards the slot machines. All the spots were occupied for the moment so they had to stand in line.

"I tell you," Singer said, rubbing his hands together, "I'd much rather visit a good casino than a bad museum. Don't you agree?"

"I don't know. Although I've seen plenty of bad museums, I've never been to a casino."

"What! And you have the gall to call yourself a philosopher! Every philosopher should gamble at least once—just to know what it's like to have absolutely no control over events. The real truth to life." He laughed. "Sometimes I actually believe that—but only until my next gas stove sale."

Serratura looked nervously behind him, then quickly turned back. He'd spotted what must definitely be his putative dinner partners walking down the corridor towards the Clock: a slightly disheveled man with white hair and thick glasses; a young woman wearing asymmetrical earrings and torn jeans and her hair the colour of pink flamingoes; and another short, dark-skinned man in an Indian kurta.

Zweck, Seppanen and Matlab. Serratura had never met any of them, yet he felt as if he knew them intimately: Bruno Zweck, with whom he'd exchanged a number of letters before the phone call, always gracious and slightly formal; Kianta Seppanen from the University of Helsinki, a disciple of mathematician René Thom and one of the leading authorities in Catastrophe Theory, that strange amalgam of metaphysics, symbolic logic and geometry that had been all the rage in the seventies; and Girgit Matlab, who laboured in relative obscurity at the University of New Delhi but whose most recent book, *Modality And The Individual*, had become extremely influential with its attempt to link possible worlds and the concept of necessity—even though he liked to say that all he did was pick up the crumbs left over from the big boys at Harvard and Oxford.

All three looked intense and ready for action. Seeing them strengthened the decision Serratura had made not to come forward and identify himself, not to join them for their working dinner, a dinner that, he knew from past experience, could easily lead to indigestion. And the strange thing was that he didn't feel the least bad or guilty about it. Anyway, if it came time to defend himself, he could always blame Singer's Restaurant Supplies for leading him astray.

"Ah, here we are at last," Singer said, patting the slot machine tenderly—like a long-lost friend. "Would you like to have a first go at it?"

"Okay. But you know I've never done this before. Is there some special trick to it?"

"Nothing at all. Just insert some of your hard-earned money and yank." Serratura slipped a coin into the slot and pulled the lever. "That's the spirit. Cherry, cherry . . . come on, come on! Lemon! Tough luck. Those lemons will get you every time. Oh, by the way, I don't think we've been properly introduced. As a matter of fact, you know my name but I don't know yours." Serratura told him his name. "Serratura, Antonio. *Alore, sei Italiano! Mi fa piacere di fare vostra conoscenza.*"

"*Grazie,*" Serratura said, struggling to remember his Italian. "*Anche lei parlo l'Italiano?*"

"Let's just say I hack at it and leave it at that," Singer said laughing. "Chop it up and regurgitate the pieces. Actually,

BERLIN

I know a few words from my business dealings in Milan. It seems to impress the buyers and increase sales when you know how to say *cucina a gas* or *macinino da caffè* in the customer's own language. I only wish I knew more—or had more practice at it."

"I'm not very fluent in it myself," Serratura said as he put another coin in—with the same results. "My parents spoke their dialect at home and I learned that. But I was born in Canada so I never had any schooling in proper Italian. And, as I'd rather play street hockey on Saturday morning, I didn't show any interest in it until it was too late. Although I did a few courses at university." He laughed. "Sort of my exercise in underwater basketweaving. Now, I can read it fairly well but speaking it is a chore."

"Languages, my boy, are both a blessing and a curse," Singer said, wagging his finger as if delivering a classroom lecture. "I can make myself understood in about five of them, not to mention various very practical hand signals I've picked up along the way." He made some quick—and obviously nasty—motions with his hands, causing Serratura to laugh. "But sometimes I envy the backwoods country boy from Idaho who can barely speak his native English and has his naked toes buried in a steaming pile of horse manure."

"I get the drift," Serratura said. "At least then the bull shit is quite easy to spot, isn't it?"

Singer laughed and slapped a coin into the machine. Serratura glanced back once more to see what the professors were up to. They were seated on a bench beneath the Clock, clearly waiting his arrival. Zweck kept staring at his watch and occasionally giving it a tap, as if he were trying to speed it up. The other two were huddled close together, deep in animated conversation. Seppanen shook her head several times as Matlab tried to make a point by smiling and pressing a finger into the palm of his hand. It was obvious they wouldn't miss Serratura—and that made him feel even more secure in the decision he'd made. After all, he had plenty of time to catch up with the learned gossip on the following day.

"Eureka!" Singer exclaimed as a handful of coins came flying out of the slot machine. "It looks like I still have that old Vegas touch."

"You certainly do. No lemons for you."

"You know what they say about being lucky at cards, don't you? Well, that's me. As for love, four divorces attest to either a general failure of nerve or an inability to distinguish quality from quantity. Or, come to think of it, both at once."

He placed several more coins in the machine—and won each time, dumping the money into his pocket.

"That's amazing," Serratura said. "You could earn a living this way. And gas ranges be damned."

"Wouldn't that be something! But, after a few more flips, my luck invariably runs out. I guess I'd have to get married and divorced again to keep my lucky streak going a little longer."

"Doesn't sound like such a high price to me."

"Spoken like a man who hasn't yet had the pleasure of matching wits with an irate woman and a divorce lawyer on commission." He looked at his watch. "Oops, it's almost time for the history lesson. Come, Anthony—you don't mind me calling you that, do you? Professor Serratura sounds so formal."

"No, no. Anthony is just fine."

"Good, good. And you can call me Zeke. It's short for Ezekiel—which makes me sound like some prophet from the Old Testament. A profitable prophet, I guess you could call me."

Singer took Serratura's arm again and led him up one

of the glass escalators. The professors had given up by then and Serratura caught their backs heading away down the corridor that led to the outside. He wondered if Zweck would try to call him. It didn't matter. No one at the *pension* knew where he'd gone.

"I see you're admiring the Clock again," Singer said. "It's not very old, you know. Five years at the most. It was designed by a French physicist. Gitton, I believe, was his name. Anyway, he's in all the tourist brochures."

"Incredible," Serratura said. "The way it goes from the continuous action of the water to the ticking of the hands."

"To me, it's like magic. God as the master magician, hypnotizing us into believing that time does actually exist—and that it's a flow of something or other. She, I presume, sees the illusion, having created it in the first place."

"That's a very apt image." Serratura reached out to touch a hanging fern on the other side of the escalator. It was real. "While we're busy watching his—or her—left hand where time flies and winds down to nothing, we don't notice her right, the steady hand of eternity and the only one that truly counts when it comes down to the cosmic crunch."

"Cr. . . u. . . n. . . ch," Singer said, stamping his foot. "Is that a goose step I hear?"

"Now, now. God might be a petty bureaucrat and paper shuffler but I wouldn't go so far as to call her a crypto-Nazi. At least, not to her face."

"True, true," Singer said. "After all, he's the one writing the history, isn't he? That makes him the good guy."

The Multivision Theatre was pretty much what Serratura had expected, a capsule of history concentrating mostly on events from 1920 on: from the Golden Age of the city as one of the world's greatest metropolises to its present-day reincarnation. The one surprising thing was the fact the producers didn't gloss over the rise of the Nazis and the devastation of the city during the Second World War, a devastation that made modern Berlin all the more amazing.

"A veritable phoenix, isn't it?" Singer said, as they stepped out of the dark amphitheatre. "It makes one proud of the human spirit, a spirit that bends but can't be broken. Or perhaps a better image is that of an extraordinary plant cut right at ground level, left with only its roots intact. Seemingly dead, it will eventually sprout new shoots when it feels the time is right."

"Only to be cut again."

"Ah, my dear Anthony," Singer said. "You're too much the pessimist. Or perhaps it's your philosophic training, the concentrating on the overview and the long-term at the expense of the particulars. I think the particulars are just as important, don't you?"

"Depends on what you mean by particulars."

"There you go again. Particulars, you know. You, me, them. The stones. Whatever." He patted Serratura on the back. "Come on, my philosopher-friend, let me buy you a drink."

"Thank you," Serratura said, shaking his head. "But I think I ought to be heading back to the *pension*. I still have work to do on my paper before the conference starts tomorrow morning."

"Bah! One drink won't kill you. Come on, I know just the place to lift your spirits—and I won't take no for an answer. It's just down the street on Marburger Strasse. No one leaves Berlin without a visit to the Kabarett Chez Elles. It would be like going to Paris and not climbing the Eiffel Tower, like a trip to Rome without stopping at the Colosseum, like a journey to India and avoiding the Taj Mahal, like—"

"Okay, okay." Serratura held up his hands in defeat. "You win. Chez Elles, it is."

"Fantastic!" Singer exclaimed. "I knew you'd see it my way. I promise you you won't regret it."

Chez Elles was a dark, gaudy place bathed in a scarlet glow from a pair of spotlights that kept whizzing about the room and occasionally going into strobe mode. They came in between shows. A silver, glittery, tinsel-like curtain had been drawn across the stage. The doorman, who had greeted Singer as a long-lost brother, led them to one of the few empty tables. It was quite close to the stage, almost right up against it, in fact. Most of the others were occupied by shadowy couples who didn't bother hiding the obvious affection they had for one another. A few tables over Serratura caught a glimpse of a hand brazenly sliding up the inside of a thigh before the image vanished again; on the other side of them a pair seemed fused at the lips and doing exploratory work with their tongues. Others were seated at stools before a bar that stretched the width of the room. A true Berlin club, Serratura thought. Images straight out of a modern-day *Cabaret*.

"How do you like it so far?" Singer asked, face half in shadow. "Intimate, yes? Not the normal teen crowd and yet at the same time not overly sedated—although I hear they do have a wheelchair ready."

"It's . . . it's . . . unusual," Serratura said, squinting to bring things into focus, only to be stymied by the recurrent flash of the lights.

"If you think this is unusual, wait until you see the show! It'll knock your socks off." Singer was becoming more and more animated, as if shedding layers of reserve. "I've visited every cabaret and night club in Berlin—quite a feat in itself as there must be several hundred. But I can say without possibility of contradiction that this is the best of the lot. And tonight's show is super-special." He was now squirming with excitement in his seat. "Hans, the doorman, told me it's in honour of our friend Ronnie Reagan's visit tomorrow."

A waitress came over. She was wearing nothing but a leather bikini and a little jewel in her belly button. The jewel sparkled in the occasional light.

"Hey!" Singer said. "If it isn't my most favourite waitress in the whole wide world. How's it keeping up?" The waitress shrugged, holding the tray loosely under one arm. "So, Anthony, what'll it be? No! Cancel that. Let me order."

He said something in German. The waitress nodded and left, making her way nonchalantly to the bar.

"Not to worry," Singer said. "I asked for the usual. Nothing but the very best for my good friend the philosopher. After all, we only get to visit the night club of life but once. Unless, of course, you're into Eastern mysticism." The spotlight, before moving on, formed a halo against the back of his head. "Isn't it interesting that this tick-tock society, this clockwork nation of punctuality and preciseness has had periods where it has orgiastically embraced the blatantly nonrational? *Steppenwolf*, for example. *Sidhartha*. And we mustn't forget *Death in Venice*."

"Nor the Nazis."

"Nor the Nazis. Precisely. Is a dark romanticism merely the other side of the rational coin? Does everyday enthusiasm and gung-ho-ness lead to ultimate pessimism about the fate of the universe? We mustn't forget that Norse mythology says that good will not triumph and calls for the final defeat of the gods. How does it go? Let's see if I can remember it now. Oh yes:

'The sun turns black, earth sinks in the sea,
The hot stars fall from the sky,
And fire leaps high about heaven itself.
The gods are doomed and the end is death.'"

60

"For someone who calls himself an ignorant gas range businessman," Serratura said, "you're quite well-versed."

"Why, thank you. I had a brief—and, I may add, uncon-summated—love affair with the mystic, the deep heart of the unknown."

"Strange. For some reason, you don't strike me as the mystical kind."

"Oh but I was. You must believe me." He clapped his hands together. "Here it comes, my life story. Hope you don't mind—and stop me if it gets too boring."

"Promise."

"I guess I became interested when the shock of still be-ing alive wore off. That was in the early fifties. I was one of the lucky ones who had been allowed to emigrate to the U.S. after the war, thanks to some kind—and fairly well-off—patrons who paid a king's ransom for me. The very same people who were good enough to give me their name, as I've never known my real one. I suppose I should have been grateful but—ah, here come our goodies. Something to revive our spirits."

The waitress brought over a bottle buried in a bucket of ice. At first Serratura thought it was champagne but then he saw the shot glasses.

"This, my fine-feathered philosopher friend, is a par-ticular specialty of the house," Singer said, holding up the squarish bottle and pouring the clear thick liquid into the glasses. "It's an *eau de vie* we call *Korn*. Some folks drink it; some folks prefer to use it as lighter fluid. I personally don't smoke so I have no choice but to chug it."

"Oh dear," Serratura said, pulling away as he caught a whiff from the glasses. "That's some powerful."

"Now, now," Singer insisted, pushing the glass towards him. "You can't back out. That would be considered an in-sult not only to me but to this establishment. You wouldn't want to cause a scene, would you?"

"No," Serratura said, laughing. "I'm terrible at scenes."

"Good. To friendship then," Singer said, clinking his glass against Serratura's and downing the contents in one shot. "It wasn't always endless night in endless winter in those northern parts, you know. In fact, there's an appropriate passage in the *Elder Edda* that reads:

'I once was young and travelled alone.
I met another and thought myself rich.
Man is the joy of man.'"

"You're right. That's quite upbeat for those dour Norsemen," Serratura said, imitating Singer's example and almost choking on the burning fumes.

"It is, isn't it?" Singer refilled his glass and reached over to do the same with Serratura's. He protested but Singer wouldn't hear of it. "You must drink to appreciate my story. Or else I'll be forced to call Hans—the ex-wrestler—over to have a talk with you. Now, where was I?"

"You had just come to the States," Serratura said, feeling the warmth of the drink spread across his chest and down to his stomach before heading back up to befuddle his brain cells.

"Oh yes. Well, as I said, I must have been in shock during those early years because the reaction only came after I'd finished university. Here I was with a valuable commerce degree and I suddenly couldn't understand why I was alive. It seemed to me the most atrocious, senseless act of all. So I told my adopted family I was hitting the road. They were hysterical. They tried everything to dissuade me—from pleading to bribery to threats. They even succeeded in fixing an arranged marriage—the first and most painful of my four failures. But my mind was made up and I never even slept with my new wife before taking off with nothing but a knapsack. It was while hitch-hiking across the States that I discovered Norse mythology—in the form of a book of translations from the *Elder Edda* that I found in a little second-hand bookstore in the backwoods of Maine. It may sound silly now but I had this idea of being one of the ancient heroes on a quest. Do you know what I mean?"

"I think so, yes." This time Serratura cautiously sipped his drink.

"He knows he's doomed to failure but has no choice because the quest is predetermined for him. Norse Mythology is big on predestination. Anyway, he must carry out the quest or languish semi-human. It was all so pure and clean under those stars. I slept within the magic ring of stones; I bathed in ice-cold streams; I rolled through scorching dunes. I was the scorpion and the pack rat, the mountain laurel and the everglade magnolia, the crumbling sandstone and the sharp-edged quartz. I was everything and nothing. And I came out of it a completely different person, yet unchanged. On my return, my relatives greeted me with open arms, broke the news that my wife had divorced me, and found a high-level spot for me in the family appliance firm. And here I am, more than thirty years later, still able to spout some choice words of wisdom—even if they no longer have much meaning."

He laughed and poured both himself and Serratura another drink. Serratura was about to say something—probably about the slackness in his use of the word "meaning"—when the music started up, the curtains parted and they found themselves in the middle of an Indian attack on a circle of covered wagons.

"The Wild West comes to Berlin," Singer said, slapping his thigh and letting out a yelp. "Or Annie Oakley meets Brynhilde and cuts her off at the fjord."

It was indeed the Chez Elles rendition of *Annie Get Your Gun*, the cast got up in stylized cowboy and Indian outfits with their lower halves in the form of horses. They chased each other about the stage tossing tasseled lassoes and yip-yip-yippying. Then Annie herself came out, a sultry, hip-swinging gal with a wig in the shape of a Mohawk haircut, her jacket opened down to the navel and both guns firing. After blowing her pistol smoke away and winking broadly at the audience, she broke into *You Can't Get A Man With A Gun*.

Maybe it was the German accent or the fact she stomped about the stage and took several turns firing from between her legs, but the song suddenly assumed some very strange undertones Serratura didn't think were in the original: a combination of kinky sex and martial exuberance that would have had the audiences in the U.S. screaming sacrilege. Then, after several more scenes during which Buffalo Bill put on his Wild West show topless style and Sitting Bull puffed on what looked suspiciously like a hookah pipe, Annie herself sat astride a chair to face the audience and burst into a full-pelvic rendition of "Doin' What Comes Natur'lly."

> Still they raised a family
> Doin' what comes natur'lly
> There he is at ninety-three
> Doin' what comes natur'lly
> She gets all her stockings free
> Doin' what comes natur'lly.

"Isn't that fucking wild?" Singer shouted, so enthusiastic he forgot he was pouring again and managed to spill a good deal of the drink on the table. "That's okay. That's okay. Plenty more where that came from. Hey! Another round."

Serratura wanted to protest that they'd both had enough but somehow he couldn't work up the energy. So he slumped in his chair and stared at the drops of thick liquid sliding back down the inside of his glass.

"Serratura, my boy," Serratura said, out loud but mostly to himself. "I think you're about to get drunk. And you shouldn't, you naughty boy."

"What's that?" Singer yelled, bringing his face close to Serratura's. The same pleasant after-shave smell, now mixed with alcohol. "Did you say something?"

"Nothing, nothing," Serratura said, licking up the drops with his tongue. "Bring on the other bottle!"

"That's the spirit! Isn't that Annie just great?" Serratura nodded, looking back towards the stage. Annie was now doing a slow bump and grind with Buffalo Bill while a dozen Indians whooped around them, waving tomahawks in the shape of double-headed dildos. The waitress brought another bottle of the eau de vie which Singer immediately cracked open. "You should know Annie's a good friend of mine. Hans says she'll come over to our table after the show. That's right, my boy! You're going to meet a genuine star of the cabaret circuit."

"Oh goody," Serratura said, clapping his hands in what seemed slow motion. "I can't wait."

But Serratura must have fallen asleep after that because the next thing he remembered was Singer shaking him and telling him to wake up—and then seeing this blurred Amazonian figure standing beside him, hands on hips.

"Anthony, Anthony," Singer said, laughing. "Is that any way to treat a lady? This is Annie, our Annie."

"Annie? Oh hi, Annie." Serratura tried to stand up to take her hand but couldn't. Everything was coming from far away—even his own voice. "Sorry about that. Won't you sit down."

She plopped down in the chair next to him. Her perfume was overpowering. She kept staring at him, eyeing him up and down. Like a prize of some kind.

"I can tell Annie thinks you're cute," Singer said. "Very, very cute."

"Why, thank you." Serratura looked from one to the other, not quite knowing what was happening. "Tell her I think she's cute, too."

"Don't take this the wrong way, Anthony, but Annie has a proposition for you. I told her what you do and Annie thinks intellectuals are very attractive. They stimulate her—if you know what I mean."

"Intellectuals, yes," Serratura said. "I think I understand. Brain power and all that."

"That's it! You got it. Annie's turned on by brain power and thinks you ought to go home with her."

"She does, eh?" What am I doing? Serratura said to himself. I'm drunk and I'm flirting—and I like it. Louise, you're fading badly, melting into an undifferentiated puddle. No, that was from another musical, wasn't it?

"So, what do you say to that?" Singer said, patting him on the knee.

"What do I say to that?" Serratura slurred. "Sure, why not. Has she got some etchings to show me—or what?"

"Etchings?" Singer laughed. "She's got something a lot better than that."

Annie had taken Serratura's hand by this time and placed it on her shoulder. For lack of something better to do, he started rubbing her bare flesh. Without wasting any more time, she was up against his face, her tongue darting in and out of his mouth. Serratura felt a jolt in his mid-section—and it didn't matter much if something kept telling him a married man shouldn't be doing this. He responded, tasting the lipstick, the hot mint in her mouth. Then, she took his hand and slipped it under her dress, urging it up the inside of her thigh and pressing it firmly against her crotch. It was at that point that he felt the thick, hard lump there, the unmistakable outline of the penis beneath the dancing tights. He pulled back as if he'd been stung. Or had placed his hand directly into a fire.

"Oh God," he said—and bolted straight up in his chair. Sat up much too quickly because the blood rushed from his head and the room started to go in and out of focus, appearing and disappearing with the strobes.

"Is something the matter?" Singer asked, the concern on his face coming through as a cross between a grimace and a leer. "You're not going to be sick, are you? You're as pale as a ghost. Tell me if you're going to be sick. It wouldn't do to get sick all over the floor."

Serratura's head was whirling. He shut his eyes tight. That helped for a moment. But then he saw blobs of red behind his eyeballs—the strobes flashing by. And Annie reached for him again, causing him to snap open his eyes. All around him couples were fondling one another in tender foreplay. Or dancing slowly, languidly across the floor. There was the waitress—who, Serratura could now see, was really a waiter—with his hand on the bare chest of one of the Indians. And Hans the doorman leading Buffalo Bill in a fox-trot. And. . . .

"She's . . . she's. . . ," Serratura stuttered, pointing in every direction in turn—at Annie, at Singer, at the couples on the dance floor, at the chipped cupids on the ceiling. "They're all—"

"What!" Singer exclaimed, roaring with incredulous laughter. Roaring so he had to hold his stomach. "So you think they're. . . . How boorish!"

He turned to Annie and said something in German. Both of them were now laughing and Annie stood there shaking her head and waggling her finger.

"You poor man, you," Singer said, patting Serratura on the head. "They're not, you know. Not at all what you think. Just having a little fun, that's all. Just having a little fun."

The words echoed through the club; the laughter spread—as if the joke, the misunderstanding, the faux pas was being passed from person to person. Either through word of mouth or more direct sexual contact. And the sound of that laughter—the roar of that laughter getting louder and louder—was the last thing Serratura heard before he collapsed face first onto Annie's lap, cheek pressed firmly against her bulge.

Postscript II

It was very late in the evening when Ryle finally turned off the computer, having in the meantime made two separate copies on diskette of Chiavetta's recovered files. Just in case those mysterious after-images decided to pull their vanishing act again, this time possibly forever. He had read the file labeled **Friday.Doc** twice. Apart from the account at the beginning of the main character's father and the last few very odd pages describing the homosexual-transvestite encounter in the bar, the document seemed a straightforward retelling of a trip to Berlin before the wall had come down.

Not one to make hasty judgements, Ryle didn't immediately jump to any conclusions about a connection between Giulio A. Chiavetta and Antonio G. Serratura (except for the obvious one of author and creation, of course). At the same time, as a psychiatrist, he couldn't very well ignore the possibility of some such connection—even if only in Chiavetta's mind. He told himself he'd sleep on it. And, now that he had doubles of Chiavetta's files, he could inspect them at his leisure in his own office.

But, before he settled down for the night, Ryle couldn't help taking a look through Chiavetta's other files. Or profiles, rather. The ones kept in the hospital's newly computerized library system. Ryle called them up now on his own terminal. Previous to Chiavetta's breakdown, diagnosed by Ryle himself as a prolonged schizophrenic episode with cataleptic symptoms and severe hallucinatory side effects, the patient had been employed as a stationary engineer in

69

the boiler room of a Montreal-based multi-national food-processing plant.

In fact, Chiavetta had been a model employee, having performed that task efficiently and without complaint for nearly 20 years—straight out of vocational training school. Until, that is, he suddenly stood up and wandered off in the middle of a night shift two years before, leaving the boiler room unattended for the first time ever. As well, he was single, resided in a one-room flat above a hardware store in the Montreal suburb of Verdun and had no living relatives—at least none that had come forward on this side of the Atlantic. That was the information obtained through his medical and employment records. And through speaking to his bosses, co-workers and his landlord, the owner of the hardware store.

However, when asked to fill out some standard forms during his admittance to the hospital, Chiavetta had scribbled next to "Occupation": Circus Performer, Freelance. And for "Civic Status," he'd marked: Married, One Child. As well, when Ryle had asked why he thought he'd been brought to the hospital, Chiavetta had answered in his matter-of-fact way: "Why, don't you know? I killed someone. I wasn't myself at the time but I still killed someone. And this is where they put people who kill people. Isn't it?" Ryle inquired who it was he'd killed. Chiavetta had responded with a snicker: "My wife and child, of course. Who else would I want to kill?"

There was one problem with Chiavetta's self-accusation: no proof was ever found that he'd actually killed someone—let alone a nonexistent wife and child. When he was confronted with these inconsistencies, Chiavetta continued to insist—even leading police and hospital staff to a house where the murders were supposed to have taken place. The startled occupants—an engineer and his wife—knew nothing about any murders. But, after the situation was explained to them, they allowed Chiavetta to lead the police to the master bedroom.

"There," he said, pointing to the bed. "There's your proof. I slit their throats. The blood soaked all the way through the mattress."

Ryle had tried to tell Chiavetta there was nothing there. Chiavetta retreated into silence. At the time, the doctors had taken this confession, this insistence he'd committed a hideous crime, as part of his schizophrenic episode, a more or less permanent hallucination. These new files, however, provided Ryle with another approach, another way to handle the deep-seated delusion. Perhaps, they might even be the key that would finally unlock the mystery that was Giulio A. Chiavetta. Perhaps he could get to Chiavetta through Serratura.

Ryle rubbed his hands together. He could hardly wait to get started. He even had the title for his paper all laid out: *Literary Allusion or Literal Illusion: Identity in the Schizophrenia Between Fact and Fiction.* Or perhaps *Fiction and the Real World* might be a better dichotomy. In any case, all he needed now was for the police to find Chiavetta and bring his patient back to him in a neat little bundle. And that was simply a matter of time. Chiavetta couldn't possibly cope for long on the streets of Montreal. He was just too noticeable. From his ripped hospital gown to his deliberate, tightrope walk, there was no way he could blend in for any period of time. Not to mention the fact the temperature was hovering close to the freezing mark.

What Ryle hadn't counted on, however, was the natural cunning of the unbalanced. Of the single-minded. Giulio A. Chiavetta, ex-stationary engineer and self-styled freelance circus performer, hadn't simply rushed onto the streets of Montreal, arms out awaiting crucifixion. Nor had he done anything else that might attract attention. Instead, he had edged along the waterfront boardwalk, making sure to stay in the shadows and avoiding all contact with other human beings. Once off the boardwalk and onto the streets, he navigated the back alleys, slithering among the garbage and the thick-headed cats preparing for another winter.

Now, he was down inside an underground locker storage area used by train travelers at Central Station. Except for a few drunks and people sleeping on their bundled belongings, the place was deserted. Chiavetta searched up and down the aisles, his finger following the numbers, until he found the locker he was looking for. He then unclenched his left hand. The key, along with an impression in his flesh, lay there, all sweaty. He inserted the key in the locker and pulled it open. Inside was a large green garbage bag.

Chiavetta grinned. The bag contained clothing, a wallet, a passport, keys and a name tag. Also inside the locker was a brown leather briefcase with the initials "A.G.S." on it. From there, Chiavetta proceeded to the nearest washroom, entered a stall and changed into the clothes he'd picked up from the locker: a grey, pinstriped suit, expensively lavish tie and polished patent-leather shoes. The pants were a little baggy on him, the result of two years of hospital meals. But, with some belt-tightening, it wasn't very noticeable. In fact, it might even be fashionable.

He placed the torn and charcoaled hospital robe in the garbage bag and the wallet, passport, keys and name tag in his jacket pocket. Then, briefcase in hand, he re-emerged from the locker storage area, nonchalantly tossing the locker key down the grating of an air-circulation vent. Once back outside, Chiavetta looked for an appropriate men's clothing store. The nearest one turned out to be Pete's Shop: Ordinary Clothes For Ordinary Folks. He smashed the front window with a trash can and, ignoring the alarm, grabbed one of the display mannequins, which came complete with suit, shirt and shoes. In an alley a few blocks away, while police sirens headed for the scene of the crime, Chiavetta took out his hospital robe and threw it on the ground. Then, he stripped the mannequin and placed the stolen suit inside the bag before losing himself in the maze of tunnels and underpasses that perforated this section of the city.

In the morning, police reported back to say that, though they still hadn't found Chiavetta, they'd made some definite progress in their search. A robe with the name of the hospital stitched on the inside of the collar had been found— along with a mannequin. And not two blocks from where a men's shop had been burglarized and a single suit stolen: a brown, mohair job with corduroy patches on the elbows. The kind professors like to wear, the policeman added.

Sounds like our man, Ryle said, again rubbing his hands together as he glanced up from the computer screen. That's our poor, deluded fellow alright. Just look for someone wearing that type of suit and wandering around the city as if he's in a total daze. Should be easy. Only please be gentle with him when you pick him up. He's completely harmless to everyone but himself. He wouldn't hurt a fly. Or, at least, he's never given any indication of wanting to hurt a fly. This last part Ryle said to himself, not wanting to confuse the policeman. After the policeman had left, Ryle turned and went back to reading Chiavetta's files. He was anxious to get to the second part of Serratura's adventures.

11: File—Saturday.doc

Serratura: "Towards the end, my father began to slip bad-ly—as if someone had suddenly greased the slope. Or had tilted it close to a 90 degree angle. He took no more inter-est in the hobbies that had so intensely anchored him down from the time he was a child—his wine-making, his garden-ing, his construction of wooden boxes and spoons. And he no longer came up to the other levels of the house to join in daily life, preferring to remain in his basement fortress. He ate all his meals there, slept there, listened to his grand operatic excerpts there, performed his toiletries there.

"Our biggest fear was that he would die—and we wouldn't know it. That we wouldn't be there for his final release from a bitterness which we could sense was like a coiled spring inside him, wound so tightly it no longer re-sembled a spring so much but a solid block of rusted iron, a fused mass of twisted resentments. So, we made a pact. As far as humanly possible, one of us would try to visit him at least once a day. We took turns on a weekly basis: myself, my brother and my sister—with our mother checking on him when no one else was available.

"Except for the memories of what once had been, it wasn't an onerous task. While the operas played themselves out in the background like a low hum, my father sat on his favourite sofa and talked. All that was required of the com-panion was to nod on occasion, though no one was really sure he even noticed that anymore. He talked about what-ever came to mind. It was as if all the neural connections had been loosened and one thing led to another with the greatest of ease. The words metamorphosed till they became unrecognizable, the products of an interior echolalia, perhaps, lost in their convoluted journey to the surface.

"Often, when it was my turn, I tried to figure out what exactly my father was saying, how the various words—and parts of words—fitted together. And what was the sense of it. I did it partly out of filial concern and partly as basic material for my own researches into language structure and the nature of logic. But it turned out to be an impossible task. The only common thread I could make out was that my father was falling further and further back, that his memories were becoming longer-term, more dense and subterranean. And that some of them had shifted onto different planes so that they collided with others that had had absolutely nothing to do with them in the first place.

"What came to mind was "cross-linking"—like when two totally different files in a computer having nothing to do with each other suddenly find themselves sharing the same space. With disastrous consequences. I knew the term because it happened to me once—resulting in an unholy marriage between a paper on Quine and one on Chomsky.

"During all this time, the one thing my father held onto was the box filled with his mementos of the war. He kept that by his side on the sofa, one arm always protectively across it. Any attempt to remove that box would lead to a horrible agitation, a terrible outcry, like that of a cat being tortured. Even that, however, was nothing compared to when we tried forcibly to carry him out of the basement one day—to take part in the party we'd planned for his seventieth birthday. He threw himself on the floor and began to scrabble about with his hands and knees, as if he were digging. As if he were trying to make himself vanish beneath the linoleum and carpeting. Occasionally, he stared up at us with a look that sought approval, with a look that said: 'You can't take me away now. I'm doing all the right things to stay here. I've fulfilled all my obligations. I'm happy where I am. Believe me. You can't take me away now.'

"There was no way any of us had the courage to pick him up again, to remove him forcibly from that dimly lit world he'd created for himself. It would have been the height of cruelty. Besides, we would have had to tie him in his chair to keep him from dashing down into the basement again. We would have had to listen to his anguished moaning as the rest of us sang 'For He's A Jolly Good Fellow.' We would have had to stuff birthday cake into his mouth. So we just walked back up the stairs and went our separate ways, leaving our mother to weep—and sweep—in the kitchen."

The next morning, you awake with a start and find yourself back at the *pension*, lying face down across your own bed—in nothing but socks and underclothes. Or rather one sock, to be precise, and shorts. You look up, squinting. A shaft of light slants through the window and directly onto your face. The brightness hurts your eyes so that you have to squeeze them shut again. Your stomach is queasy; your mouth dry and furry. There's a constant pounding inside your head, like the thwacking of a stone over and over against a rubber-lined wall. It becomes even less bearable when you try to sit up on the edge of the bed. The room is spinning, leaving you with the sensation you're floating away from yourself, abandoning parts of yourself.

You look around, gripping the walls for support. There are clothes scattered all about: trousers on the floor; tie on the door-knob; shirt on the window sill; second sock hanging from the desk lamp. You realize you're in the throes of a massive hangover, something not experienced to this extent since your early undergraduate days of all-night tavern crawls and tequila-guzzling contests. The days when you had decided all you wanted to do was punish your father for his lack of any displays of affection.

For a few seconds, you sit staring out the window, watching the dust-laden sunlight across wilted flowers and struggling to reconstruct what had happened the previous night. The parts that come percolating to the surface are not very reassuring. Or pretty. Had you really ended up in a transvestite bar after inexplicably standing up your sophisticated dinner companions from the philosophy conference for a supplier of gas ovens whom you hardly know and who is "into mysticism" as he so proudly proclaims? Had the pistol-packing "heroine" of *Annie Get Your Gun* made a crude pass at you? Or had you made one at her? Him? Whatever. Had you danced with someone with a five o'clock shadow and the taste of mint chewing gum on his breath? Better yet: How had you managed to make it back to the safety of your room when you could hardly stay awake, let alone walk? And where had you been between your collapse onto Annie's lap and your collapse onto the bed?

Oh God, you mutter, holding your head. Careers had been shattered, rendered null and void, by cracks and perceived moral slips no wider than a hair's breadth. This is a lacuna that threatened to swell to the size of the Grand Canyon. Stay tuned tomorrow for the next unpredictable episode of *Serratura: Not So Young but Still Quite Restless.* Wherein the protagonist—respectable philosopher and respected teacher by day, wild and crazy gambler-sexpot-pervert by night—once more sheds his petty bourgeois inhibitions for a turgid psycho-sexual display of Gargantuan proportions, a display seldom before witnessed in this corner of the universe and videotaped in whole or in part for your exclusive pleasure. Just send $9.98 to: The Chairman, Committee for the Investigation of Non-Rational Behaviour by Supposedly The Creme de la Creme of Rational Beings, Deviant Acts

Division. And then after you've finished getting your jollies, expedite the tape to the personnel file of your local philosophy department head—anonymously, of course, for the best effect.

You're babbling—and you know it. Whatever had been in those drinks is probably still coursing its way through your veins. What you need now is a shower to clear the cobwebs—the colder the better. Followed by a hearty breakfast. Besides, you tell yourself, it couldn't be as bad as all that. Here I am, in a strange city, amid strangers. No one knows me from Adam here. No one cares what I do—or what the sexual preferences of my companions may be. All they want from me is my logic paper—and that isn't due to be read until tomorrow.

You stand up to test your legs. They're still wobbly and you have to lean on the bedpost for support. But—thank God for small mercies—the room is no longer spinning. The musical alarm on your wrist watch goes off: no simple Mickey Mouse tune this but a synthesized version of Beethoven's *Fifth*. This is one time though when you aren't in the mood to hear it all the way through. Not really in the mood at all. You struggle to click it off—and check the time. Ten o'clock. At least you haven't overslept. The first reading at the university is to take place at noon. A very civilized hour. That gives you plenty of time to shower. Perhaps even to get rid of your headache.

As you stumble about searching for a change of underwear, the mystery of how you made it back to your room is cleared up. On the writing desk, next to the logic paper and your father's little black book, you spot a hand-scribbled note:

"Anthony, old buddy. I think it's safe to call you that now, isn't it? Especially after what we've been through together. Sorry you missed what turned out to be one hell of a lovely time last night. After you decided to snooze, we all got up on stage to do an encore of the show. I played Sitting Bull—should've seen my horns and peace pipe—and we wanted you for Buffalo Bill. But, even though we put the cowboy hat on you and tried just about everything to spur you on, we just couldn't get you to wake up. Silly boy. So Annie and I took you home—after we had our way with you! Just kidding. No need to get upset. We're all honourable people here. All kidding aside though, Annie would dearly like—no love—to see you again. I can't understand it myself but you seem to have made quite an impression on her. Must be all that brain power.

"P.S.: If you're wondering why you're wearing only one sock, it's because you wouldn't allow us to take it off. You kept yelling something about a deformed toe—a piggyback toe, I think you called it—and how embarrassed you were to let anyone see it. P.P.S.: Annie's one hell of a sweet, fun person once you get to know her. I mean, *really* get to know her. Her number is the same as the one on my card as I stay with her when I'm in Berlin. In case you've lost that, it's 883-50-62. Call her anytime—day or night. Or you can always catch her doing her thing at Chez Elles most evenings. She's performing in *Show Boat* next. If you think she made a great Annie, you should see her vamping her way through 'Where's The Mate for Me.' Ciao, baby. Hope to see you again soon.

"Your friendly restaurant supplier. Kisses and love."

What have I got myself into? you say, rubbing a fist against your throbbing skull. What exactly am I doing? This is crazy, absolute lunacy of the first order. Make that second order. No time for silly jokes. You crumple the note and throw it in the wastepaper basket, determined never to set eyes on Singer or his weird friends again—even if Berlin **is** a small place where all the dirt roads meet. Besides, what was the idea of referring to Annie—or whatever his real name is—as a "she"? Why can't they at least come right out and spill it? Are they that afraid of admitting to themselves who they really are—especially in this day and age when no one really cares anymore? Or has the delusion become so deeply ingrained it has taken on the air of reality?

The two bird-like old ladies you bumped into the day before are just finishing their breakfasts as you step out of your room, barefoot and wearing only a bathrobe. You smile politely and nod in their direction. They bob back, pursing their mouths, and continue to spread marmalade on their toast. Your stomach rumbles. It strikes you the last time you've eaten is on the plane. No wonder the drinks had hit you so hard. You're almost tempted to join the ladies at the table. Yes, why not?

But, as you approach, you see the small sign on it that reads: "Breakfast period over. Service is now regrettably unavailable." Ha! It seems to be aimed directly at you, placed there expressly no doubt by good old Fritz. Breakfast is on the fritz this morning. Or not on the fritz. No matter. The university will most likely serve up some coffee and doughnuts for the invited guests. So Fritz be damned. You turn down the corridor—and halt for a moment to orient yourself. Why do you experience a feeling of vague foreboding here, as if you were running a gauntlet? The doors, of course, the doors that don't quite fit, that make it possible for someone to come bursting out, to come rushing at you without warning. *The Cabinet of Dr. Caligari*, that's it. That's what it reminds you of. Visions from the days of your McGill University Film Society membership.

It doesn't help that the linoleum—in alternate patterns of black and white squares—is cold and clammy beneath your feet. You surmise that it has just been washed and hasn't had time to dry in spots—especially where the plywood has worn through. Your hypothesis proves correct as you catch a glimpse of a wet mop disappearing into one of the rooms. Frieda, no doubt, who doesn't need brains because she can do wonderful housework and has a nose for dirt and punishment. At the same time, you can hear music from the far end. A woman's operatic voice—high-pitched, crystal-clear and piercing—struggles to make itself heard above the clash of cymbals and thunder of drum rolls.

You hold your head as the noise reverberates inside it. Not really what you need just now. It feels as if someone is probing your brain with the tip of a sharp knife, flicking at the nerve endings just for the fun of it, just to see what connections could be made—and unmade. The music grows louder, more insistent, as you approach the washroom. It's coming from the same room you'd passed the previous day, the one where harsh, grating voices had been repeating something—a name or a phrase—over and over again. Only this time the door is open.

A tiny wizened old man—a midget really no more than four feet high—goose-steps mechanically out into the corridor. Everything he wears is oversized: from the military cap that bobs as he marches to the embroidered jacket whose sleeves reach down to his knuckles; from the trousers that drag on the floor to the boots that push up into his crotch. The entire ensemble gives the impression he's shrunk without realizing it. He reminds you of a cross between a parade soldier and a member of the Salvation Army standing on a street corner at Christmas. His hands wave in the air before him, as if he were conducting an orchestra, as if he were the one responsible for the music.

"*Guten Morgen,*" you say, taking the opportunity to get in a little language practice. "*Ich heisse* Anthony Serraruta. I mean Serratura! *Wie geht es Ihnen?*"

Without ceasing to conduct, the old man midget turns

slowly towards you, looks you leisurely up and down several times and then, without in any way acknowledging your presence, turns away again. Finally, after staring at the wall directly in front of his door for several seconds, he does an about face and heads back into his room. As you cross the open door, you can't help but look in. The room is dominated by a huge, four-poster bed. It's larger even than the one in which you'd seen the old woman lying the previous day. The old man is standing with his back to you next to an old-fashioned gramophone—the kind you wind up with the speaker in the shape of a cornucopia.

The gramophone has been placed on a low, very ornate chest decorated across the front with what you quickly realize is an elaborate, gold-coloured swastika. The swastika glitters in a menacing way, as if it were about to fly off, a whirling four-edged scythe to decapitate unbelievers and others with racial impurities. On the other side, a film projector whirs, sending blurred images in black and white up against the drawn curtain that serves as a screen. You catch a glimpse of a huge crowd waving in unison towards a speaker who's ensconced on a high pedestal and exhorting them on.

There must be several hundred thousand people in that shadowy crowd, all doing the same thing—like flowers in a windswept field. You can see their mouths opening and closing but no sound comes out until the old man midget puts a new record on the turntable and gives it a whirl. You recognize them as the same scratchy voices you'd heard the day before. Only now you can understand what they're saying. They repeat the words "*Sieg Heil!*" over and over again. The old man midget lifts his own arm in jerky salute, slicing across the projector image, and removes his cap. Then he turns abruptly towards you and he, too, begins to repeat the words in a respectful tone that seems to combine pride, longing and regret. No, you see that he's only mouthing them, not actually saying them. A wisp of white hair falls across his forehead. He brushes it back. There are tears in his vividly blue eyes, tears he allows to flow down his cheeks and then wipes abruptly—and angrily—with the back of his hands. You, not knowing what else to do, smile sheepishly and continue down the corridor.

Obviously a nutcase, you say to yourself. One of those *idée fixe* people that Singer had mentioned on the plane. One of those trapped in his own vision, a vision that won't allow him to move forward because it's circular in shape and constantly keeps looping back on itself, onto the point that makes it real. Thank God they've been rendered harmless in the world of today, you tell yourself. And for the same reasons they can't escape the past: outmoded weaponry and less than deadly aim.

Right, you say with a hint of bitterness. Neat and tidy. Almost gift-wrapped in its symmetry and ease of analysis. And look who's doing the talking, look who's doing the analysis. No kinks in your primrose path, eh Serratura? Nothing undermining your straight and narrow. No disturbances to make you hesitate in your well-ordered and quantified universe. Snap out of it, Serratura, you say to yourself. This is a bad time for doubting of any kind, let alone professional skepticism, something you've always despised in your colleagues.

You're about to enter the washroom when Fritz comes down the second corridor. One of his hands supports the woman you'd seen in bed the day before; the other holds jewelled leashes for the two dogs. They start yapping the moment they see you, an intensely irritating howl that makes you want to kick them both through the first convenient set of goal posts.

"Ah, Der Professor," Fritz says, fawning. Then he turns to the dogs. "*Dumm! Blodsinn! Halt's Maul!*"

They yelp one last time and then scurry to hide behind the woman, obviously their protector, elegantly dressed in a long, flowing gown and with a black veil across the top half of her face. The whole affair topped by one of those turbans that had last been popular during the 1920s.

"Professor Serraruta—"

"It's Serratura," you correct.

"Sorry, sorry," Fritz says. "I have difficulty with foreign names." He grins. "At any rate, I would like to introduce you to my mother. We are going for our daily stroll. It is how we prefer to start off each day. Excellent for the heart." He pounds his chest.

"How do you do?" you say, holding out a hand which she shakes limply. "Lovely morning for a walk."

"*Enchantée*," she says in a high-pitched voice that seems on the verge of breaking.

"No, mother," Fritz says, yelling right up against her face. "He is Canadian, not French."

"Ah, Canadian," she says. "*Güt, güt.* Toronto, *ja?*"

"No, Montreal," you say. "And I do happen to speak some French."

"*Güt, güt.* Toronto *ist* nice."

"My mother is a little hard of hearing," Fritz says. "You must excuse her."

"No need to apologise. My mother is, too. At least, when she wants to be."

"So, are we feeling a tiny bit more like it this morning, Herr Professor?" Fritz asks, the hint of a smile on his face.

"More like it?" you repeat, putting on your best possible blank look, the one reserved for students who asked impertinent questions in the middle of a lengthy and complicated proof. "What do you mean?"

"Ah so," Fritz says with a theatrical wink. "I understand to perfection. We will keep it a tiny little secret between us and the mouse, yes. As long as one has enjoyment, is that not so? I, too, would like to go out more often but with my mother and sister to look after . . . well, you know how the affair goes."

"Not really," you say curtly, hoping to cut off the conversation then and there.

"Ah, you are so very lucky," Fritz says. Do you detect a note of condescension, a conspiracy among thieves? "To care for invalid people is very burdening, is it not?" He waves his hand in dismissal. "But enough of my troubles. Tell me. Have you known your friends long?" When you don't answer right away, he continues: "I am making reference, of course, to the two gentlemen who were so kind to bring you home last night."

"No, no—and they're not my friends," you say, thinking: Oh God, he saw me with them. What'll I do now? Tell the truth, of course. Or as much of it as I could safely get away with. "No, not friends of mine at all. I just met them for the first time last night. At a club I went to. Strangers, really. Perfect strangers."

"Ah, I am very glad to hear that," Fritz says, leaning close to you in order to whisper. His breath smells of mints. You note that it seems a common Berlin scent. "I do not wish to alarm you but I feel I should tell you. Or I would not forgive myself if something should be wrong. You know that they are, without a doubt, *Schwuler*—ah, how do you say it in English?—faggots. Queers. Bumsen boys. I have a nose for such things." He touches his nose. "I say this as your friend, you understand. We must protect our visitors to beautiful Berlin. We cannot give them an impression of error. We must not let them think that it is a city of deviations. Although a man may be in need of a good whore on the occasion to keep the spirits up. Is that not so? And of those we have more than enough. Even I am mildly aware of several—if I may ever be of service."

For a whole host of reasons, this man irritates you, who are normally good-natured and slow to anger despite your severe demeanour. Perhaps it's just Fritz's general presentation and manner. Or that "nod, nod, nudge, nudge, wink, wink" approach to life. A perpetual sneer like a slimy film covering everything it surveys or touches. Whatever, you want to quickly disabuse him of any ideas he may have of forming a bond between the two of you.

"Some of my closest friends happen to be gay," you say, wondering where the transition has taken place so that Singer and "Annie" suddenly qualify right up there with "some of my closest friends." "And I don't think they really enjoy being called faggots, queers or any other pejoratives you may come up with in your spare time."

"That is so, *ja?*" Fritz says, unveiling a crooked grin to go along with the impish tilt of his head. "In that circumstance, the best of luck to you. You will be in need of it."

"What do you mean by that?" you demand. "What are you trying to imply? I'll have you know—"

"Nothing, *Herr* Professor Serraruta," Fritz says, holding up his hands. "I wish to imply nothing in the extreme. If you do not mind, I will take my mother for the walk now. Come, Dumm. Blodsinn. *Raus!*"

He yanks the two dogs viciously, the whole time with that grin on his face. They come skittering across the floor, sliding by you like two rags—but not before leaving a pair of dribbles next to your shoes. You barely have a chance to swing open the washroom door when Frieda comes dashing, slipping, sliding out. She overshoots her mark and has to turn back. Then, she slops a wet mop onto the linoleum where the dogs have peed. Head down, kerchief tight, she scrubs, completely oblivious of the fact you're standing right there, watching her. Then she gives out a sigh and vanishes again, reversing her entrance act. Maybe she does have a head for nothing but cleaning up after all, you say to yourself, as you shut the door behind yourself. And immediately feel the uncharitableness of that thought—acting, God forbid, just like the despicable Fritz.

After a quick shower and shave, during which you think up more retorts to counter Fritz's redneck comments (and to do penance for your own trespass against "poor Frieda," as you've taken to calling her in your mind), you dress, slip on your earphones, pick up your briefcase and head for the nearest U-Bahn station. On your way there, you catch the very end of the demonstration to protest U.S. involvement in Central America. Outnumbered and herded along by a line of riot police, the last of the marchers—a small group wearing skeleton body suits and skull masks—stagger down the street, pulling a cart with a coffin on it that has been draped in an American flag.

A troupe of musicians brings up the rear. One plays the flute while several others beat on a variety of drums and tambourines. It's a lively tune—evoking snow-capped mountains and deep, golden pools of water—and not at all in keeping with the sombre mood. The same dichotomy exists between the ribald image of Ronald Reagan hanging in effigy—a huge red, white and blue penis bouncing before him—and the dirty, yellow-coloured steam that's rising from the various sewer outlets, rising with a gloomy hiss as if, somewhere, safety valves for the spirit are being released. I wonder if that's the methane gas, you think, before descending into the station. But of course not, you correct yourself. Methane is supposed to be odourless—and this stinks most foul.

You flip the tape and turn the machine on at the appropriate place:

"Tourists will find that the most amazing thing about the Berlin subway is that it works on the honour system. That is correct! There are no ticket booths and one-way gates. Helpful attendants are there only to give directions, to reunite parents with their strays and, if lucky, to prevent the occasional suicide. Though this is a pretty difficult task when the extent of the system is considered. On occasion, because this is, after all, the modern world, inspectors will go from car to car checking to make sure passengers have their tokens properly stamped and issuing 50 deutschmark tickets to those who have sneaked on. Naughty, naughty. But Berliners, for the most part, pay as a matter of course. We all take immense pride in a clean and efficient transportation system that effectively blankets the city.

"Before boarding, please study a map of the U-Bahn network to find out where you are going. Or ask one of the attendants, some of whom even speak English. It is virtually impossible to get lost. As an aside, the names of the U-Bahn stations provide a quick read of the not-so-subtle differences between West and East Berlin. In the West, you will find Kaiserdamm and Bismarck-strasse; in the East, Rosa-Luxemburg-Platz and Leninallee."

You emerge at the Oskar-Helene-Heim station—easy to remember as it comes right before Onkel Toms Hutte. You wonder how popular Harriet Beecher Stowe's novel is in Berlin to have a U-Bahn station named after it. Once on the Freie Universität campus in suburban Dahlem, it's even harder getting lost than it was on the subway. Large bright signs announce the conference and give directions to the university's main auditorium where the opening day ceremonies and the more important readings are to take place.

It strikes you that using such a large auditorium is a bit optimistic on the part of the conference's organizers—especially as, in your experience, the summer sessions tend to attract fewer participants than any other time of year. Back in North America, even at the height of the winter term when students are looking for a warm place to park themselves, most philosophy seminars would be happy to fill a 25-seat reading room. Unless, of course, the university is able to nab one of the really big stars of the circuit—a Chomsky, for example. Or a Derrida. Then, they'd move to one of the mid-sized halls.

But, despite the lack of a superstar draw, the people in charge of the First Wittgenstein World Symposium on The Realism/Anti-Realism Debate in Contemporary Philosophy obviously know what they're doing. The auditorium is packed to the rafters—with several hundred students filing in and battling for spots. Most have brought lunches and are obviously planning to settle in for the duration. Ushers carry portable chairs to place along the side and back walls. Those who can't find seats are stretched out in the aisles.

There's a buzz in the air, a sense of excitement and expectation that you've seldom before felt at one of these dos. Not only do these people take their politics seriously but they don't do a bad job with their philosophy either. You check the brochure for the day's roster, hoping that will give you a clue of some kind. Following the opening comments by Zweck, the conference is to lead off with *Meaning, Bivalence and Anti-Realism: Can Classical Logic Be Preserved or Must We Toss out the Baby with the Bath Water?*—or at least the German equivalent. Ah, the old true or false, take-it-or-leave-it gambit—no ands, ifs, buts or maybes about it. Next comes *A Marxist Interpretation of the Wittgensteinian "Criterion" Dilemma.* Now, that's a real rabble-rouser, a guaranteed drawing card, you say with a laugh. Or how about: *Intuitionist Logic: A Constructivist Approach to Non-Existent Objects?* Right. If that doesn't get them, nothing will. Yeah, right.

"Professor Serratura," a voice calls out from the front of the auditorium. "Over here."

You look up and recognize Zweck, the kindly host. He's waving at you from a table next to the podium. You wave back. Zweck motions that you should make your way down to the front.

"Do you always get this many people for the opening of a philosophy symposium?" you ask after pushing through the crowd and nearly tripping several times over the legs of those in the aisles.

"I would dearly love to say yes," Zweck says, smiling while taking your hand and squeezing it between both of his. "But unfortunately it would not be the truth. It is customary to get a good attendance—but nothing at all of this magnitude."

"Oh," you say, spotting Seppanen. She's already seated at the table with a dozen or so other invited guests. Matlab paces nervously back and forth in front of her—occasionally stopping to say something or to make a point of some kind. After Seppanen shakes her head several times, Matlab abruptly turns and leaves. "A mystery guest, then. Who is it? Putnam? Hallett? Travis?"

"No, no," Zweck says, laughing, "nothing like that. And we do not offer door prizes either—although it might be something to seriously consider in the future. No, this is the brainstorm of one of our first-year lecturers. From the graduate school at the University of Buenos Aires, if you must believe it. She gave the suggestion that the beginning students be made to attend—in order to listen to the papers being presented on opening day. For papers being read in English, translations will be made available—and vice versa. And, to make things more interesting, the essays produced by the students on the proceedings will be enumerated for 50 per cent of their marks."

"Brilliant!" you say, looking around at all the students sitting with notepads or tape recorders in one hand and roast beef sandwiches in the other. "That guarantees not only attendance but attentiveness as well."

"Yes," Zweck says, taking the opportunity to direct traffic. "I had the intuition it was an excellent idea. And a little smack of blackmail never hurt anyone. Come. Take a seat. The others are already in their places and we are just about set to roll the ball. I hope you do not mind but I have taken the liberty to put you next to Seppanen. We call her Our Lady of The DayGlo Hair. I believe it is purple this morning but that may change before the day is out. The advantage, of course, is that she is a perfect speaker of English, having done most of her graduate work at Harvard. Have you met by any circumstance?"

"No," you say. "At least not officially. But that's her sitting over there, isn't it?"

You point towards the table where Seppanen sits sipping coffee nervously from a Styrofoam cup.

"Yes," Zweck says, shaking his head, as you walk in her direction. "Kianta Seppanen does stand out, does she not?"

"Very. Like a furry and well-striped candy-cane."

Zweck lets out a guffaw and leads you to the empty place beside her.

"Ah, here we are," he says, pulling back the chair. "Professor Seppanen, may I introduce Professor Serratura."

"Hello," you say, sitting down. "I've been so looking forward to meeting you."

"You stood us up last night, isn't that so?" Seppanen

says, gulping the last of her coffee and staring down into the dregs as if seeking an answer there to her question.

"Now, now," Zweck says as he walks away. "Do not be too hard on the poor boy. I am sure he had his reasons."

"New-found girlfriend, perhaps?" Seppanen says, still not looking at you. "Whore? They were lined up barely a few metres apart along the Ku'Damm last night, whispering sweet nothings at the tourists. Not even the violent demonstrations could drive such dedicated free enterprisers away for long."

"Zweck was right," you say, pouring yourself a cup of coffee from the pot and reaching for a delicious-looking, jam-stuffed pastry.

"About what?"

"You do speak perfect English."

"I see. You don't wish to talk about it. Or, perhaps, standing people up is the latest New World fad. Something you do all the time."

"Ouch! That hurt!" you say, taking a bite of the pastry. "Normally, I'm an extremely punctual man who honours his every commitment. But—"

"But this time," Seppanen says, overturning the empty coffee cup onto the table, "being a long, long way from home and responsibility, you felt that catching up on sleep was more important than your dinner engagement."

"Sleep?" You're looking at her crucifix earring, swinging back and forth hypnotically. "How do you know I was asleep?"

"We have our ways. Call it psychic airwaves. Call it the ability to intuit the fluidity of events from a fixed point in time. Call it Doctor Zweck's insatiable curiosity."

"Aha. They don't call Berlin the spy capital of the world for nothing."

"I would have left it at that but, when you didn't show

up, he insisted on calling your *pension* from the Europa Centre. The girl who answered said she couldn't wake you although she knocked on your door several times."

"Sleeping soundly is one of my better qualities," you say, glad that Seppanen has made the assumption, thus saving you from an outright lie—or a twinge of conscience to pour out the unadorned truth.

"Well," Seppanen says, twisting the cup back and forth, "I think you've come to the right place to practice."

"What!" you exclaim, raising your eyebrows. "Did I hear correctly? Was that a *sotto voce* comment on the calibre of the speakers?"

"Oh no." She lifts the cup. It leaves behind a brown circle. "The speakers are excellent. My colleagues are nothing if not excellent orators. It's the speeches themselves that usually leave something to be desired. The speeches, mind you. Not the speakers."

"Tell me," you say, as you reach for a second pastry to quell your rumbling stomach. "Do you always speak your mind?"

"Only to strangers—and people who stand me up. And they usually end up being one and the same."

"Oh dear." You're starting to enjoy yourself. The kind of repartee you fancy yourself good at. "I'd hate to be a stranger. Must I do punishment to get back into your good books?"

"Not at all. Sitting through this symposium will be punishment enough, let me assure you."

"Cynicism is very unbecoming in a professional philosopher," you say, half seriously. "In the case of a Catastrophe Theorist, someone who's supposed to lead the rest of us out of the desert of self-doubt and into the Promised Land, to the unraveling of the universe as it is, cynicism comes close to being illegal."

Seppanen turns slowly and looks you straight in the face for the first time. Her eyes are a clear, liquid green. Relentless. Unperturbed. You can see the retinal patterns behind them—like the upside-down roots of hydroponic trees.

"Come with me," she says abruptly, standing up. "I'd like to show you something." You sit there, startled. "Come on. We haven't got all day. The conference is about to start—and you wouldn't want to miss that."

You get up at last. Seppanen leads you out a side door with a sign indicating washrooms and then down a slick, white-tiled corridor that has just been washed.

"What—" you begin to say.

But Seppanen hushes you, motioning that you should simply follow. You go past the two washrooms. At the far end of the corridor is a large closet which holds mops and buckets and other cleaning equipment. Seppanen steps inside the closet and pulls shut the opaque glass door once you enter.

"Now," she says, quickly lowering her torn jeans to reveal she's wearing nothing underneath. "Fuck me."

You freeze. You can smell the heat rising from her pelvic area. It mingles with the odor of Javel water—and somewhere that hint of mint.

"What are you waiting for?" she says, spreading her legs and pushing her hips forward. You can see her pubic hair has been carefully shaved in the form of a target, with the concentric rings dyed black and yellow. "We don't have much time, you know, considering the German mania for cleanliness."

With that, she grabs your trousers and pulls them down around your ankles. Then, she jerks you towards her, easing herself onto your penis and slipping a finger into your rectum at the same time. You feel a shock of hot electricity, a spark from your anus to the tip of your penis. Your mind goes blank—shorted out. It's all over in a matter of seconds. You slam her against the wall, thrusting until a stream of semen shoots inside her and then dribbles down her leg. And the whole time you're unloading into her, the whole time you're slapping frantically against her stomach, she stares at you, unblinking, passionless. Almost bored. The only things pulsing are those upside-down roots deep inside her eyes.

"Do you believe in rebirth?" she asks as you scramble to pull up your pants and she leans back to light a cigarette.

"Rebirth?" you stammer, almost catching the tip of your penis on the pants zipper. "You mean like in life after death." She nods. "No . . . I don't think so."

"Well, you'd better get the fuck out of here then." She blows out a ring of smoke and pokes it with her finger. "You've just had sex with the dead."

She shoves you out, propelling you down the corridor and past a couple of startled students just emerging from the women's washroom. When you look back, she's still leaning against the closet wall, casually smoking her cigarette with one hand and hoisting up the jeans with the other. You stumble back out into the auditorium and make your way to the seat. You can still feel where her finger had penetrated, had pushed against the inside of your anus— and the short bursts of semen that had fired in automatic response. And it brings back memories of something similar you'd done as a child. Squatting in the bath-tub and masturbating as you slipped a toothbrush as far up your rectum as you dared.

There's a loud screech from the microphone. The symposium's about to start.

"*Damen und Herren,*" Zweck bellows amid frantic motions from the sound technician that he should move back from the mike. "*Das ist sehr laut, nein?*"

"*Ja,*" the students shout back.

You look for Seppanen. She hasn't yet returned. But why would she do such a thing? With you? To you? You look over at her seat. No clues there. The coffee cup has left a brown ring on the table where she'd rubbed it. And the identification badge with her name on it is on the chair. You hold it up to the light and twirl it around. A sharp pin gleams. Without thinking, you put it in your pocket. A souvenir perhaps. Or a trophy.

Maybe there's some explanation in the package before you. But no. Simply a list of the papers to be read and English translations of those written in German. As you go down the list, you notice Seppanen's name under the title *Cusp Geometry and Doubly Infinite Series in Deterministic But Random Effects*, a paper which is to be presented later this afternoon. Unlike your offering, her material is to be showcased in the main hall, a keynote paper. People actually come to listen to her speak.

You search for her paper. It isn't there. Of course not. Just like yours isn't. You have the option of holding on to them and working on them till the last minute. And, in the case of symbolic logic papers, they're sometimes held back for security reasons. If translations are requested, they can be made later—after the mad scientists at the military installations have gone over them with a fine-toothed comb.

"*Damen und Herren,*" Zweck begins again, after the technician finally shows him how far away to stand so he doesn't burst any eardrums. Speaking in both German and English, he welcomes everyone to the opening of the symposium, lists the other rooms where seminars would be taking place during the course of the next two days, introduces the first speaker and then sits back down.

Let's hope they're all like that, you say to yourself. Maybe, Seppanen is wrong about the punishment. Maybe this is one symposium that proves the exception to the rule. The thought of her brings back in sharp relief that closet wall. You feel your penis swelling once again—so much so you have to slip a hand in your pocket to push it to one side. Where is she anyway? Her absence bothers you more than if she was right there on the table in front of you, taunting you with glimpses of her spread-open, bull's-eye labia. You look towards the side door leading to the washroom. It remains closed.

The first paper is in German. You bury your head in the translation before you and hardly look up again until the speaker has finished some 45 minutes later. The paper is extremely dense and technical—having to do with a rebuttal of Putnam's assumptions against a form of metaphysical realism. Can Brains in a Vat ever know they're Brains in a Vat? And, if so, is it the Brain speaking or the Vat? Or neither? Both? You enjoyed it immensely—and a pat on the back for having erased the reference in your own paper. You glance up at the auditorium. A good three-quarters of the seats are now empty. Aha, you say to yourself, the students have quickly come to the conclusion there's no need to stay for all the readings. Not if they have the transcripts of the papers with them. Or as many as they need anyway for their course work.

And then, out of nowhere, the thought: Oh God, she has AIDS. And this is her way of spreading the disease. The greatest cynicism of all. Lured into unprotected sex in a bathroom closet. By a professor of symbolic logic, of all people. You begin to sweat. You try to remember if you have any cuts on or in the vicinity of your penis. What about the finger in your rectum? Could she have transferred tainted fluids from herself to you? Had she rubbed herself first? Had she inserted a finger into her vagina before easing it into your anus? Most likely as it would have been the best way to lubricate it. Yes. That's what she must have meant about fucking the dead. She was pronouncing sentence. Your throat constricts; your penis shrivels.

The second reader is introduced and approaches the mike. This time the paper is in English: *Was Anti-Realism Consistent with a Creationist View of the World?* You lean back and shut your eyes, hoping to immerse yourself in what's being said. But you have trouble concentrating. No, you say to yourself, she might be crazy—but not crazy enough to deliberately give me AIDS. And yet you realize that's a silly statement. A statement not backed up by facts. Except for a few papers of hers you've read, you don't really know Seppanen from . . . from a hole in a closet wall.

You play the whole thing over in your mind—from start to finish. The improbability of it all. Would a sane person have risked unprotected sex with a stranger? Who are you talking about here: Seppanen or yourself? It's almost as if you had no choice in the matter. As if you were seized by the balls and led to that closet without once stopping to think about it. Literally allowing your gonads to do your thinking for you. And then you remember your palms against the cold, clammy wall. Your sweat-oozing palms as you thrust into her, a primordial rutting animal without the least insight into what you were doing—and not giving a damn about it either. And it hits you that you probably would do the same thing again if offered half a chance. Talk about not learning from history when you can't even learn from personal experience.

You open your eyes and glance up. More students are making their way out of the auditorium. The speaker drones on. You try to follow the gist of what he's saying. Something about the fact that, if we assume an anti-realistic view of the past, it would make no difference whether the world had come into being four billion or four thousand years ago. We would never have any direct proof of it. Even videotapes and films could be easily doctored. Nor would we have direct proof of the Holocaust once the last living witness was gone, you say to yourself. Nor of yesterday. Nor of a minute ago.

That's an interesting idea—a kind of continuous fashioning and refashioning of lives that owe absolutely nothing to what had happened even a split second before and that are thus completely random, that couldn't be predicted in any way without taking into account the rest of the universe down to its last subatomic particle—and beyond. Whatever that means. But what about the predictions that *are* made— and quite often proved true, especially those we like to call the Laws of Nature, always spelled with capital letters? Why, simple. Those predictions are fashioned after the fact, are created along with a past that doesn't really exist to bolster a future that never actually arrives.

So the only thing you can assume is that you are here in Berlin at this very moment—or can you? Isn't the assumption of your being in Berlin made a split second too late? Never mind that. Isn't the assumption of your being anywhere a split second too late? The washroom closet, for example? The firm pressing of a finger against your rectum? The releasing of sperm, squid-like into the inky ether? But, if you can't assume that you're somewhere, then where are you? Could you consistently create yourself? Or are slipups and incongruencies inevitable, a fact of anti-realistic life, like novelists who forget basic details or describe the same room in two different and contradictory ways?

And what do you know about yourself really? Are the patterns that you see, that you make your own, actually the ones working in your life? Or are there more mysterious structures, deeper meanings that operate behind the scenes—like clusters of properties, for example, that inevitably draw what seem totally unconnected events together. Watches and werewolves? Windows and Wahnsee? Sex and Seppanen? Sex and Singer? Sex and Louise? Louise. She appears before you, hands on hips. She's there in the closet, observing your rutting frenzy. It's her reflection in Seppanen's glassy eyes. There's that familiar martyred look, the slightly disheveled hair, the grim tightness of her lips and . . . and. . . . No! You squeeze your eyes shut to make her go away. You push her back away from you as you take aim once more at Seppanen's bull's-eye. Still smiling, Louise falls . . . she collapses . . . then she rises . . . ascending beyond you. . . .

Polite clapping snaps you back to the auditorium. The speaker first shuffles his papers and then shuffles off the podium. Zweck announces a 15-minute break before the next reading. You breathe a sigh of relief. Concentrating has become impossible. For the first time in your life, you aren't able to follow a logical discussion. What the hell is happening to you? Distractions aren't allowed in your world—not if you want to advance the cause of logic in a mad universe. And advance yourself in the process—as the carrier of this sanest of messages.

"Professor Serratura?"

"Yes?" You turn to look behind you. A short man in a kurta waits politely. "Ah, Professor Matlab." You stand up. "An honour to meet the man who believes in the best of all possible worlds. How are you?"

"*Namaste,*" Matlab says, holding his hands out before him as if in prayer. "I am fine. Very fine—even if the search for those worlds is not going too well. And you?" He gestures to the room. "How is my respected colleague enjoying this beautiful symposium so far?"

"Well-organized, I must say. And impressive. The speeches are short and everything's on time—especially the gravy train. Or at least the coffee and pastries."

"Yes, yes. The famous German mania for clockwork." Matlab looks around the auditorium. "Tell me, have you seen Professor Seppanen?"

"Seppanen? Why yes—" Should you tell him? You'll find her in the washroom closet, you say to yourself. If you hurry, you might get a quickie out of her, too. You try to imagine Matlab having sex standing up. All you can envision is a short rotund man with his kurta over his head. Maybe in some other impossible world. No, best to feign ignorance.

"She was here at the start of the symposium," you say, looking at her seat. "I'm sure of that. She may have gone to the washroom. Or she may have decided the topic wasn't to her liking. A bit too vague and undefined for her rigorous mathematical tastes."

"Yes," Matlab says, unaware of your attempt at irony. "She is extremely meticulous in her own research. Doesn't stand for any slackness." He looks around again. "I must locate her. Her paper is due to be read within the next two hours."

"A touch of stage fright maybe," you say. And what a silly thing to say. Stage fright? From someone who doesn't think twice about lowering her pants in a washroom closet. And sticking her fingers into strange crevices.

"No," Matlab says with a smile that reveals several teeth in need of work. "That would be very much out of character for Professor Seppanen. In fact, unlike the rest of us shadowy bookworms, she is one of those who may be said to revel in the spotlight. To actively seek it out and exploit it. In London several years ago, she read her paper as part of a magical act—while she was being sawed in half."

"I heard about that!" you say. "But I always thought the story was apocryphal. You know, the kind of mythology built around someone who claims to communicate with spirits and wears clothing more suited to a rock and roll dance hall than the study hall."

"I don't blame you." Matlab looks about the auditorium. "But I myself was a fascinated witness at the event. She pulled bunny rabbits from a hat while explaining dissipative systems and caught knives with her teeth in the midst of initial point trajectory mathematics."

"A woman of infinite talents," you say, picturing once again that quick lowering of jeans and thrusting forward of pelvis. Only this time followed by her being pinned to a spinning wheel while knives hurtle towards a blurred black and yellow target. Or fly out—it's hard to tell.

"Nonetheless, a not very happy person," Matlab says.

"Yes, I noticed that from our little talk."

"She's dissatisfied with her work," Matlab says. "We discussed it last night. You were supposed to meet us, were you not?" You nod reluctantly, not sure where this will lead. "She was most anxious to meet you and to question you. She wanted to know more about the logic you study, how it connected to the world, as she put it. And then again today before the conference. She was agitated and even threatened not to read her paper."

"Well, that explains it, doesn't it? She obviously doesn't feel her paper is up to scratch."

"Up to scratch? On the contrary, she fears her work is going too well."

"Now you've got me confused."

"She is too honest," Matlab says. "When she saw the full realization of the implications of Catastrophe Theory, she wished to reverse her research, to go back to the beginning."

"But we all know that's impossible. No one can go back to the beginning, as you put it. How do you erase the knowledge you've acquired?" Mental Varsol, you find yourself thinking. Removing the palimpsests, the obscuring flesh. "Memory-erasing machines are science fiction—at least for the time being. Besides, what good does it do for her to go back to the beginning when there are hundreds of others working on similar projects?"

"Yes, you are absolutely right, of course," Matlab says, tilting his head and smiling again. "It is becoming a very popular field with ramifications that go much beyond philosophy. I have heard that even the Pentagon has expressed interest and that the Soviet Union is on the verge of conducting experiments on the effect cusps have in triggering pivotal events. It may come in handy on the battlefield someday—or in the political arena." He sighs. "Perhaps, it is time to reevaluate. Or to drop it altogether."

"Reevaluate, yes, Professor Matlab. By all means. But dropping it? What could you find to replace it? Mysticism? Contemplation? Spiritual solace? All-embracing faith?"

"I would not dismiss Tantric Yoga out of hand," he says. "Perhaps it works with a logic of its own."

The microphone rings out again, feedback from Dr. Zweck's voice shattering the myriad conversations going on in the auditorium.

"Seems we're about to begin again," you say.

"Would you do me a favour?" Matlab asks. "Would you help me find her? At least that way we will have satisfied ourselves."

"Well, I—" You want to tell him you have better things to do than look for someone who may have tried to infect you with the AIDS virus—while you were busy satisfying yourself. But that would be just a little bit difficult to explain. "Sure. We can't have our keynote speaker going AWOL, can we?"

"Splendid," he says. "I'll check outside. She may have gone for a breath of fresh air. Why don't you try the washroom area?"

"That's right," you say. "Might be a simple case of nose powdering."

Or recharging the anal finger weapon for her next victim.

You watch Matlab climb the auditorium stairs towards the front exit. Then you push open the door to the washroom area. Seppanen isn't in the corridor. You don't expect her to be in the men's washroom—but you never know and check anyway. The only other place you can think of is the women's—and you're not about to go barging in there. Instead, you stand at the door and call her name several times. A moment later, another woman comes out. You recognize her as a participant in the symposium.

"Excuse me," you say. "Do you speak English?"

"Yes. A little."

"Is there a woman in the bathroom? A woman with a ring in her nose?" You gesture with your fingers to indicate a nose ring.

"No," she says, looking you up and down with some distaste. "There is no one else at the moment."

"Thank you."

She walks away. You're about to follow her back into the auditorium when the closet door creaks slowly open behind you. You turn—and there she is, still half-leaning, half-sitting against the wall. I should've guessed, you say to yourself. She's not through yet with her demonstrations. She's getting ready to lure another unsuspecting victim into her trap.

"Professor Seppanen," you say, approaching her. "They're looking all over for you. It's almost time for your—"

That's as far as you get. The left sleeve of Seppanen's shirt has been rolled up and a tourniquet applied above the bicep muscle. A used syringe lies on the floor beside her, drops of clear liquid lingering on its tip. Fuck, you say half-aloud as you fall back. When you get up the courage to look at her again, you can see that her eyes are wide open. But the eyeballs, with their eerie retinal images, have turned inward. And she isn't breathing. She definitely isn't breathing.

You start to back away from her and out of the closet. That's when you notice a piece of paper folded on her stomach. You reach forward slowly and lift it gently off her as if afraid to disturb her. It's a neatly typed note and it reads: "The shattered crystal is stable but unstable. The smallest, most minor of changes in the external system can lead to catastrophic results in the inner system. Why? I've got to find the answer. Good bye."

You drop the note back on her stomach and back out, in your haste tripping over a bucket filled with scummy water. The water spills out onto the floor, racing across the floor. You want to cry out for help but the words stick in your throat. You end up making a croaking sound, somewhat like a crow. It doesn't matter anyway. There's no one in the washroom area at the moment.

You push open the door into the auditorium. Another paper is being read—in German. The small band of professors and philosophers that remain have migrated towards the stage and now sit huddled together in the first few rows—almost as if to protect themselves from outside influence. As if to form a circle keeping infidels and heretics out. Should you shout it out? Shake them out of their state of hand-on-chin bemusement? That's probably the way Seppanen would want it. A grand entrance even in death. Her final performance, ladies and gentlemen. A slight miscalculation but one hell of a way to go. But it just isn't in you to do that sort of thing. Instead, you look for either Zweck or Matlab. They need to be told. Zweck is at the head table, nodding intently as he listens to the speaker drone on. You decide he shouldn't be disturbed. But where is Matlab? Must still be looking for Seppanen.

You climb the auditorium stairs towards the exit. You spot Matlab right away in front of the building. He's looking around in a distracted fashion, perhaps hoping that Seppanen will suddenly materialize from the warm, sunny air—just another of her magic tricks. You almost hate to break the news to him.

"I've found her," you say, fighting hard to stay calm—at least on the outside.

"Splendid!" he says. "I was getting worried for a moment. Thought perhaps she'd actually carried through her threat to go home." He looks at you. "My dear fellow. Is something the matter? Your face has been drained of colour."

"She's . . . she's dead," you say, unable to suppress a shiver.

"Dead? Professor Seppanen?" You nod. "Come now." He laughs. "She put you up to this, didn't she?"

"No!" you say. "I'm serious. This is no joke." You want to stop talking but you find you can't. "She's in the washroom broom closet. And she's dead. Drug overdose. Or that's what it looks like anyway. There's even a suicide note. A note that makes no sense at all."

"I see," Matlab says. "Seppanen has taught you how to keep a straight face."

"For Chrissakes," you say. "I'm telling you she's dead. I saw her myself. If you don't believe me, go see for yourself."

"Oh well," Matlab says with a sigh. "I guess the only way to put an end to this nonsense is to let Seppanen have the last laugh." He heads back inside, then notices you aren't following. "Come on. Don't you want to have some fun as well? Get some laughs at my expense when she jumps up?"

"No," you say, sitting on the steps. "I need some air."

BERLIN

Matlab shrugs and goes in. After all the practical jokes Seppanen has pulled, you can't blame him for not believing you. And you want to believe yourself that it was all a hoax. But you saw it. You saw her body twisted and sprawled on that slimy floor. You saw the syringe beside it—something slithering and evil, an inanimate object with a mind of its own. And you saw the note, the confirming note.

Suddenly, you have a strong urge not to be there when the body is found. Not to be anywhere near the place when they open the door to that closet and make their grisly discovery. You decide it's time for a little sightseeing. Time to visit the Wall. The infamous Wall. You take out your map of the U-Bahn system and follow the coloured lines with your fingers. The Wall is all the way across the city. That's it then. A trip to *der Mauer* to help clear your head. And also so you can tell the folks back home you were there—at the spot where East meets West and the two snarl at each other in eternal enmity. Or make faces like two children who've decided they dislike each other and there's nothing they can do about it.

When you emerge from the Hallesches Tor station in the Kreuzberg area, you find it hard to believe you're still in the same country—let alone the same city. In contrast to the broad boulevards around the Ku'Damm and the wide-open green spaces of the Freie Universität campus in Dahlem, starkness and a feeling of being closed in are the order of the day here. Rundown apartment buildings and flats edge right up against narrow, litter-filled sidewalks and streets; stores and factories are boarded up: some gutted by fire, others simply collapsed under their own weight (or the weight of history—who really knows?). Everything is pale and streaked with grey—like clothes that have been washed once too often. Even the sun helps create the mood by vanishing behind a thick, dirty layer of clouds.

Yet at the same time, you sense a street life here that's both vibrant and dangerous. A dip into chaos. Shaven-headed punks spilling out of a basement bar, black on black, bottles hidden in brown paper bags, playfully pushing one another and slam dancing their way down the alley. Old men in turbans sitting at the front of a Turkish pastry shop and fingering prayer beads, their eyes fixed on other, warmer worlds, other, less confusing market squares. A storefront artist with his half-painting half-sculpture creations—each and every one a study of Christ on the cross, the thorn-haloed and bloodied face emerging in three-dimensional anguish from a flat background. And, looming behind it all, you see the Wall, almost like a magician's illusion gone wrong with its dead-end streets and the belief that someone with enough faith could drive right through, could make it immaterial.

You've read somewhere that, if placed end to end, the barbed wire used on the Wall and surrounding barricades would encircle the Earth at least once at the equator. And, in a strange way, it all seems familiar to you. For isn't this how you'd envisioned Berlin before even setting foot in the city? Yes, despite Singer's enthusiasm and fascination for the society that had practically tortured him to death (to life?), this is what a part of you wants the city to be like. Here is that famous German *Angst* (what a great, perfectly apt word! you think), forever fixated on the past, forever recreating that past in its malcontented youth who roam the streets looking for something to destroy. Here are the three-story-high wall paintings (one in particular that depicts a naked reclining woman with a piece of cement sprouting from her belly button and covering her vaginal opening). And here is its Checkpoint Charlie, bristling with armaments and mutual hatred. Maw signaling the end of the world or narrow gateway to freedom?

BERLIN

At the crossing itself, you climb the elevated wooden platform that allows the curious to look over into East Berlin. To peek into the frontiers of the Evil Empire. The bleakness continues undiminished. The immediate area behind the wall has been razed entirely of buildings and replaced with spider-like observation towers. A series of barbed-wire fences—cutting off fields where tufts of grass struggle to break through foot-thick concrete—completes the impression that this is one of the prime battlegrounds in the Cold War arena.

A small group of people demonstrates in front of the border crossing. You can tell they're habitual, daily practitioners of this strange rite. One of them carries a placard with a blown-up poster of a young woman on it, a young woman who might have had the face of a Madonna—except that half of it has been blown away. The others hold up graphic drawings of people being impaled on the barbed wire or being shot by caricatures of the hated Vopos, the East German border guards. Save for the squeak of new running shoes, the group is silent in its protest, lending an air of unreality to the proceedings.

Arm in arm, a young couple make their way briskly up the wooden steps of the platform. Clean-cut, both blond and light-skinned, the standard Nordic type, they stand on either side of you, hands against the railing and taking deep gulps of air. Immediately, you picture them in uniform, singing "Tomorrow Belongs to Us" in the sweetest, clearest, most angelic voices possible. And ready to march off to the end of the world for the right leader. Dare you say the right *fuhrer?*

"Someday we will rebuild the Thousand Year Reich, *ja?*" the woman says in a clipped German accent—but oddly enough in English (for your benefit, no doubt). "We will purify the race once again. Do you not agree?"

"There is no question," the man says, also in clipped English. "Absolutely none at all. We will bring the German people together again under one nation, under one flag, under one leader." At that point, he turns to you and asks: "Is it not so, sir?"

"I beg your pardon? Were you speaking to me?"

"Brr, she's danged and miserable cold, ain't she?" the man says smiling. He has suddenly developed a nasal twang. You've heard such an accent once before—at a philosophy conference in Atlanta, Georgia. "Never this freakin' cold where we comes from. You?"

"I don't. . . ," you say, startled. "I. . . ."

"Honey, now don't you go botherin' the man," the woman says, with the same nasal twang. "Can't you see his English ain't so hot?"

"Ah jeez, I was just asking about the weather, is all. Ain't nothin' wrong with being sociable."

"Come along, Dickie. This here view is mighty depressing—especially for a baby." She pats her stomach.

"You're right. I don't rightly know how our boys over here can stand it. Even if they are protectin' the free world and all that."

"And to think," she says, "they sent my poor old Elvis over here. No wonder he got hisself all screwed up."

You watch their backs as they start to walk away.

"Now there I think you're wrong, honey. Elvis what got sent to Hamburger—or one of them places."

"Hamburger, Berlin. It's all mighty foreign and mighty queer to me. All enuf to make a downhome boy screwed in the head."

"Ain't that the truth," the man says as they hold hands and descend the platform stairway together, feet clip-clopping on the wood. "Ain't that the whole livin' freakin' truth."

BERLIN

You shake your head. What on earth has just happened? How have you managed to mistake a couple from the Southern U.S. for members of Hitler's Youth Corps—even if only for a few seconds? It's the city, you tell yourself. No doubt about it. There are ghosts around, ready to pop up at the snap of a synapse. Long-dead ghosts; ghosts on short notice; ghosts created by the second; ghosts ready to come together with the first deviant thought, the first inappropriate phrase. But how do they fit in? What have they to do with Seppanen, for example, who is foremost on your mind? Ah, the Great Tailor in the Sky, no doubt, with his made-to-measure world. Suitable for all occasions and yet full of surprises—and the occasional hole where you least expected it.

You are heading back to the Hollesches Tor station when you spot a sign: "Haus Am Checkpoint Charlie—Es Geschah An Der Mauer" and below it, in English, "Checkpoint Charlie Museum—It Happened at the Wall." More ghosts? You step inside. A notice above the ticket counter gives the admission fee as 3.50 deutschmarks for regular visitors, 2.50 for students and free for residents of Poland, Czechoslovakia and the GDR. Freedom's ticket tier, no doubt. The "museum" claims to be an historical record of all the more ingenious escape attempts out of East Berlin. It includes photographs of those who've made it across as well as some of the vehicles and tools they used: false-bottomed cars, hot-air balloons, gliders, hollowed-out cable drums, pulleys, mini-submarines and tunnels.

Even for you, who come from the privileged zones of North America, the implications are painfully obvious. When it comes to fleeing oppression, human ingenuity recognizes no bounds and it's clear everyone knows which way the osmotic flow is going. There are also photos of the "martyrs," of those who didn't make it, of those hung up on the wire or shot within a stone's throw of freedom. The most effective is a painting of a priest in East Berlin who'd set himself on fire to protest the closing down of his church.

Despite your claims at objectivity, you can feel the emotional tug of it and the urge to split the world neatly in two: us and them; the friend and the foe. But, professor of logic that you are, you have other questions you wish to ask here, questions the Museum, with its single-mindedness and one-track message, ignores. Or refuses to acknowledge. For example: what has happened to the thousands who've succeeded in fleeing? Do they look back on that moment as the most important in their lives, a tight-sphinctered, emotional high never to be reached again? Are they tempted perhaps to sneak back across so they can try it once more, caught forever in that cycle of escape? And finally: do they find the freedom they're so desperately seeking, so willing to leave families behind and risk lives for? Or are they now simply on the flip side of the coin, the mirror image that still holds them prisoner, outside it all?

You remember what your father liked to say when he still talked a modicum of sense: "It's right that Germany should be divided. We can't trust those people as a nation. The Russians know what they're doing because at the bottom of the German soul lies breathing the germ of Nazism." Like a sediment, perhaps, that filters out when everything else is processed and balanced. Or maybe the two Germanys are like two halves of an extremely powerful, extremely sensitive, extremely volatile chemical-bacteriological, psychological-emotional weapon. As long as the halves are kept apart, the world is safe. Thus, the Wall is a small price to pay, a tiny scar left from a major operation. And will probably stay up forever, you find yourself thinking, as solid and as buttressed as hatred of all things foreign.

BERLIN

At the end of the tour, you buy a package of Berlin Divided postcards—photos of the Wall from its "temporary" beginnings in 1961 to the vinyl-covered structure of 1987. One of your passions is sending unusual postcards to fellow logicians around the world. These will be great. You also pick up several posters you feel will go well in your office, including a reproduction of the wall painting depicting the woman with the cement piece wedged between her legs. The painting is entitled: *Gesetz Des Beton*. The Law of Cement. Or perhaps The Concrete Law to give it its full measure of ambiguity. What happens when flesh meets unyielding solidity.

Now that you've had a chance to study the print more closely, you find it really disconcerting. The cement seems not foreign but an outgrowth of the flesh itself, an organ added on to combat some alien disease. The disease of technology. Or an organ created by the disease of technology. To combat what? So that human flesh would fight itself, turning more and more of itself into concrete, into the building material for future walls? There's significance then in the fact that it starts with the female reproductive organs. "The next time you try to fuck me," it seems to be saying, "this is what you're going to run up against. This is what your dick is going to bounce off."

You shudder and roll the print up again, snapping the rubber band around it. A vivid picture of aborted intercourse pops into your mind, followed by that of a foetus unable to get out of its mother's womb, trying to wail but forced to remain silent with that cement stuck like a bit in its mouth. In any case, hung facing out, it's certain to raise a few eyebrows in the staid halls of the philosophy department.

You look at your watch—and suddenly realize you aren't wearing it. Odd. You could have sworn you had it on this morning. Of course. Hadn't it played the *Fifth* to accompany your pounding headache? You must have taken it off for your shower and then forgotten to put it back on.

Despite the lack of a watch, you know it's time to return to the symposium—and the fallout from Seppanen's death. You can't avoid it for much longer. With that thought, your headache returns. For a moment, you seriously contemplate heading straight to your room where you can slip into bed and pull the quilt over your head. But there might also be other things waiting: Singer, for example, lurking about, all set to lead you once again into strange practices. And, if not Singer, then Fritz with his lurid "I-told-you-so." Innuendo Fritz. Fritz The "Nod Nod" Hinter. Besides, Zweck and Matlab will be wondering where you've gone to—and might even fear the same fate may have befallen you. The same darkness that overtook Seppanen.

So you rub your temples and descend one more time into the U-Bahn. As you sit in the nearly empty train facing backwards, the swoosh of rubber tires and the flash of tunnel lights bring on an hypnotic lethargy, a sensation of floating free. You find yourself reflecting upon Seppanen's death, asking questions usually mumbled in funeral parlors: How would her family back in Helsinki take the news of her suicide? Did she have family? Was she married? What about children? Somehow you doubt it. Would her friends walk about saying: "What a catastrophe!"—and in that way unconsciously mimic Seppanen's work? And just what had her suicide note meant—if anything?

As you step out of the subway station, you notice a bank of telephones along one wall. You have the sudden urge to hear Louise's voice again. The phone rings, crystal clear. But again the answering machine picks up and it's your own voice you hear—breezy and friendly but also a little metallic. You wait for the signal beep and leave another message: "Hello, Louise. Not having much luck catching you in, am I? Oh well. Nothing important. I think you'd like Berlin. Maybe one day we'll come here together. Just the two of us. Give my love to Cathy and I hope my mother isn't giving you too much trouble."

You debate whether or not to tell her about the suicide but, in the end, decide against it. No need to frighten her while you're so far away. Louise is a great believer in the idea that tragedy is catching—like a virus. Or perhaps it's the Domino Effect of human emotional states. You'll tell her everything once you get home. Once you're back in your own study amid the familiar, comfortable objects of married life.

You arrive at the auditorium to find it empty and, in the late afternoon sunlight, particularly sombre. No, it's not completely empty. Zweck and Matlab are still there, sitting across from each other at the head table. But everyone else has vanished—melted perhaps into the fake woodwork and ready to reemerge when everything is straightened out. When the coast is clear. When the scent of suicide has been scrubbed clean. Matlab looks up as the door opens but Zweck remains with his head in his hands. You begin to walk down the steps to the front; Matlab rises to greet you halfway.

"The police were here," Matlab says, whispering. "I did not inform them that you were the first to see the body."

"Why not?" you ask. "I've nothing to hide."

"No, no," he says. "It is not a question of that. Simply that they would have demanded to know where you were. And why you left so suddenly. That might have led to complications."

"I understand," you say. "Thank you."

You walk towards Zweck who still hasn't moved. He finally looks up. He's holding a piece of paper in his hand.

You recognize that paper. It flashes onto a belly button—the naked sprawl of a hand turned upwards, fingers open.

"*Sie ist Tod,*" Zweck says. "*Sie ist Tod.* Our Professor Seppanen is dead."

"Yes," you say, her body floating before you again. "Horrible!"

"Terrible," he says. "And what does this mean?" He waves the paper in the air, then passes it to you. "What does this mean? Can you tell me?"

You look at it—the suicide note. You pretend to read it—even though you know it by heart.

"I don't know," you say, shrugging, after you place it back on the table. "Perhaps, it was one of her practical jokes gone awry. Or an experiment."

"Mein Gott!" Zweck says, pounding the table. "A practical joke! On herself, yes? What a terrible way to die." He shakes his head. "She took her own life. I do not understand. A brilliant woman. I do not understand."

Zweck stands up and wanders off, still talking to himself.

"What about the symposium?" you ask Matlab.

"The rest of today's papers have been cancelled," he says. "We can't very well have the ghost of Professor Seppanen hovering over the proceedings, now can we?"

"No," you say. "That wouldn't do."

"As for tomorrow's sessions. . . ," Matlab shrugs. "We shall wait and see what Dr. Zweck decides on the matter."

"When I saw her body being taken away," Zweck says, returning to the table, "it made me realize the closeness of her friendship. It made me want to forget everything. And yet, there were several times this afternoon when I entertained some very uncharitable thoughts. I asked myself: 'How she could have been so selfish? So miscaring?' She must have had the realization that her suicide would jeopardize the entire symposium. Something on which I have worked for nearly five years. And now I am in a terrible quandary."

He leafs through some papers and then walks off again.

"Did she do it on purpose?" you ask Matlab. "Did she kill herself to scuttle the symposium?"

"Perhaps," he says. "You must remember that the show was everything for her. On the other hand, she may have just come to the end of her rope. Or something that happened in the last two days may have triggered the death wish—which I know was never too far from the surface."

"Years of planning," Zweck says, looking around the auditorium. "Months and months of work. The bureaucracy alone was staggering. The coordination. The struggles with the Ford Foundation who wished to turn this into just another ringing endorsement for democratic ideals American-style. You cannot imagine. I have thought of nothing else. Nothing else. And now this. . . ."

"Tomorrow's another day, Doctor Zweck," you say. "I'm sure things will look better then."

"Ah," Zweck says as he shakes his head, "the optimism of youth. We had that once, too, didn't we, Matlab?"

"I would like to think I still maintain mine," Matlab says with his enigmatic smile.

"Besides," you say, "youth is a relative term in this instance, isn't it? After all, I'm no spring chicken."

"Come," Zweck says, "this place no longer elates me. Let us continue this at my home, shall we? It is not at too great a distance."

"Well . . . I'm not. . . ," you begin to say. And then ask yourself: You're not what? Not in the habit of intruding in other people's lives. "I have. . . ." You have what? Other plans? With Singer and friends perhaps? Or an intimate rendezvous with Fritz?

"Come, come," Zweck says, taking you by the arm. "I insist."

"Yes," Matlab says, taking your other arm. "You managed to escape us last evening—but we have you now."

"Alright," you say. "Lead me away."

You pick up your briefcase with the poster folded across the top. Then the three of you walk out of the auditorium arm in arm—like old university chums meeting again after many years apart.

"We'll take the shortcut, shall we?" Zweck says, stopping in front of a playing field where a boy and girl chase each other in circles. "I don't see any dangerous ruffians about."

"Dangerous ruffians?" you ask.

"He means footballers," Matlab says.

"Footballers?" you say. "Oh, you mean soccer players."

"Yes," Zweck says. "They have a tendency to run you over first and apologize later."

Still arm in arm, you cut across the field. Walking through that field is, for you, like being caught in a sudden space warp. You have to remind yourself that you're in suburban Berlin and not back home in Montreal's N.D.G. district: the same early-evening sunlight slanting onto the same gently waving trees and solid but modest brick homes; the same air of peacefulness mixed with a feeling that things aren't really anchored down all that well and could float off at any time; the same gut queasiness of being almost lost, of being slightly out of focus, of fading in and out; the same apprehension as your hand reaches for the door knob . . . reaches for something solid . . . reaches for self-evident proof that everything is alright . . . reaches for. . . . You stop, shuddering to regain your equilibrium. The others stop with you.

"Something the matter?" Zweck asks.

"No," you say, shaking your head. "Just a. . . ." Vision? Prescience? "I was just thinking."

"About earlier in the day?" Zweck asks. You nod, not wishing to have to go into long explanations. "Yes. Our curse, isn't it? Homo Philosophens. Like what dogs do with a bone. What is the expression in English?"

"They worry it," Matlab says.

"They worry it," Zweck repeats. "Very appropriate, is it not?"

"Yes, very," Matlab says. You begin to stride forward again. "Sometimes they worry it to death."

"A curse," Zweck says as you climb up the front steps of his house. "There is no better word for it than that."

"The voodoo of higher consciousness," Matlab says. "There is no reference without self-reference."

Zweck throws open the front door on which has been placed some sort of wreath. Already in mourning, you say to yourself. But no. It is a stalk of wheat, braided and intertwined and covered in some sort of lacquer. You enter the front hallway—and another shock hits you. The cottage could be a mirror image of the one you left behind in Montreal, complete with an oak staircase running up to the second level. There are differences, of course. Yours is carpeted; this one has been stripped to the hardwood flooring. The lighting isn't the same; the walls are painted a different colour; the furniture of another period. But the similarities are still disconcerting—including a print of Picasso's *Guernica*.

"Celine?" Zweck calls out. "Are you there? I'm home." He turns to you and Matlab. "Still at work, I suppose. Oh well." He gestures vaguely. "Come, come. Make yourselves at home."

He leads you into the living room—exactly where you predict it will be—and points to the sofa. A large picture window looks out onto a back yard and beyond that to the playing field.

"If memory serves," Zweck says, "you don't drink, do you, Girgit?"

"Not spirits, no. They give me the hiccups."

"And you, Professor Serratura? Sherry? Or would you prefer something a little more potent?"

"Sherry will be fine," you say, as you sit down and place your briefcase by the side of the sofa.

Zweck reaches into a cabinet and pulls out a bottle of sherry. He pours you a glass and then one for himself.

"Cheers," he says, taking a sip. "Ah, nothing like a refreshing glass of sherry after a bruising day. You don't know what you're missing, Girgit."

"Kianta hated sherry," Matlab says. "In fact, she hated anything sweet. Said it reminded her too much of all the saccharine shit we have to swallow in our daily lives."

You start at the word "shit"; would never have predicted it coming from Matlab. Just like you can't imagine him having sex with Seppanen.

"Professor Seppanen was a woman of violent likes and dislikes," Zweck says, finishing off his sherry. "Contrary to the Greek call for moderation in all things, there was no middle way for her. No safety net."

"Yes," says Matlab. "Her entire life's work was based on that: to take things to the absolute limit."

"Not just her work," says Zweck. "She was reckless and undisciplined in all things—from her eating habits to her sexual practices."

You choke back on the sherry, trying hard not to cough as it burns down your throat.

"A long string of lovers of both sexes, I hear," says Matlab. "And no precautions. Hard to imagine in this day and age."

"A true gambler," Zweck says. "What was it she liked to say: 'Precautions are for sissies and the muddle-headed.

If catastrophe is inevitable, then it's no use trying to hide from it.'"

"I guess she took one chance too many," Matlab says.

"I'm sorry," you say, feeling the perspiration in your armpits. "I don't quite understand that. What do you mean by taking one chance too many? I thought she committed suicide."

"How familiar are you with her work?" Zweck asks, refilling his glass—and then yours.

"I've not made any close study of it," you say. "Only that she was working on refining Dissipative System Theory. Trying to pin down the precise cuspal point of no return."

"Exactly," says Matlab, and lowers his head.

"Oh my God," you say. "You're not implying . . . an experiment of some sort?"

"It does make a certain sense," Zweck says. "It is not something for which one asks for volunteers."

"Gruesome, nevertheless," Matlab says.

"Yes, I agree," Zweck says. "One would think that death, of all things, would be spared the reduction to an equation."

You stand up suddenly and walk to the window. You're feeling feverish, unable to shake the vision of Seppanen's body. As much as you desire pulling her back to the point where she's at least standing up against that clammy wall, you always end up having sex with her on the floor. Fucking the dead—isn't that what she had said?

"Oh dear," Zweck says. "We seem to have upset Professor Serratura."

"No, no," you say, turning towards them. "It's nothing you said. I haven't been feeling myself for several days now."

"Air travel," Matlab says. "Always makes me feel as if I am in two places at once."

"Have you been eating?" Zweck asks.

"Not the way I should, no."

"But there you have it!" Zweck says. He comes over and pats you on the shoulder. "You must stay for supper."

"No, I couldn't possibly," you say. "I don't want to impose."

"Impose! Nonsense. We have a few . . . remains? . . . leftovers, I mean. A bit of *boeuf Bourguignone.* You have not lived until you've tasted Celine's heavenly *boeuf.* In fact, there is only one person in the entire universe who refuses it."

"Only because it is against my religion," Matlab says. "But the temptation is devastating."

"It's settled then," Zweck says, rubbing his hands together. "*Boeuf* for Professor Serratura. As for you, my dear Girgit, let me see what I can find in the refrigerator."

Zweck heads for the kitchen; you turn back to the window. Two boys are dribbling a soccer ball back and forth. When they get to the near end of the field, they turn around and head back. At the far end, you see a young woman carrying a brief case overflowing with books. A student, no doubt. She walks briskly along the sidelines, full of purpose and determination. As she approaches, you can see that she is very attractive and poised—long and thin, with short blond hair and wearing a yellow blouse and a black ankle-length skirt. She could easily be a model rather than a student. Or a top executive in a corporation. But no. That wouldn't explain the books.

"Admiring the view?" Matlab says, standing beside you.

"Huh? Oh yes. Pleasant, isn't it? Reminds me of the view from my university office."

Halfway across the field, the woman looks up, smiles and waves. Matlab waves back.

"You seem to know each other," you say.

"I should hope so." He grins. "That is Celine. Mrs. Zweck."

"Mrs. Zweck?"

"You sound surprised," Matlab says. "Not quite what you were expecting?"

"Will lentil soup do?" Zweck calls out from the kitchen. "If not, I can always prepare something else."

"No need to put yourself out for me," Matlab says. "Lentil soup will be just fine."

You continue to watch Celine approaching the house—now making out the fine details of her face. High cheekbones; huge eyes; full lips. All the ingredients of the classic beauty.

"Actually," you say, pulling yourself away so it doesn't seem like you're gawking, "I mistook her for a student."

"You would not be the first," Matlab says. "Either a student or a model."

The front door opens.

"Ooof!" Celine calls out, her voice made more exotic by the hint of a French accent. "What a day. What a day."

There's the sound of a briefcase being dropped to the floor. Then, she appears at the door of the living room.

"Girgit!" she exclaims. "What a pleasant surprise!" She holds out her arms for Matlab to hug her—then turns to you. "And you must be Professor Serratura. All the way from Canada."

"Hello," you say, reaching out to shake her hand.

But she hugs you as well, enveloping you in the scent of her perfume. You feel slightly faint.

"Canada is a lovely, enchanting country," she says. "I did it—how do you say it? *Sur le pouce.*"

She sticks her thumb up and moves her arm back and forth. The delicacy of her actions makes you want to reach out and touch her.

"Hitch-hiked," you say, trying to keep your voice steady but only half succeeding.

"Yes! I hitch-hiked across it one summer long ago when I was still wild and fancy-free. It is very wide, yes?"

"Very," you say. "*Et plein de moustiques avec un appetit pour le sang.*"

"Ah!" Celine exclaims, clapping her hands. "*Vous parlez le français!*"

"*Un peu,*" you say, struggling to get the words right. "*Je suis loin d'être bilangue. Mais je suis capable de demander un assiette de boeuf Bourguignone.*"

"That is very good," Celine says.

"Ah, Celine," Zweck says as he comes in from the kitchen, holding a wooden spoon with sauce in it. "You are back at last. I was about to send the dogs out for you."

"He's a jealous old man," Celine says to you as she goes over to give Zweck a kiss.

"A lot of good it would do me if I were," Zweck says. "You move much too fast for my poor old eyes to follow."

He holds the spoon up for Celine to taste.

"Perfect," she says.

"Good," Zweck says. "Perhaps you can carry it to the table while I fetch a bottle from the cellar."

"And he likes to boss me around," she says as she heads out for the kitchen, spoon in hand. A moment later she peeks back in, wearing a pair of oven mitts. "There is someone missing, non?"

Zweck and Matlab look at each other.

"Kianta," Celine says. "Where is Kianta? I cannot have three males at the dinner table without some counterbalance."

"Kianta—Professor Seppanen," Zweck says, clearing his throat, "is . . . indisposed this evening."

"What a shame," Celine says. "Oh well. I will have to make do. Be forewarned, however. The battle will be difficult."

She turns and heads back into the kitchen.

"Best to keep it to ourselves for now, do you not think?" Zweck says in a low voice to you and Matlab. "They were wonderful friends. It would upset her horribly."

Both of you nod.

"*Le souper est prêt,*" Celine calls out in her singsong voice.

"Excellent, excellent," Zweck says, patting you on the back. "Now, why don't the two of you go into the dining room? Make yourselves at home, as the English like to say. I will get some wine."

"And a bottle of mineral water for Girgit," Celine shouts.

"Yes, yes," Zweck says. "Mustn't forget our teetotalling colleague."

Matlab and you walk into the dining room. Dimly lit and framed in dark mahogany, it exudes a warmth that acts like a pleasant sedative on you. The hypnotic effect is increased by a window in which has been imbedded a stained-glass angel—with the early evening sun deflecting blue-green light through it. You reach up to pass your fingers along the ridge of the angel's wings, which seem less pristinely white than the ones you're used to seeing in church.

"A beautiful piece, is it not?" Matlab says.

"I don't normally believe in angels," you say. "But I could make an exception with this one."

"And here we are!" Celine says, carrying a steaming casserole dish. "Professor Serratura—"

"Anthony," you say. "Please call me Anthony."

"Anthony, then," she says with a smile. "Would you be so kind as to slide that pad over? Bruno would never forgive me if I scorched his mother's antique table."

With her chin, she indicates a wicker pad at the far end of the table. You reach past her, brushing her arm in the process, and position the pad so she can lower the casserole dish onto it. This time you get a good whiff of her perfume. Perfume has never been high on your list of priorities and the sultry advertising come-ons have left you cold. They just don't stand up to logical analysis. But, trite as it might seem in the saying, this one actually defines her in some way, actually says: "Celine." You can't imagine it on another woman—and you can't imagine her using something else.

"We were admiring your angel," Matlab says.

"Yes," you say. "It looks so . . . so human."

"Lucifer," she says, as she exits again, trailing seduction. "Before the fall."

You shake your head clear and continue to look around the room. At about eye level is a wooden ledge on which have been placed dozens of clear-glass figurines: deer, more angels, unicorns, dragons and a host of other creatures all exquisitely shaped and carved in fantastic detail.

"Switch on the other light if you wish," Celine says from the kitchen.

Matlab reaches for a switch. The wall opposite you lights up, revealing a recessed area filled with framed pictures of various sizes, some no more than two inches square, others up to a foot or so in height. For the most part, they're family portraits: young couples dressed in the style of an earlier era; older people at anniversary parties; children standing stiffly at attention. But at the centre and dominating the rest is a gigantic painting of Zweck and Celine, she in bikini, he in knee-length bathing trunks. They seem to be on a tropical island somewhere, holding hands and staring at one another. Even the most hardened of cynics would have to admit that the glint in their eyes is one of pure, unadulterated joy. You feel a twinge of jealousy. You have never before seen such identical looks on two people: a combination of trust and intelligence, a distilling of essentials, of something that needs to be identified and savored. You struggle to come up with words for it—but they elude you.

"Maddening, isn't it?" Matlab says.

"Sorry?" you say.

"Every time I see that painting, my heart sinks. As if the rest of the world dims slightly. Loses its colour. Fades in the washing." He looks at you and tilts his head. "Am I making any sense?"

"As much as you ever make when you get mystical on us," Zweck says, clutching two bottles, one wine and the other mineral water.

"We were dissecting your painting," Matlab says.

"Not literally, I hope," Zweck says.

"Please, be seated," Celine says as she enters. "Supper is served."

She places a steaming bowl of fettuccine on the table, along with a plate of lentil soup. Then she sits next to Zweck so that she's directly opposite you.

"They were talking about our painting, dear," Zweck says, patting her hand.

"A curse," Celine says, frowning. "As all ideal things eventually become when you have to live in the real world, *n'est-ce pas?*" She looks at you, her eyes twinkling. "Next, you will ask me how Bruno and I met."

"How did you—?"

"ESP," Bruno says. "She has ESP."

"A guru in the making," Matlab says, spooning up his soup.

"*Pas vrai,*" Celine says, laughing gently. "Just the laws of statistical probability analysis."

"I beg your pardon?" you ask. You understand the words. It's just that this isn't something a model is likely to say.

"Simple," Celine says. "Nine of ten people ask that question when they realize Bruno and I are—how do you say it?—a couple." She lifts some fettucine from the bowl and deposits it on your plate. Then she does the same for Bruno and herself. "They look at my silver-haired husband—distinguished, highly intelligent, respected—and then at me. And they ask, usually with narrowed eyes: What does he see in that anemic *épouvantail*—in that scarecrow?" She ladles out the *boeuf* onto the fettucine. "Aha! It must be the Pygmalion Complex! He wishes to teach her the proper table manners, no? Either that or poor Zweck has slipped into his *dieuxième enfance* and the vixen is taking full advantage."

"*Oh mein Gott!*" Zweck says. "Soon, she will have me playing the violin on the street corner. You should know, my dear professor, that, as well as possessing all the beauty and youth, she is actually the brilliant one in this family. Isn't that right, Girgit?"

"Of course," Matlab says. "For too long she has been hiding her light under a bushel."

"*C'est pas vrai!*" Celine says, holding out her wine glass for Zweck to fill. "I am but a disciple at the feet of my masters. A student eager to learn. An apprentice—"

"Listen here, Professor Serratura," Zweck says. "My good wife Celine is pulling your leg. True, she doesn't concern herself with questions such as the existence of God, free will and Kantian categorical imperatives. They're too simple—and trivial for her liking."

"Now, you are going completely overboard," Celine says. "You'll soon have our guest believing I teach nuclear physics."

"That's exactly what my dear Celine does," Zweck says. "And not just any nuclear physics. No sir. Her research specialty is quantum electrodynamics. Or QED, as the insiders prefer to call it. Gluons and quarks and other exotic creatures of the subatomic world that no one has ever made visible."

"That is more than enough, dear," Celine says. "I think our guest is losing his appetite."

"Not at all, not at all," you say excitedly. "This is fascinating. I've tried to read several of Richard Feynman's attempts to simplify the QED concepts. But the truth of the matter is they have done little for me except make me feel thick-headed and very unintelligent. Do you actually understand those things? I mean, properties such as half-spin and charm and flavour and anti-colours?"

"*Mon Dieu!*" Celine says, slapping her forehead. "This man not only wants me to be an expert but to understand as well. Now that is asking a bit much. No, no, no. That is too much!"

"Yes, extremely presumptuous of him," Matlab says. "One does not ask a master to explain herself."

"*Exactement!*" Celine says.

"A thousand pardons," you say. You raise your glass. "May I offer a toast then. To Celine—and subatomic physics."

"That's better," Celine says.

You clink glasses.

"So," you say. "How *did* you meet?"

"Oof!" Celine says, throwing up her hands. "At the Paris Inter-Disciplinary Conference for Scientific-Philosophical Debate on Heraclitus and Sub-Atomic Particles. Where else would two geniuses meet?"

"Again, she pulls your leg," Zweck says. "We met truly at a Club Med in Guadeloupe. I took one look at her and said: 'At last, someone who is not going to waste my nights arguing about Hegelian synthesis and the search for the ultimate Good.' Was I ever mistaken!"

"He should complain," Celine says. "He led me to believe he was part owner of a gold mine in the Amazon and had made his fortune as the inventor of the commercial jam-peanut-butter swirl. You can imagine my shock when the magic swirl turned out to be an on-the-bread mix with which he so disgustingly starts his mornings. As for the gold mine, that was nothing more than a damp, shadowy Plato's cave deep in the Black Forest."

"Ah," Zweck says, caressing her arm, "but you found that cave not only mossy but quite enticing, didn't you, my dear?"

"We'll not get into that now, Bruno," Celine says. She turns to you. "Und so, as the Germans say, have you had a chance to see some of our *wundervoll* Berlin in this year of its 750th anniversary?"

"Well, I made it to the Wall," you say. And saw two members of Hitler's Youth Corps from Alabama, you want to add.

"Ah yes," Celine says, twirling her fettucine. "*Die Mauer.* Our world-famous landmark. And what did you think? Did it live up to what you expected of it?"

"To tell you the truth, I don't know. I can't say that I really had any expectations. It was certainly odd to see this two-and-a-half metre cement barrier splitting the city in two. But, at the same time, it also seemed . . . natural."

"Natural?" Matlab asks. "How so?"

"Well, maybe, that's not the right word. What I mean is that it reminded me of the suture between two tectonic plates caught in a test of wills, if you'll allow me a mixed metaphor. They grind up against each other and, in the grinding, raise a wall. Or a barrier. After a while, the quote-unquote natural landscape that was there before the wall tends to adapt itself to the new reality. Buildings, some cut in half, are razed; the ground is scorched and cemented over; barbed wire grows like crabgrass; the area turns grey, leeched of its colour. And then that itself becomes the norm, the expected nature of things."

"That is a very vivid and frightening image," Zweck says.

"But you are right. We do get used to it."

"But I've also had a chance to walk up and down the Ku'Damm," you say. "To visit the Europa Centre and, of course, the Freie Universität campus. Those could be in any city in the world. So I'm not sure how much Berlin actually suffers from the wall."

"The Europa Centre, *c'est quelche chose fantastique!*" Celine says, clapping her hands. "It is my favourite place in the whole universe. I go there whenever the gluons threaten to come unglued—and that is quite often."

"My wife is an inveterate gambler," Zweck says. "She loves me but banco is her true passion. That and the Dead Kennedys."

"The Dead Kennedys?" you say, a doubtful look on your face. "You mean she prefers John and Bobby to Ted?"

"No, no," Celine says, bursting into laughter. "The punk group. Have you never heard "California Uber Alles?" You shake your head. "*Mon Dieu! Quelle deprivation culturelle!* How about "Nazi Punks Fuck Off?" Surely you are aware of that seminal anthem in which Jello Biafra, the Dead Kennedys' genius leader, says: 'You still think swastikas look cool/The real Nazis run your schools/They're coaches, businessmen and cops/In a real Fourth Reich you'll be the first to go.'"

"No, I'm afraid I haven't had the pleasure," you say, trying to decide whether or not she is putting you on. "J. S. Bach is more my speed."

"Well, at least you are not one of those baby-boom boys who thinks New Age music soothing for the soul," she says. "That I find makes me want to vomit. Gag me with a spoon, as your Valley Girls say. It is Madame Guillotine—whoosh—for them."

"You must forgive my wife," Zweck says. "She does take her music seriously."

"As a matter of fact," Celine says, "Kianta and I are going

to a concert this Monday evening. A Tribute to the Dead Kennedys. Not the real thing—but it will have to do, no?"

Zweck and Matlab look at each other once more.

"Oh, how I wish she were here!" Celine says. "Now, what could have been so important that she couldn't make it? Doesn't she know I need her?"

"*Gott,*" Zweck says, slamming his napkin down. "I cannot take this any longer."

"Bruno, what on earth is the matter?" Celine asks. "*Qu'est-ce-qu'il passe?*"

Zweck pushes his chair back, stands and hurriedly leaves the room. Celine turns to Matlab.

"She is dead," he says. "Kianta is dead."

"What? What are you saying?" She laughs nervously. "Is this a joke?" She looks at you. You shake your head. "Surely, you are joking."

"It should be," Zweck says as he returns. "The ultimate joke. The joke to end all jokes, *nein*. But it isn't."

"Most assuredly not," Matlab says.

After Zweck explains what happened, Celine collapses onto the living room sofa. Matlab and Zweck sit on either side, trying to comfort her. But it doesn't help. She sobs uncontrollably. The tears stream down her face. Her eyes are rimmed with red.

"I loved Kianta," she says, taking deep breaths. You can't help notice the swelling of her breasts each time she does so. "I loved her with all my heart and soul. We were supposed to go to the concert together. Remember, Bruno?" Zweck nods, blowing his nose. "A tribute to the Dead Kennedys." She sobs again, burying her face in her hands. "I need a drink, Bruno. A stiff drink."

Zweck pours her some brandy in a large snifter. The bottle says "Fin Champagne" on it. Celine holds the glass with both hands—then gulps it down, tilting her head back

132

as she does so. Her throat is like a swan's.

"Kianta! Kianta!" she suddenly cries out. "How could you?" Without waiting for Zweck, she refills her glass and swallows the contents. "It's like losing someone from your own family."

"Perhaps I should go now," you say.

"No, no," Celine says, standing up. "You must stay!" She wipes her cheeks and then smiles through her tears. "We must celebrate Kianta. We must render homage to her passing. It's what she would want. Is that not right, Bruno?" Zweck nods glumly. "Come, come. Give me a smile." Zweck smiles. "That's better. Now, fill up those glasses!" Zweck fills your glass as Celine holds up hers. "To Kianta!"

"To Kianta!" the three of you repeat.

You and Zweck sip your brandy; Matlab drinks mineral water.

"Music!" Celine shouts. "We must have some music."

You expect something funereal, something in keeping with the occasion. She puts on the Dead Kennedys—and sings along lustily as they scream incomprehensible lyrics. Then, without warning, she starts to stomp across the room, legs high in the air and then thumping the floor like pistons.

"Slam dance!" she shouts above the music. "Kianta's favourite. She showed me how."

As the music speeds up and becomes increasingly frenetic, so does she—going about the room faster and faster, bouncing off walls and furniture.

"Come on!" she yells. "Get up here!" Zweck and Matlab shrug their shoulders, indicating they're unable to partake. Celine turns to you. "Come on! Let's show these old geezers how it's done."

She takes your hand and leads you to the centre of the room. Then, she lowers her head and stomps towards you.

You stand there as she bounces against you and almost knocks you down.

"Come on! Come on! Come on!"

Again, she stomps—and again bounces against you. This time you're prepared for her and hold your ground, leaning forward. You feel her breasts yielding, flattening, before she pulls back to circle the room again.

"Stomp!" she says. "Stomp, damn you!"

You begin to stomp your feet, awkwardly, tentatively, like a recruit on his first maneuvers.

"No, no," she says. "You have to mean it. You have to let the world know just how angry you are." She stops and goes to the record player. "Here—listen to this." She lifts the needle and brings it down on another part of the album. She sings along, harshly: "I am Emperor Ronald Reagan/ Born again with fascist cravings/Still, you made me president."

She howls. Then she takes a run at you, stumbles and falls over the sofa to the ground. The three of you rush to her aid but she's laughing. Rolling about the floor and laughing.

"Celine," Zweck says. "Why don't you—"

"Oh God," she says, sitting up. "Kianta—what have you done?"

With that, she lowers her head and bursts into tears. Zweck helps her to her feet.

"Come, dear," he says. "You need to sleep. You need to get some rest." He leads her away. "You will feel better in the morning. I am sure of it."

"A shame," Matlab says after they've left the room. "One wonders if Kianta considered all the possibilities when she went ahead with her experiment."

"You persist on calling it an experiment," you say. "Isn't it possible it was just a mistake? A tragic miscalculation?"

"No," Matlab says, shaking his head. "Kianta did not make those kinds of mistakes. Each and every one of her moves was calculated beforehand—down to the finest detail."

"I think she will sleep now," Zweck says, coming back into the living room. "I have provided her with a mild sedative."

"They must have been very close," you say.

"It was love at first sight," Zweck says. "As if they had been meant for each other from the very start. As if they were two sides of the same coin. Isn't that so, Girgit?"

"Yes, yes," Matlab says. "True love."

"Kianta gave Celine what I could not," Zweck says, perhaps noticing your puzzlement. "The excitement of youth; the thrill of mutual satisfaction; the blaze of pure physicality." He turns to you. "Do you see what I mean?"

You're not sure what to answer. Does he mean they were lovers in the bedding-partner sense? If so, how can he be so calm and matter-of-fact about it? Or were they simply kindred souls? In the end, you just smile and nod.

"After a night with Kianta," Zweck says, "Celine would always return recharged. Ready to face life again." He sighs. "Professor Serratura, would you care for another brandy?"

"Ah, no," you say, images of your encounter with Professor Seppanen now flashing through your head. "It's getting late." You check your watch. Past 10. Your watch? Back on your wrist? You pull your shirt sleeve over it—then check it again. It's there, alright. Ticking away.

"Something the matter?" Zweck asks.

"No, no," you say, picking up your briefcase. "Just a little tired, that's all. And I have a feeling tomorrow's going to be a long day."

"Yes," Zweck says as he walks you to the door. "A long and perhaps unpleasant day—if we do not get the symposium back on track."

"If there's anything I can do," you say, standing on the front steps.

"No," Zweck says, shaking his head. Then stops. "Actually . . . a favour. . . ." He stops again. "No, no. I dare not ask."

"What is it, Doctor Zweck?" You smile. "The worst that can happen is that I say no."

"True, true," he says. He looks at Matlab, who nods his head. "It has to do with Professor Seppanen's paper."

"Yes?"

"I would like you to read it," Zweck says. "Tomorrow. At one of the seminars."

"What! But—"

"I do not expect you to defend it," Zweck says, holding up his hands. "Or even answer questions on it. Really, I just want to be able to say that the paper was first read at our symposium. It would be quite the coup."

"Well, I don't know," you say, looking first at Zweck and then at Matlab. "I would have to think about it."

"Of course, of course," Zweck says. "Here, let me get it for you."

He goes back inside.

"The moon is something tonight, is it not?" Matlab says, face turned to the sky. "Almost makes you want to believe in gods and goddesses."

"Yes," you say. "Gods and goddesses." You look at Matlab. "Tell me. Why doesn't he ask you to read the paper?"

"You should take it as a privilege," Matlab says, still staring at the moon. "An initiation step perhaps into the inner sanctum."

"Here we are," Zweck says, handing you Seppanen's paper. "I hope you will consider it carefully."

"I will," you say. You put it in your briefcase. "Are you headed in my direction, Professor Matlab? Perhaps we could share a taxi."

BERLIN

"Girgit is my guest," Zweck says, taking his arm. "He'll be staying here this evening."

"The inner sanctum," you say.

"I beg your pardon," Zweck says.

"Yes," Matlab says, laughing. "The inner sanctum."

It's nearly midnight when you open the front door to the *Pension Aryana* and tiptoe in. Only the desk lamp is on, casting elongated shadows across the hallway. You fumble for the key to your room and have to turn it twice before it works. As you step inside, you feel something crumple beneath your feet. You bend down to pick it up: a piece of paper, folded in half. You switch on the light. Your name is written in large letters across the front of the paper: "*Herr* Professor Serraruta." Misspelled as usual. You unfold the note:

> "You will notice Frieda performed a new cleaning of your room. To me it was more of a mess than it was necessary for it to be and that would make it customary to demand an additional accounting. But I will leave it be this time. In future, please to keep your stockings from the lamp. A Mr. Singer telephoned for you. I do not normally take messages—but I have granted an exception this time. Mr. Singer says he is sorry about the tragedy that befell you and your colleagues earlier in the day. If you wish to call him to talk about it, he is available all day tomorrow. Or, if you wish, you may visit him at the address on his calling card. In any case, he would like to see you again before you depart Berlin. Telephone message received at: 8:23 p.m. Berlin time. Also, I hope you do not wish to stay further than Monday. The room has already been reserved for another—and we have no others available. Truly yours, Karl (Fritz)."

137

The little twerp, you say to yourself. I wouldn't stay here a moment longer than necessary. Besides, after tomorrow, I won't need your ratty *pension*. It's Doctor Bruno Zweck's inner sanctum for me. You reread the note. How could Singer have known so quickly about Seppanen? But then it wasn't so quickly, after all. Her suicide had taken place between one and two. In six hours, there would have been plenty of time for the news to spread. It may even have been on the local newscast.

You sit down on the bed and prepare to remove your shoes. Suddenly, out of nowhere, you feel your bladder about to burst. You pride yourself on your control. Often, as a child, you would hold back the whole night before finally seeking blessed relief. But there's always the danger that you have to rush out in the middle of the night, legs squeezed tightly together. Best to get it over with.

You walk as quietly as possible past the desk lamp and down the corridor, dimly guided by a pair of night lights. No matter how softly you tread, however, the floor crackles and squeaks beneath you. As you inch by, you can imagine heads popping up from beds like a series of jack-in-the-boxes. And then falling back onto their pillows. You've almost made it through when a door opens ahead of you. Oh God, you say, freezing in the hope whoever it is will go right back in. No such luck. A head sticks out and peers down the hallway. It's the old man midget, still dressed in his oversized uniform. He crooks his finger at you and motions that you should approach.

By the time you reach his door, the midget is sitting up on his gigantic bed, feet rocking back and forth as they don't quite touch the ground. Next to him and directly under a lamp is the trunk with the glittering swastika on it. Only this time it's opened. You notice a very rudimentary eye-and-hook catch for such an elaborate trunk. Where have you seen a similar catch before? You feel it's very familiar. But then again they're very common. The midget motions once more, indicating you should come in.

"Hello," you whisper as you cautiously enter. "What can I do for you?"

The midget jumps off the bed and, pulling you forward, closes the door behind you. Then he scurries, crab-like, back to resume his position on the bed. He pats the space beside him. You sit down, gingerly. You're not quite sure what all this means but are secure in the knowledge you can defend yourself if it comes to that. After all, you outweigh the other man by at least 50 kilos. As if to emphasize that fact, the mattress creaks under the additional weight.

Without wasting any time, the midget dips into the trunk and pulls out a yellowed photograph, torn at the edges. It shows a group of soldiers posing awkwardly in front of a tank and holding their helmets against their chests. The midget points to a tall blond soldier at the end with a wisp of hair before his eyes and a wide grin—then at himself.

"That's you?" you say, unable to keep the surprise out of your voice. "Are you saying that man is you?"

The midget nods vigorously, then reaches up and pulls a strand of white hair across his forehead as if in imitation. He puts the photo back and takes out a scorched medal hanging from a tattered ribbon. He holds the medal up for a moment and then, after placing it around his neck, offers you the opportunity to examine it.

"I see," you say, fingering the medal. "You were not only tall and blond once but a hero for the fatherland. Is that the implication? Is that what you're trying to say? Do you even understand me?"

Once again the midget nods and, after kissing it, returns the medal to the trunk. The last thing to come out of the trunk is a small black book with a mottled cover. The moment you see it, you snatch it out of the midget's hands without thinking.

"What are you doing with this?" you demand as the midget covers his head in fear of being struck. "Where did you get this? That's my father's book. You've been sneaking around in my room, haven't you?" The midget shakes his head. "Of course, you have. Where else would you have got this? I'm going to report you to the management. I hope you haven't damaged this or you'll pay dearly. I'll see that you go to jail. There are laws against taking other people's property, you know."

You open the book—and realize it isn't yours after all. Oh, there's similar handwriting in it—and it too may have been a phone or address book at one time. But the writing is in German, not Italian. You stare at the book, then at the grinning midget. This isn't possible. Something is definitely not right here. You let the book fall on the bed. The midget picks it up and drops it back in the trunk. Then he closes the trunk with the latch. Now, you recognize the latch. Now, you remember where you've seen one just like it: in your father's basement, holding down the lid on his box. His precious memorabilia.

What does all this mean? You don't know. Perhaps there isn't an explanation. Perhaps it's just pure coincidence. The midget jumps off the bed and tugs at your sleeve. You allow yourself to be pulled towards a mirror on the far wall. A shaving mirror perhaps. You stand in front of the mirror, staring at yourself. There's a look of disbelief on your face—as if you've been stunned. The midget pushes a chair against the wall, then gets up on it and unhooks the mirror. He hands the mirror to you, suggesting you should place it on the bed. You stare at your face in the mirror the whole time you're carrying it to the bed. The midget indicates you should come forward. He points at the space from which the mirror has just been removed. There's a small hole at the centre of that space on the wall—a perfectly round hole obviously done with a precision instrument.

The midget, still on the chair, puts his eye to the hole first. Then, rubbing his hands together gleefully, indicates you should do the same, offering you the chair. But you don't need the chair. You lean forward tentatively, not knowing what to expect—a poke in the eye perhaps or a practical joke shot of flour. The hole turns out to be the opening for a wide-angle lens, providing a distorted, almost hallucinogenic view of the next room. You pull back; look about the room for a moment as if checking to make sure no one else is spying on you. The midget makes lewd gestures with his hands, forming a circle with two fingers and poking a third through it. You put your eye against the lens again.

Fritz is lying face up, spread-eagled and naked, on a bed frame with no mattress, no sheets, no pillows—only metal springs cutting into his back and buttocks. He's gagged, a metal muzzle fitted in his mouth. At the edges of your view, his hands and feet are tied to the bedposts with leather thongs. He struggles to free himself but can't and only succeeds in digging the springs deeper into his flesh. All the while, he keeps shaking his head and looking towards a corner of the room, his face a mask of fear. Finally, a shadow emerges, carrying a folding wooden chair. It's Frieda. She's also naked, all except for the familiar kerchief on her head. Her flabby breasts flop in opposite directions; the flesh on her upper arms and stomach sags; her feet slap loudly across the floor.

She opens the chair, places it with its back to Fritz and then straddles it, legs wide apart and hips thrust forward. As she does so, her swatch of pubic hair parts in the middle, exposing a thick pair of labia so bright red it seems they've been painted. Slowly, she lifts her sagging breasts and rests them across the top of the chair. Then, she grins. There seem to be more teeth missing. Someone is knocking them out. One by one. She stands up and does a handstand on the chair—both hands at first, then one only. She rolls away, for a moment out of the line of your vision. When she returns, still walking on her hands, she has an open switchblade between her teeth.

With a backflip, she lands on the edge of the bed, sending the springs bouncing up and down—and cruelly biting into Fritz's back. Like any decent human being, you want to scream, to sound a warning. But, at the same time, you feel mesmerized, your eye the only part of you that's able to move, flitting back and forth between Frieda and Fritz. Still balancing on one hand, Frieda takes the switchblade from her mouth with the other hand and brings it close to Fritz's testicles. She makes a downward motion, as if to slice them. Fritz tries to pull away but can only go so far before the leather straps restrain him, cutting into his wrists and ankles. He is shaking his head frantically, eyes about to bulge out.

Frieda laughs and flips backwards off the bed. She lands perfectly, her feet slapping as one on the floor. The switchblade has become a feather, a long, curving peacock feather with an iridescent eye at its centre. Fritz relaxes for a moment, breathes more easily. The knife has vanished; the danger passed. Frieda, standing provocatively before him, one foot on the chair, uses the feather to tickle herself. She starts with her breasts, circling each one several times. Then, she works her way down her stomach, curves the feather until it covers her labia. She waves it back and forth like a fan before slipping her other hand beneath it. She rubs her fingers back and forth, making exaggerated moaning and heavy breathing sounds while at the same time rocking on the balls of her feet.

Fritz's penis stiffens, quivers like a bow. With a "Ta-Rum!", Frieda drops the feather and pulls a syringe from between her legs. You gasp and hold your breath. You want to look away. You can't look away. She places the syringe sideways on the tip of his penis and balances it there, cold plastic on foreskin. Fritz is staring down the length of his body, the muscles on his neck about to pop. He dares not move as Frieda runs the syringe along the side of the penis to the scrotum—and then back up again. She pulls the foreskin back and holds the needle point right above the eye of his penis. One small jerk and she can jam it down the urethra. Or snap it sideways so that only the needle remains inside. But she pulls back at the last moment, runs it once again down the side of his penis to the scrotum. There, she pushes the tip against the wrinkled skin where the testicles are trying desperately to shrink back into Fritz's body.

A drop of blood trickles slowly down the inside of his thigh. He gags. You can hear his scream—his silent scream. As Frieda pulls the syringe back up his penis, Fritz arches up in one stiff motion and ejaculates forcefully, the bed springs squeaking to the violent shaking of his body. Frieda leaps off the bed and takes a bow, backing away until she disappears from your line of vision. You remain pressed against the peephole, glued to it. Eye darting frantically back and forth. Hoping perhaps for an encore. The midget yanks you away at last, indicating he wants to replace the mirror. You stand aside as he climbs the chair. Now, you're looking at yourself once more.

"*Alles ist kaputt,*" the midget says in a hoarse, raspy voice that seems to come from deep inside his throat, as if it isn't really him speaking.

You allow yourself to be taken unresisting by the hand and led towards the door. Then, when you just stand there,

looking back at the mirror, he gives you a shove and pushes you out, locking the door behind you. You find yourself back in the corridor, unable to remember what you're
doing there, what brings you there in the first place. The
room next to the midget's, that's it. You must find out
what's inside that room, what awaits you there. No! Best to
go about your own business and not to interfere in someone else's. You take several steps past it. But then you can't
resist. You reach for the door knob and try to open it. It's
locked. Naturally, it would be. They wouldn't want someone to come barging in. You place your ear to the door.
Not a sound.

You're about to knock when you suddenly stop, your
hand already in the air. Frieda has a switchblade, you remind yourself. And a syringe. And, from the looks of it, she
knows how to use them both. You could easily be her next
victim on that bed—and this time she might not turn the
blade away at the last moment. She might not simply prick
you with the tip of the needle. You shudder. That thought
reminds you of why you left your room in the first place.
Something is applying unrelenting force to your bladder.
You make it to the bathroom and just manage to pull your
trousers down before exploding.

The first shot of urine goes almost straight into the air
and barely misses your face. In order to direct the stream
into the bowl, you have to double over and push down hard
on your penis. It's hard and tumescent—as if you too had
been on the verge of ejaculation. You clean up the mess
and then sit on the bowl, trying to get up the courage to
make the trip back to your room. You curse yourself for
not turning around the moment you heard that first slap
and scream, on a morning that seems an eternity ago. Now,
who knows what might happen to you. There are perversions going on here, you tell yourself. Deadly perversions,

undermining the most basic taboos. If those taking part in the acts ever discover that you saw them . . . that you could bear witness against them. . . .

And the midget. The midget knows. He might tell Fritz everything. They wouldn't think twice about doing away with you in your sleep. You would vanish forever amid Berlin's thick, odoriferous vapours, part of the yellow mist that rises from the sewers. You would. . . . There's a sudden knock on the door. Your heart thumps.

"Yes?" you call out in a falsetto.

"*Bitte*," a muffled voice says. "*Ich muss zu dem Klosett gehen*. Please, I am to go to the toilet."

"One moment please."

You take a deep breath and open the door, prepared to do battle with whoever dares face you after their display of incestuous sexuality. But it's only Fritz's mother, the two Pomeranians huddled in her arms, ready to snarl.

"You must pardon me," she says, squeezing her legs together. "But I cannot help what is about to happen. Old age is a curse. An evil curse."

"I understand," you say, noticing the beginning of a wet spot on her nightgown. "Good night."

You wait for several more minutes at the far end of the corridor, hardly daring to breathe. Then you walk briskly through it, determined to ignore every temptation to look left or right. And especially not to pay any heed to superannuated midgets in military parade uniforms. You make it back to your room without any further incidents. Once safely inside, you check that both the window and the door are locked—and the catch is on. But what do I do now? you say, sitting on the bed. This is surely a matter for the police. Or is it? What exactly were Fritz and his sister doing anyway? And was it against the law? You shudder. Circus sex. High-wire S & M. The sight is still vivid before you.

MICHAEL MIROLLA

Despite a strong sense of revulsion, you feel yourself becoming excited, almost to the point where the syringe seems to be pressed against your testicles rather than Fritz's. You get up and switch on the desk lamp. There, on top of the desk, is your father's little black book. At least that's safe. Or is it? You leaf through the pages. Yes, it's the right one, written in the right language. You sit staring at it until it starts wavering before your eyes, until it starts floating away. Strange, shouldn't it become more real the more you stare at it? Perhaps not. Perhaps it'll simply vanish one day from lack of attention. From the loss of witness. I've waited and I've waited, you say, and for what? For just the right moment? For a signal from on high? Well, the wait is over. This is as good a time as any. Besides, I don't think I'll be able to sleep anyway. You look at your watch. It's one a.m.

You rub your eyes. Then you take a portable dictionary out of your suitcase—the *Dizionario Garzanti Della Lingua Italiana*, bought just for this purpose—and place it on the desk beside the diary. On the other side, you stack a thick pile of lined sheets.

You centre yourself perfectly in the light. Then, you open the diary to the first page. It begins: "*Ecco le torture inflitte dai tedeschi ai martiri politici. . . .*"

Postscript III

After reading and re-reading the file marked Saturday.doc, Ryle frowned and then began to tap a pencil repeatedly against the side of the computer. There was definitely something wrong here, something that didn't connect. It was a suspicion that had been reenforced with each word, phrase and sentence Ryle had read. He may not have been a literary critic or even a trained grammarian, but Ryle did know one thing: Giulio A. Chiavetta, vocational school graduate and former stationary engineer, wasn't likely to possess anywhere near the vocabulary and wide-ranging knowledge demonstrated by the author of *Berlin*. Nor was it likely he'd be able to move from subatomic particles to cusp geometry, from Wittgenstein to possible worlds theory.

On the other hand, Ryle was well aware that stranger things had happened and the idea of a self-taught polymath with a talent for writing fiction wasn't so uncommon as to be dismissed out of hand. Especially in the dimly lit world of schizophrenia, a world even he had to admit was rarely penetrated by therapeutic flashlights and mental probes—at least with any consistency. So, even if highly unlikely, he was nevertheless willing to entertain the possibility that Chiavetta had hidden talents and *had* actually written this.

No, what really worried Ryle was the tone the manuscript was taking, the sense not so much of an imagination gone wild but of illness so deep and dense nothing would ever drag it back into the open. Into the light of day. While reading it a second time, Ryle had jotted down some brief notes, the psychiatrist's automatic reaction when confronting a stubborn patient:

"Hallucinatory episodes. Loss of contact with reality. Inconsistent parameters of judgement and other higher faculties. Yet totally capable of decision and action (or a facsimile thereof). Highly lucid one moment; strangely delusive the next. Lucidity—symposium; Checkpoint Charlie Museum; supper at Zweck's. Delusions—closet sex with Seppanen; Hitler Youth; Fritz-Frieda. Question: Is Chiavetta aware of this side of Serratura as not being your standard model, not your typical character study? Or does he assume all this to be part and parcel of the normal furniture of life, something we all possess in one form or another?"

In either case, the equation had suddenly become much more complex and the psychiatric decoding would take a great deal longer. If Chiavetta had actually sat in front of the computer for two years to produce this, then Ryle would have to drastically revise his diagnosis of the calm, placid, almost comatose patient he had come to know. And he was certain now that what he was reading would provide him with a startling insight into Chiavetta's mind—and into those like him. But was it an insight that would do either of them any good? And, just as important, was the mind he had to unravel that of Giulio A. Chiavetta, real life ex-stationary engineer claiming to be a circus star? Or that of G. Antonio Serratura, philosophy professor and chiaroscuro character in a novel? Or both at once—working in tandem so that what one did and said and thought would automatically affect what the other did and said and thought?

Meanwhile, Ryle had a more pressing problem: the whereabouts of Chiavetta himself. When his patient had vanished from the hospital grounds the previous evening, Ryle hadn't been overly concerned. He knew it was only a matter of time before the police caught up to him—especially as they now had a clear description of him and the clothes he was wearing. And he had assumed his patient would be back under his wing by now: once again tranquillized; once again lying curled in his bed.

Now, however, Ryle was no longer so sure. Chiavetta was either extremely lucky to have avoided capture or more cunning than he'd let on. On the assumption Chiavetta had written the *Berlin* files, Ryle was ready to entertain the latter. In fact, "cunning" might be too mild a description. Twisted was more like it: abnormal; corrupted; heteroclitic. The rat who learns more about the maze as he scurries through it than did the researcher who set it up, despite the researcher's decades of study and planning.

Ryle put on his coat and went outside. Snow had fallen the night before but it was a sunny, if crisp, afternoon. He retraced Chiavetta's steps, now leaving his own footprints in the snow. The hole in the fence had been immediately sealed. Just in case there were others like Chiavetta. Others waiting for a signal to trigger their escape reflex. Ryle doubted it but why take chances. He walked towards the front gates, to where Chiavetta had tried so desperately to scale the fence.

It was there that Ryle remembered something he'd failed to mention to the police: his brief conversation with Chiavetta, the one in which his patient had off-handedly said he was on his way to Berlin. Another of his delusions obviously. Which explained why Ryle hadn't thought it important enough to report. After all, how did Chiavetta ever hope to get from Montreal to Berlin? Even if it occurred to him to make his way to Mirabel Airport, he had no money and, more importantly, no papers. To make doubly sure, Ryle checked the files where patients' birth certificates and other ID cards were held (for the day they were pronounced cured). Chiavetta's were all there—including an expired passport.

But, what if Chiavetta *thought* he could go to Berlin simply by walking onto an airplane? Wouldn't the airport be a natural place to set a trap for him? Or at least to alert the airport security to be on the lookout for him? Ryle called the airport police and, after identifying himself, told them about Chiavetta. He then gave them a description of what Chiavetta was wearing. He also told them that the patient was harmless and should be held until he could collect him. Finally, just in case Chiavetta had found some way to actually pay for a ticket, he asked when the next flight to Berlin might be. He was told there weren't any direct flights—but one to Frankfurt with a connecting flight to Berlin had left within the hour. The security officer said he wasn't allowed to give out the names on the passenger list but did say that a Giulio A. Chiavetta definitely wasn't on board. Good, good, Ryle said to himself, before asking when the next flight would be. The following day, the officer said.

Ryle felt a sense of relief when he put down the phone. The net had to be tightening around Chiavetta. With the police keeping an eye out in the city and the airport security alerted, where else could he go? He had no relatives, no friends. The charities and the shelters would quickly spot him. My friend, your cord can only stretch so far, Ryle said. Soon, I'll have you back safe and sound where you belong. In the womb of your surrogate mother. And, armed with all this new data, I'll have you cured in no time. I'll have you back manning your boiler room station, once more a productive member of society. Or you can practice your high-wire act, provided the safety net is securely in place. What do you think of that, my friend?

Ryle was right about one thing: Chiavetta wasn't on the

plane to Frankfurt. No one knew where he was at that moment. Perhaps not even he himself. But the plane did carry a dapper-dan, spiffy-looking passenger with a far-away look in his eye and a brown leather briefcase on his lap. And, as Antonio G. Serratura pulled out some reading material from the briefcase—a paper or thesis of some sort, he felt secure in the knowledge that he possessed all the appropriate documents to quietly slip through customs in Frankfurt.

III: File—Sunday.doc

Serratura: "My father guarded his little box of mementos as if it were his life, as if nothing else in the universe mattered: neither his increasingly distraught wife nor his permanently on-the-back-burner children. He took the box with him wherever he roamed in that basement suite, lugging it back and forth between sofa and bathroom, sofa and workshop, sofa and wine cellar. He had long before stopped making wine himself but, somehow, he didn't seem to realize that. Somehow he thought the wine was still being made. Somehow. And he would raise an unholy fuss if he happened to run short—accusing those around him of stealing it.

"So we were given the task of keeping his wine cellar stocked, of sneaking in while he slept to empty store-bought product into his well-worn containers. He would toddle into the cantina and comment on how clear, how fine, how pure the latest vintage had turned out—and then give some date forty years in the past for that vintage. He would go through all the motions of transferring the wine from the large demijohns down to gallons and finally bottles. And all the time, the box was beside him, not far from his sight. Ready to be clutched at a moment's notice.

"When he was still lucid, he used to often talk about his war experiences. At first, he told us about his duties as an orderly on a field ambulance and then about being rounded up by the Germans and taken to a P.O.W. camp. About the struggle for food and dignity. About the deadly work in a foundry that came under daily Allied bombardment. About his own efforts to escape that work—once slamming his own foot with a sledge hammer so that it ballooned and became infected. But he had always related these incidents in a cold, clinical manner. Clipped and precise. Without wasted breath or emotion. As if they had happened to someone else or were part of the articles he constantly read about that period. Articles which he cut out of magazines and kept on a chair beside him where they eventually curled and turned yellow. Articles about Mussolini and his mistresses and the betrayal of the Italian royal family.

"But now, as he slipped away, he seemed to be inside those experiences once again, not recalling them so much as reinhabiting them, carrying on one-sided conversations and giving heated answers to questions no one else heard. Thus they became even more incomprehensible to those around him. There was no way for him to explain to us what was happening, so why even bother to try? He was trapped—and the box was either the key to that trap or the ball and chain that held him securely in place. That prevented him from escaping to some better space.

"My own feeling for that box went from an intense desire to ransack it and claim it for my own to a wish to destroy it utterly, to toss it into the nearest fire and leave only the ashes and metal bits behind. Several times, I pretended to pry it away from him, joking that I was taking it off to be cleaned. Or to be repaired as there seemed to be a few screws loose. But he only grunted and held on to it even more tightly. His bony hands would turn white from the pressure and he would squeeze his eyes shut, perhaps thinking I would vanish if he only wished it hard enough.

"If I had wanted to, I'm sure I could have tricked him into giving it up. Or I could have waited till he fell asleep and substituted another for it. Or I could have simply forced it out of his grasp. After all he was just a feeble-minded, feeble-bodied old man by this time, wasn't he? How could he have possibly known the difference? And yet, to this day, there's no doubt in my mind that he would have sensed it at once. And also no doubt at all that any such attempt would have killed him on the spot."

At first, I can't believe what I'm reading in the last few paragraphs of my father's diary. There must be some mistake, something I'm missing, I keep telling myself, as I search frantically through the Italian dictionary for alternative meanings to what have been till now harmless, familiar words. The fault must lie with my poor Italian, my execrable grasp of the language. I thought I could understand it well enough, thought I knew a fair number of its nuances and idioms. But now I realize that's not the case. I must be placing the accents on the wrong syllables, translating the words improperly, interpreting the sentences in ways they weren't meant to be interpreted.

They're supposed to be taken ironically, thick tongue solidly in cheek. It's all a satire, a vision of black humour revealing the damp and crumbling foundations of the human soul once it has surpassed its limits, once it has been pushed beyond all endurance. No, it's allegory. That's it. That's the ticket. He's reenacting Everyman, Original Sin, the Burden of Guilt, the Egress from the Garden of Eden, Innocence Versus Experience, Mechanical Man at War with Himself, the Grinder into Dust of the Free Spirit. The symbolism's what counts, the underlying universality of the statements.

Then, when I realize that won't work, that it's only a smokescreen and a poor one to boot, I start checking the physical material itself. Perhaps I can spot some subtle variation in the paper's age or composition that will allow me to say: "Aha! This was most certainly written by an impostor, by my pretend-father!" Or: "This was inserted later without his knowledge." Or even: "Sure, that's it. Every night while he slept fitfully on his hard, thin bunk, oblivious to the bed bugs and splinters, some fiend, aware of the diary's importance and its hiding place beneath a pair of loose planks, came in and added to what my father had written during the day. His additions were, naturally enough, in invisible ink, and the bogus writing would only materialize upon my father's death, when he could no longer rise to defend himself."

But, of course, search as I might, I can find no variation in age or composition, no sudden deformation in t-crossing or i-dotting, no deviation in style, no tell-tale signs of cut-and-paste. From beginning to end, it's of uniform quality: ink, paper, writing. Even to the occasional misspellings. And, no matter how many times I read it, no matter how many different translations I make, filling, at times, entire sheets with versions and variations of one single sentence, the result always comes down to the same thing, to the same inescapable conclusion.

Conclusions. Now, there's something I know all about. They're supposed to be my specialty, my bread and butter, my *raison d'être*. I can get my teeth into those without any problem. And premises. I mustn't forget premises. Necessary for reaching conclusions. But what has this train of thought to do with what I'd seen in the diary? Nothing, you stupid son of a bitch. Absolutely nothing. With a sweep of my arm, I scatter the sheets to the floor, cradle my head on the desk and try to get some sleep.

This time there's no sleeping, however, no slipping off into blessed unconsciousness. Only a state of total immobility and enervation, suspended in a space that has no dimensions, no boundaries, no Cartesian grip. I feel as if I'm being drained of some vital fluid, a fluid needed absolutely for my functioning. I feel as if I'm being sapped while doing nothing at all, while just lying there with my head beneath the circle of the desk lamp. Wherever I turn, the words are there ahead of me, flashing before me, iridescent and grinning wickedly in the dark. It's impossible for me to shut them out: *"Sono tradito i miei amici."*

I've read those words over and over God knows how many times but I still can't understand them. Or pretend not to. They come following a dozen pages where my father has carefully (and with growing passion, I feel) described the torture and murder of political prisoners; the medical experiments that left victims begging to be put out of their misery; the indiscriminate gassing and cremation of men, women and children; the mass graves dug by those still strong enough to wield picks and shovels; the monstrous tractors used to pile them up and bury them; the sudden breakthrough of the Americans that left the S.S. task of extermination unfinished; the discovery of the survivors who huddled naked and unbelieving in their bunks, thinking it was one more horrible trick being played by their sadistic keepers. All the things, in fact, that had been witnessed, catalogued and numbered so many times before for use as evidence in the eventual trial and punishment of the perpetrators. Not to mention *la gustizia divina* that everyone so fervently prayed for, the cleansing, purging, destroying right hand of God, the one that always had time on its side and sooner or later would descend on the leering wicked.

But these descriptions—the cries of horror and disbelief at the Nazi atrocities and the pitiful renderings of their victims—only make the final words of betrayal even less understandable. Even more of a hammer blow to the head. My father writes towards the beginning of the diary (my translation of sections "C" to "F"):

"When the Americans overran Buchenwald, some of the German citizens from the nearby town were brought by force to the concentration camp to witness the indescribable, the war-time monstrosities committed by their compatriots. German men and women were forced to view the crematorium ovens where over 200 had been incinerated daily. In some of the ovens, one could still make out a few half-charred cadavers, all twisted like pieces of driftwood on some dark beach. The more squeamish among the Germans tried to cover their eyes not to observe that macabre scene. But the American military police told them to lower their hands. They wanted them to see face on the horrendous deeds done by their fellow citizens, the extent of the cynicism and criminality without parallel in human history."

In the same vein, he puts down towards the end—at least of the sections "X" and "Y" that can still be deciphered:

"Most of the women over forty were sent directly to the ovens. A few were 'spared,' but only at the whim of the examining doctor. A small number of these were recruited to do forced labour while the majority of the ones saved from the ovens ended up as medical experiments, alongside dogs, rats and guinea pigs. The cruelty of these experiments is unimaginable, beyond the level of the human mind to grasp. A measure of that cruelty can be felt in the fact that, in the end, many of the women begged to be gassed. Anything was better than the torture they were undergoing in the name of medical science, the mental and physical abuse that reduced them to mounds of quivering flesh, like jelly fish responding to the prod. They wanted to anesthetize and cut away the parts of themselves that hurt, to expel them from an all too brutal consciousness."

It's a full-fledged condemnation of what he's seen, heard about and experienced, a judgement seemingly well-merited. But, then, out of the blue, when it comes time to sum up, to come down as hard as possible with that hammer of divine justice, the tone changes abruptly. The last paragraph—written in section "Z"—reads:

"We're all traitors, each and every single one of us. We're all mass murderers. We've all compromised to stay alive, to scrabble out our measly, miserable existence, to chew on our potato skins and grub-infested cabbages. Only those who did themselves in at the very beginning managed to escape the stain of guilt and complicity. I have betrayed my friends. I have betrayed them over and over again daily. They know not who it is who betrays them, who constantly slips the knife into their backs and gives it the final twist. They continue to treat me like a friend, like someone they can trust. But I'm not worthy of their trust. I don't deserve their friendship. I deserve only to die."

Betrayed them how? In what manner? I want to scream. Why? What did you do? What did your betrayal consist of? Specifics. I want specifics. Details. Facts. Were you one of those who cried: "The horror! The horror!" while at the same time planting human skulls to see if they'd sprout? Come on, tell me. I can take it. I'm a man now. I'm no longer a child. Let me have it. I keep staring at the last page of the diary which is only half filled and ends with the date of liberation—"12/6/45"—written in giant-sized numbers across it. Perhaps I can force an explanation from the empty half, crowbar the answer from its hiding place, burn away the cloak of invisibility it has used to shield itself from the very judgement I have come to expect.

But, no matter how long I stare at it, no matter what incantations I use, nothing of the sort happens. Instead, a light comes on in the hallway, sending a sliver probing beneath my door. I rub my eyes and stretch. My back aches from my having sat scrunched up all night—and from the tension. One of my legs is asleep, the blood cut off against the sharp metal edge of the writing table. The fingers on my right hand are swollen, a result of gripping the pen too tightly. I slap at the hand, massage my leg to get the circulation going.

BERLIN

There's the clinking of glasses and cups outside my door, the shuffling of feet followed by the strong odour of coffee. I look at the luminescent dial on my watch, the watch so faithfully present once more (but who can tell for how long?). Eight o'clock. The first breakfasts are being served. That must be Frieda out there right now, padding along barefoot in her creepy-crawly way. Switch-blade Frieda with the peasant kerchief and the whiplash personality. I decide on the spur of the moment not to miss out this morning. No, I'll make it a point not to miss out. After all, haven't I paid for the meals in advance? Of course.

Feeling lightheaded from lack of sleep coupled with a confusion I've never experienced before, I open my door and step into the hallway. The two bird ladies are seated at the breakfast table, silhouetted by the first rays of sun. Ibises, perhaps, on the banks of the Nile? Or whooping cranes driving their beaks time and again into the silty mud in search of food?

"*Guten Morgen*," I say as I plunk myself down at the far end of the table across from them and nervously unfold a cloth napkin onto my lap.

"I'm sorry," the lady closest to me says in a clipped voice, the skin on her throat stretching like cracked velour. "You must have us confused with someone else."

"Oh, do you think so?" I say, smiling, looking quickly back and forth between one and the other. "And whom might that be, hmm?"

"You said '*Guten Morgen*,'" the second one takes up the chorus, frowning. "You definitely said that. Didn't he say that, Agnes?"

"Yes, Bettina, he did."

"I admit it," I say, hand against my chest. "Guilty as charged. I was under the impression that it was German for—"

"Young man, we know perfectly well what it means," velour-throated Agnes says. "There are plenty of others in this city for whom '*Guten Morgen*' would be appropriate—or at least a propos, having had the misfortune of a foreign birth. But we happen to be British. And exceeding proud of it. If you wish to address us, a simple 'Good morning, dear ladies' will do from now on, thank you very much."

She turns her head and bobs an "I-told-you-so" at Bettina, obviously pleased with herself.

"I see," I say.

I peel back a packet of orange marmalade. It's all scrunched in one corner from being left on its side. Or perhaps it too is afraid of the knife.

"You see what?" Agnes and Bettina say together, swiveling their heads sharply in my direction.

"Perhaps it would be best to remain merely nodding acquaintances," I say, slapping the reluctant marmalade onto my toast. "That way language wouldn't interfere. One nod for 'Hello'; two for 'Have a pleasant day.' And so on. Or, if that sounds a bit monotonous, we could expand the symbolic repertoire. Perhaps lift a leg as we pass each other in the corridor. Or wiggle our fingers. Or release a little gas. Just a teeny-weeny bit, you know. What do you say to that, dear ladies? Our own private code. We could change the key each night as we saw fit. Wouldn't that be—"

I stop. The ladies have gone back to pecking at their food and are pointedly ignoring me, almost as if I'm not there. Maybe it's true, I say to myself. Maybe I'm not really here. Maybe I'm somewhere else and this is just one in the infinite number of possible worlds quickly leading to dead ends, leading to places where evolution never got a chance, where anaerobic bacteria go to the head of the phylic class. Hmm, must ask Matlab if such a thing is possible. Or perhaps I could write a paper on it: *On the Logic of Things That Aren't There.*

BERLIN

I pick up a cube of sugar and plop it into my mouth, sucking at the sweetness. LSD perhaps. To help you traipse off the top of the Europa Centre without a care in the world, to float down like a feather right into the World Fountain. That would explain a lot of things. Or would it? I must test the composition of the water. H_2O or XYZ? Ah, Twin Earthians, who can tell the difference? Who can ever tell the difference? I giggle, unable to keep the joke to myself. Both ladies glance over for a moment and shake their heads in jerky unison—as if joining forces to better yank out a reluctant worm. Or Nile leech stubbornly clinging to its biblical reed.

"Patter, dear ladies, patter," I say, wolfing down marmalade-smeared bread, bread over-dripping with the stuff. "The glue that holds the social fabric together when it comes right down to it." I chew harshly, smacking my lips. "Crow's feet. Besides, how do we know who we are?" I lick my lips. "Surely, we can't be so sure of ourselves. Surely not."

"Come, Bettina," Agnes says, putting her knife and fork down with great deliberation and pushing back her chair. "I've had enough rudeness for one morning."

"Yes, Agnes. I, too, seem to have lost all appetite."

They're huffing and puffing and making elaborate preparations to leave when Fritz careens around the corner balancing a fresh pot of coffee and a plateful of muffins. I feel something tighten in my stomach. I can't avoid a glance at Fritz's crotch. The bulge is still there beneath the form-fitting, stone-washed jeans. No tell-tale splotch of red; no limp amputation.

"Ladies, ladies," Fritz says in his sweetest, most mocking voice. "You are on your way so soon this morning? Did the professor drive you off with his loose talk? He has a way with the women, does he not?"

Both ladies giggle like a pair of youngsters caught doing something naughty behind the woodshed. I can see them hovering, all feathery and bird-like, over a captive Fritz, clamping false teeth onto his nipples, depilating his nostrils, toothbrushing his anus. Toothbrushing his anus? My God, I think. That can't be me. I can't be thinking those things, coming up with those images.

"It's Sunday morning, Fritzy," Agnes says, trilling. "You know what that means."

"*Futball!*" Fritz exclaims, adjusting his cap. "The betting pool. This is my lucky day, *ja*."

"No, no, you silly boy," Bettina says, giving him a light tap on the chest with the back of her hand. "Worship. Offering thanks to the Lord for His infinite mercies."

"Yes, Fritzy," Agnes says. "There wouldn't happen to be a Church of England service in the area, now would there? Preferably Low?"

Fritz shrugs, then shakes his head. He, too, it seems, has been reduced to nonverbal responses.

"No, I didn't think so," Agnes continues. "The risk of contamination is too great with all these foreigners around. In that case, we must settle for one of the other denominations. As long as it's decently Protestant, of course. Come, Bettina. Or we'll be late."

"Tootle-loo, ladies," Fritz says, as the two of them hop off. "Say a prayer for poor little Fritzy, now. *Gott im Himmel* above knows he is most in need of it."

Fucking right, you need it, I say, barely under my breath. Perverted little bastard. And with your own sister, too.

"Did you say something, Herr Professor Serraruta?" Fritz asks with his customary tilt and sticking out of chest.

I shake my head, not bothering to correct him this time. Not a thing. What would I have to say to you anyway?

"You are up with the cock this morning, Professor," Fritz

says. "Not the usual."

"I had a little trouble sleeping," I say, gritting my teeth at the thought of being so close to Fritz. And at crotch level.

"I hope it was not the message," Fritz says as he leans over and pours me a second cup of coffee. "Your Mr. Singer insisted very much that I get it to you. He said it was very important. A good friend, *ja?*"

"He's a Jewish concentration-camp survivor," I blurt out, not exactly sure why I said that. But it feels good. Take that, you protector of Nazi villains. You wearer of bulge-revealing jeans.

"Oh, that is most unfortunate," Fritz says, replacing the coffee pot on his tray.

"What's most unfortunate, Fritzy? That he was in a concentration camp? Or that he survived?"

"Professor!" Fritz says, taking a step back as if he's just received a blow to the midsection. "That is not a funny thing to say in our country."

"Funny?" I stand up and throw aside my napkin. I start to raise my voice. "Why you sick little bastard! It wasn't meant to be funny. Not funny at all. You're hiding a Nazi sympathizer in this house. In this very *pension*. You can't deny that. I've seen him with my own eyes."

"Please, Herr Professor." Fritz holds up his hand and brings a finger to his lips. "Not so loud, please. Sunday morning. There are other guests—new guests. Important guests. And, they are sleeping."

"Is that so?" I'm now shouting. "Well, it's about time they wake up. We can't have unreconstructed Nazis running around with swastikas and propaganda films, now can we? We just can't allow that to happen again."

"You must be mistaken," Fritz says, taking a deep breath. "There is no Nazi in hiding here." He sweeps the room with his arm. "As you can detect, this is a respectable *pension*."

"Respectable, you say? You call what you were doing last night respectable. It was perversion, pure and simple. Even I recognize perversion when I see it. But, of course, that's none of my business. What families do in their own bedrooms is their affair—even if it does involve a sleazy scumbag and his dim-witted sister. Who probably can't help yourself—"

"I am sorry," Fritz says, shaking his head. "I cannot understand what you are trying to say. You must repeat. My English is too poor—"

"Now it's your English, is it? Come on, then. No need for any Quinean radical translation here. Let me simply show you exactly what I mean."

I take several steps down the corridor, motioning to a puzzled Fritz to follow.

"Come on, Fritzy," I say, crooking my finger. "Or are you afraid of what you might find? A few skeletons goose-stepping in the closet, maybe? The squeak of bed springs that just won't stay still?"

I continue to walk as I talk—then stop in front of the door where I'd last seen the midget. Fritz hovers a few feet behind me.

"Let's see you deny this." I throw open the door. "What do you call—"

I stop, my mouth wide open. Except for the four-poster bed and metal writing table, the room is completely empty.

"Yes," Fritz says, puffing up his chest and regaining a measure of his dignity. "You wished to show me something? Something not proper with the room perhaps? Although I do not see what concern that is of yours."

"There was a man here," I say, looking frantically about. "An old man. More like a midget. He . . . he wore some kind of military uniform." I scramble to check under the bed.

"He had an old-fashioned record player and a homemade trunk with a glittering swastika on it." I point to where I'd seen the trunk. "There was a film projector. He was showing Adolf Hitler at Nuremburg." I pull down the window shade—it flutters back up when I release it. "The people were shouting '*Sieg Heil!*' at one another. It's a famous propaganda film." Then I peter out and say, almost as an afterthought: "I know it. I saw it at university once."

"I see," Fritz says, hands on hips. "A man, you say? An old man but not exactly an old man. A midget, no less? Showing films of Adolf Hitler? And many people shouting '*Sieg Heil!*'? Is that correct? Did I understand you to have said the right thing?"

"That's right. An old man with white hair, sitting on the bed right there." I pat the spot, now all smoothed out. I'm having trouble catching my breath. "I talked to him. Just last night, as a matter of fact."

"That is interesting," Fritz says, straightening a corner of the bedsheet. "Very interesting." Then he turns to me. "You must know this room belonged to my father."

"Your father? Then, he's the man I saw. He did say he had fought in the war. That's right. And he even had pictures from that time. Pictures he took out of the trunk. It must have been him. Of course! Stupid me. Why didn't I think of it before?"

"I am sorry for you," Fritz says, shaking his head sadly. "You must be in complete error. My father was lost on the Russian front. *Kaputt.* We did not find—recover—his body."

"But . . . but. . . ." I suddenly notice the mirror above the chair next to the writing desk. I jump up and rush over to it. "How about this then? How did I know . . . how was I able to see you and your sister . . . the two of you doing what you were doing in the next room?"

"My sister and I?" Fritz says. He takes off his Yankees cap and scratches his head. "In the room next door?"

"Yes, yes," I say.

I climb up on the chair and tug at the mirror. I can see myself in it, slightly distorted, red-faced and yanking hard. But the mirror won't come away, screwed solidly into the wall.

"Professor!" Fritz is standing behind me, arms out in case I fall. "Professor Serraruta!"

"Serratura!" I shout, stamping my foot on the chair. "Not Serraruta. Don't try to confuse me! Get my fucking name right, at least!"

"Again, my apologies," Fritz says. "But what are you doing? Please come down from there. I do not wish for you to injure yourself. That would not be a pleasant experience for you or for the *pension*."

I feel my puzzlement growing. Standing on the chair and looking down at Fritz, I realize something definitely isn't right here. I'm being manipulated. They're playing some elaborate game to disorient me. The midget has obviously told them about my peek-a-booing and now they have to cover it all up, have to make it seem as if none of it ever happened. That sort of thing wouldn't sit too well with the *pension*'s regular clientele, especially with the bird-like ladies in search of the Church of England. Low, non-Papist Division.

"I see," I say, struggling to calm myself as I step down from the chair and brush my pants. "So I'm to assume this room hasn't been used in more than 40 years."

"We have not rented it out, if that is what you mean to say. My mother would not allow it. Never. Every morning, she cleans it, *ja*. And the bed she makes once a week. She is insistent we wash the sheets and replace them. She is—how do you say it?—fixed that my father will return one day. An old woman's fantasy. It does no harm, *ja*?"

"Right, right. Just a harmless fantasy, a way to keep an old lady happy. Correct?" Fritz nods warily, unsure of what other craziness I'm about to unleash. "And the room next door. That too, I presume, is empty."

"The room next door? No, that is not empty. That is where we keep the beds that are extra. Would you care to see it?"

I nod. Then, shake my head as I remember the gleaming switchblade, the spurt of what could easily have been blood.

"But, of course, you must," Fritz says, grinning and taking me by the arm. "Come. I insist. I will show it to you and—how do you say it?—place your mind at repose." Fritz leads me out of the midget's room. He searches through his pockets. "I have a key here for it. Aha!" He pulls out the key and opens the door. "There, you see."

I peek in, almost afraid of what I'll find. But the room is sweetly innocent in the daylight. No tell-tale signs of what had taken place the night before: no leather thongs, no glint of switchblade, no peacock feathers, no crumpled handkerchiefs stiffening as they dry. Only parts of beds piled against its walls—bedposts, headboards, springs, mattresses. And dust everywhere, floating serenely in the sunlight as if it's the only thing that matters, as if it alone gives things substance. Or permanence. The dust fills my nostrils. I sneeze repeatedly, sending waves of it streaming across the room.

"*Gesundheit!*" Fritz says with a wide grin. "I, too, find extreme discomfort with dust."

I've had enough of this. I turn and walk out of the room. Halfway down the corridor, Frieda sticks her kerchiefed head out from behind a door and smiles at me. I don't return her smile. She is, without a doubt, a willing accomplice, and probably still naked from the neck down, the switchblade-feather held in readiness behind her back. I hurry on, glad to escape the corridor before it closes in on me again. The young couple are at the breakfast table feeding one another toast, fingers going deep into each other's mouths as they lick marmalade from them. They too smile as I walk by. I nod at them. Curtly. Business-like.

Once again, the TV is on without any sound. Excerpts of the president giving his speech are being shown, interspersed with shots of people holding up cereal box tops and walking through metal detectors while military helicopters hover overhead. To one side, a group of Buddhist monks in yellow robes sits and chants—or they may be lip synching. I return to my room and lock the door.

That outburst, I realize, was a stupid thing on my part. I've allowed myself to be outmaneuvered by Fritz. Now, I feel discredited and things don't look good at all. They've managed to remove every piece of evidence that backs my claims of perversion, of boarders with Nazi sympathies, of crimes against . . . against the common good. My word against theirs—and they have the advantage of the language on their side, the explanatory power of words mostly foreign to me. The only way to prove my story is to have a forensic team comb the two rooms, looking for the slightest drop of semen. Or blood. Fibers from the midget's military coat indicating his presence. Splinters of wood from the trunk. But, even to set such a search in motion, I would need some sort of evidence. Or at the very least to convince someone in authority that I'm not delusional. And who would believe me?

I see they obviously have nothing to fear from me. I wasn't thinking straight, hadn't reacted logically, burdened as I am by my own problems—not the least of which being my father's enigmatic diary entries. Now, my disorientation is palpable. I can feel the room shifting around me, the ground tilting beneath me. And that little black book, I feel, is at the very root of it. Has managed to dislodge the anchor and leave me adrift on the seas of some terrible whimsy. Several times I come close to shredding it, to tearing it into bits so small no two words would be left intact. Several times I hold it before me, ready to let rip. But I can't go through with it. Instead, I stuff the diary into my jacket pocket.

Despite the bitter pill of its contents, I feel an ironic comfort from its mere existence, from the idea of it being there. Perhaps, in time, what's in it can be forgotten, sinking out of sight till the next unsuspecting victim delves into its deadly waters. Perhaps that person will have the courage—and the means—to refute it, to turn the *je t'accuse* around and point it once again in the right direction. For now, I satisfy myself with tearing up the translations and tossing the pieces into the waste basket.

Then, still stunned, still not quite sure of what I'm doing, I step from my room and, briefcase in hand, prepare to head out. Only to bump into Fritz who stands at the doorway with his sister a few steps behind him. She's dressed as a maid again and has a rolling pin in her hands instead of a knife. Behind her are the two old ladies, the young couple and Fritz's mother, still in her fancy turban and feather-duster robe and holding the two yapping dogs in her arms.

"What, no midget?" I say smiling, trying to regain whatever advantage I may once have had. "Is he at a political rally or something?" The others don't respond, just continue to stare at me. "No, no. Let me guess. He's on his way back to the Russian front. To battle once again the communist peril—only this time with the help of President Reagan, enemy of the Evil Empire and defender of the free enterprise faith."

They still don't respond.

"Well," I say, "if you'll excuse me—"

I try to get around Fritz but he cuts off my path—with Frieda in reserve behind him, slapping the rolling pin against the palm of her hand. The others close the circle around me, leaving me with my back to the door.

"Professor, your behaviour—," Fritz begins.

"Yes?" I say curtly. "If it's something you want, Fritz, be quick about it. As you can see, I'm in a hurry."

"I do not wish for trouble of any sort," Fritz says, looking back as if to make sure that his sister and the others are still there, ready to support him.

"I'm glad for you." I tap my foot, to all appearances simply a man in a hurry. "Now, is that all?"

"This is—"

"I know, I know," I say with an air of impatience. "This is a respectable *pension* and you don't wish for trouble. Of any sort."

"That is correct."

"Well," I say, smiling at each of them in turn, "you won't get any from me. Not a smidgen."

"That is good news, Herr Professor," Fritz says, relaxing noticeably. "There will be no more disturbances then?"

"Not a one, Fritzy my boy."

I pat Fritz on the shoulder—which makes him cringe slightly.

"Can you trust him?" Agnes asks, pointing her beak at me.

"You have my word on it," I say. "The word of an honorary Englishman from the colonies."

"Harrumph!" Bettina says. "We'll see."

"Tootle-loo," I say.

Fritz and Frieda move out of my way as I step forward and walk to the *pension* door. I open the door, then turn and wave, resisting a strong urge to give them a Nazi salute.

BERLIN

"*Auf Wiedersehen!*"

I turn once more and continue to walk towards the front of the building. I can feel the others behind me, standing at the doorway, eyes on my back, waiting for me to collapse perhaps. Or to make some move that will allow them to call the police. The moment I'm outside, out of their sight, I lean against the wall, exhausted. I'm having trouble breathing; I can barely keep my legs from collapsing beneath me; the palms of my hands are covered with sweat. I rub them on my pants.

After several deep breaths, I walk hurriedly away, worried that Fritz might decide to follow me out, perhaps leading his little ragtag band into battle with the flag of respectability flying high above them. Now, wouldn't that be an ironic twist after what I'd seen and heard in that *pension?* At the end of the block, just before turning onto Kufferstendam, I look back one last time. No one following behind me—at least no members of Fritz's little troop. And the only flag is the gold, red and black of the German Federal Republic as it flaps in the wind atop the Europa Centre.

I look at my watch: 8:35 a.m. Where to now? Too early to present myself at the symposium. Or at Zweck's home. Where Bruno is probably still trying to comfort his beloved Celine, grief-stricken over the loss of her. . . . I never did uncover the nature of her relationship with Seppanen. Perhaps I should go back to sleep. Just turn around and walk into the *pension* and announce I'm not going anywhere and that I have as much right as anyone else to be there—having paid the full amount in advance.

On second thought, I'd better not. Fritz might get it into his head to prevent my leaving again. He might detain me until he's had a chance to call the police—using his posse to barricade my bedroom door. I can just picture myself being led away, screaming my innocence in English while the policemen nod sagely and continue doing their duty—with helpful little Fritz and the bird ladies as guides. No, best to stay away for now.

A phone booth reminds me of the promise I made to Louise. I try to calculate what time it might be in Montreal. Six hours? Forward or back? Middle of the night or middle of the day? I can't do it. Silly, isn't it? But it doesn't really matter. If it's the middle of the night, then at least I'm sure of finding someone there. I search through my pockets for coins and then pull out a handful which I place by the telephone. In their midst is Seppanen's identity pin and a card with "Singer's Restaurant Supplies: We Cater to the World" written on it.

After dialing, I wait anxiously for Louise to pick up the phone. It's the middle of the night, I'm suddenly sure of it. And she's now rising drowsily from the bed. Our conjugal bed. Wondering who might be calling at this time of night. I count the number of rings. At five, the answering machine picks up. What the hell! I exclaim under my breath. Where could she be? At my mother's, of course. She's sleeping over at my mother's to keep her company. Louise has always had a heart of gold, has always put the feelings of others ahead of herself. I wait for the message beep:

"Louise. It's me again. Not much to say really. I can't wait to get home. Hope you've missed me as much as I've missed you guys. Some crazy things have happened here. Some things I still find hard to believe. But I'm alright. And I'll tell you all about it when I get there. Okay? We'll have a good laugh over the whole thing. Bye, now. All my love to Cathy."

I hang up and start to replace the rest of the coins. I hold Singer's business card in the palm of my hand. The writing's embossed in gold. There are several telephone numbers on it: New York; Milan; Berlin. I dial the Berlin number.

"Hallo," a tired, irritated voice responds.

"Yes," I say. "Uh . . . could I speak with Mr. Singer, please? I believe he is staying there." There's silence at the other end of the line. "Mr. Singer. Zeke. Is he there?"

"Ah, Singer." He pronounces the "s" like a "z." "Moment, *bitte.*"

"*Hallo,*" a different voice says after a momentary pause. "Singer *hier.*"

"Mr. Singer," I say. "Zeke. It's Anthony. Professor Serratura."

"Anthony! What a pleasant surprise! You got my messages. For a while there, I didn't think I'd hear from you again. You've been busy, right?"

"Ah . . . yes . . . very."

"So, my friend. What can I do for you?"

"Well, I'd like to. . . ." I look around. What exactly *would* I like him to do for me? Why have I phoned *him* of all people? "I'd like to see you." That's it. To see him. "If that's possible. If you're not too occupied, that is."

"I'm never too occupied for a friend." There's a pause. "Is something the matter? You sound disturbed somehow. Has it to do with that death yesterday?"

"The death yesterday?" I say. "Oh yes. Professor Seppanen. We were all shaken by it. All of us."

"I can well imagine," Singer says. "Suicides are never a pretty sight." He pauses again. "Is that why you want to come over? Need someone to talk to?"

"Yes," I say. That's it. "Someone to talk to."

"I'm here," Singer says. "I've got some business in the afternoon—no rest for the wicked, you know. Even on the Sabbath. But my morning's free. So come right on over, why don't you?"

"I'd love to," I say. "But I don't have your address."

"Of course," he says. "How silly of me. Write the address

down on a piece of paper. Then, just hand it to a cab driver."

When the cab drops me off, I don't go directly into the high-rise apartment whose address Singer has given me. Instead, I walk around the block several times. Getting up my courage, I guess.

This is crazy, I tell myself, leaning against one of the pylons for the overhead railway that runs directly in front of the apartment building. What am I doing here anyway? What do I expect out of Singer? Help? Comfort? Solace? A pat on the shoulder? A train speeds by above me, rattling loose a flock of pigeons that has sought shelter in the nooks and crannies. Several youths—both male and female—are running back and forth across the pylons, playing hide-and-seek. No, they're hurling bottles at each other. The bottles shatter against the pylons, spreading the odour of gasoline. Demonstrators practicing, perhaps. Or a new mating ritual.

I start to walk again. Across from the front door to Singer's flat, a balding man in a leather jacket squats beside his motorcycle. I can see pieces of the engine spread on a greasy cloth. He looks up at me as I walk by—then returns to his engine parts. He, too, smells of gasoline and his hands are black with grime. The would-be demonstrators let out a war whoop and disappear. After hesitating for several seconds, I finally ring Singer's doorbell.

"Come on up," the voice on the intercom says. "Turn left once you get off the elevator."

The door to the apartment is partially open. Through it, I can see Singer sprawled on a sofa, reading a newspaper and sipping a cup of coffee. I'm about to knock when I hear laughter. Loud and raucous. Then a pillow flies across the room. I knock. The door squeaks open under my knuckles.

"Anthony!" Singer says, putting down his cup and rising to greet me. "I was beginning to think you'd changed your mind. Come in, come in."

He clasps me across the shoulders and pulls me into the room. Annie is sitting on the sofa, wrapped in bedsheets. He is holding hands with a dark-skinned man wearing nothing but a fez on his head.

"I'm sorry," I say, trying hard not to stare at the man's penis, which hangs limply to one side. "Perhaps I should—"

"Nonsense!" Singer says. "You remember Annie, don't you?"

Annie nods at me—then leans over and kisses the man with the fez. Kisses him right on the mouth. He says something to the man in German and the man nods. The two of them stand up and go into a bedroom, hand in hand, closing the door softly behind them.

"You must forgive our Annie," Singer says with a chuckle. "She's madly in love again. This time she says she's through with intellectuals. No more brainy types. They're too unreliable and fickle. She wants solid working class love. She says she'll devote all her time to the Gastarbeiter and those who have entered the city illegally. I hope you're not too disappointed."

I shake my head, a trickle of sweat sending chills down my back. Disappointed? What *am* I doing here?

"Listen," Singer continues, patting me on the leg. "About the other night. I've been thinking it over and I think I owe you an apology."

"An apology?"

"Yes. It was a lousy joke. In bad taste. I should have warned you beforehand. I hope you don't judge us too harshly for it. We're just a little too fond of our jokes, that's all. Sometimes, they get a bit out of hand. We forget that strangers might react badly to them."

"Forget it," I say, standing up. "It was the alcohol, that's all. I shouldn't have had so much of that *Korn* to drink."

"You're a great sport," Singer says. "The owner of Kabarett Chez Elles says there's a free bottle waiting for you any time you want to go back."

"That's very kind of him."

High-pitched grunts and other noises come from the bedroom where Annie and the fez man have set up shop. I sit there unable to imagine how Singer and his "friends" can take this situation so matter-of-factly. Haven't they heard of AIDS? People aren't supposed to do this kind of thing anymore—at least not without some sort of protection. And I don't see any signs of that.

"Would you care for a cup of coffee?" Singer says. "I've just made a fresh pot."

"Uhh . . . no," I say. "I'd better be going now."

"Going?" Singer says. "You just got here. And you haven't even told me why you came in the first place."

"Oh, it's nothing," I say. I don't feel like telling him I really don't know why I went there. Or what I expect from him.

"Nothing? I can't believe that." He looks me straight in the face, unblinking. I avert my eyes. "There's obviously something bothering you. I could tell when you called. Did you know this professor who killed herself?"

"Not very well," I say. "I only knew her through her work." And the occasional closet job.

"It's amazing though how death binds people together," Singer says. "You watch someone being hit by a car on the street, sent flying through the air to die at your feet, and suddenly you and that person are tied by that act. Jeez, listen to me. You'd think I was the philosopher. Professor Singer: Freelance Philosopher to the World. Or the Demi-Monde, at least." He laughs. "Sounds pretty good actually.

You don't think so?"

"I'm sorry?" I say, pretending I haven't heard.

"There's definitely something wrong. On the other hand, I can't force you to tell me about it, can I? So, if you just prefer to sit here for a while, be my guest. Or would you rather come out on the balcony with me? The view from the 20th floor is truly spectacular. You can see the Wall clearly from here. Come on, let's go. A breath of fresh air will do you good."

"No!" I practically shout. I can see a body tumbling end over end—to splatter before the balding man trying to fix his motorcycle.

"Ah, afraid of heights, are you?"

"Yes, that's it," I say. "Heights."

And depths.

"No problem, Anthony. You just sit there and relax. It'll do you good. I'll get some coffee."

Singer goes into the kitchen through a swinging door. I shut my eyes. Sounds of obvious love-making come from the bedroom, intense and unconcealed: first Annie, then the fez man. I can picture them. I want to join them. I want to throw them off the balcony.

"And here we are," Singer says, carrying a mug of coffee.

Do something, I say to myself. Quick! Without thinking, I take out my father's diary and hold it up.

"Do you know what this is?" I ask.

"Well, let's see." Singer puts down the coffee and takes the booklet. "Hmm. It appears to be one of those address or phone books."

"Take a closer look," I say.

"It's a diary," Singer says, as he leafs through it. "I can make out that much because of the dates written across the top."

"Yes, a diary," I say. "My father's diary. Read the last few paragraphs."

"You want me to read the last few paragraphs?" I nod. "Are you sure?" I nod again, having trouble speaking. "Okay. If you don't mind."

Singer opens the diary up at the last page. He peers at it for a few moments, then shakes his head.

"What's wrong?" I ask, afraid that Singer has just confirmed my worst fears.

"I'm sorry," Singer says. "It's in Italian."

"Yes, of course it's in Italian," I say. "My father was Italian. What language did you expect it to be in?"

"I can't read Italian," he says with a shrug. "Except for a few words here and there. Just what I need for my business really."

"But you said—" I stand up, suddenly in a rage.

"Anthony—"

"Don't call me, Anthony!" I shout, snatching back the diary. "Bloody bastard! I bet you made up all that stuff about the concentration camps, too. What was that on your arm? A cereal box tattoo?"

"What!" Singer turns red. He makes a move towards me, then manages to calm down again. "No one could possibly make up anything about the camps." He smiles. "You, of all people, should realize that."

"That's crap and you know it!" I'm really screaming now. "People are making things up about the camps all the time."

Annie comes out of the room, naked, followed by the man in the fez. Jutting out in front of Annie is an enormous penis, held in place by a pair of plastic straps that have been Velcro-ed together between his buttocks. My mouth goes slack. I look up Annie's body. It's then I notice the breasts, tiny but perfectly shaped, completed by dollar-coin sized aureoles and nipples that project out at least a centimetre.

"You're . . . you're. . . ," I sputter, pointing. "You're not a man!"

"Obviously not," Singer says. "Is there a law against it?"

"A law?" I shout. "What the fuck's going on? You're just a bunch of fucking perverts! Nothing but a bunch of sickos! Where's the fucking SS when you need them?"

Annie shrugs and adjusts her penis so that it aims directly at me. It glistens and, for a second, I can see it moving on its own, swelling. I shut my eyes tight in the hope it's nothing more than a bad dream. Then open them again. It's still there, veins bulging.

"What the fuck is that?" I continue to scream, pointing at Annie. "What the hell has the world come to?"

The man in the fez makes a motion with his hand and flicks out a knife. A switchblade. An all-too-familiar switchblade. He glides towards me, knife weaving back and forth.

"Get away!" I shout, backing up. "Don't you come near me! I'm a Canadian citizen!"

Singer steps between us. He turns to Annie and says something in German to her. Annie shrugs again. Then she takes the other man by the hand and leads him back into the room. At the door, the man stops for a moment and flicks the knife at me again. Both Annie and he laugh before slamming the door shut behind them.

"Anthony . . . Professor Serratura," Singer says with a sigh. "I think you'd better leave now. I won't be able to hold him back the next time."

"He's already killed, hasn't he?" I ask, suddenly feeling much calmer. Composed even.

"I wouldn't know," Singer says. "But I certainly wouldn't want to test him on it."

"You're right," I say, smiling. "Hey! Maybe I'll have that

cup of coffee now." The body is flipping end over end through the air again, the ground coming up fast beneath it. "And what say we have it on the balcony."

"I'm sorry," Singer says. "I don't think that's possible. In fact, I would appreciate it if you left. I've got to prepare for a business meeting."

"Yes, yes, of course," I say, heading for the door. "No rest for the wicked. Is that it?"

"You got it."

"Before I go," I say, "would it be possible . . . I mean . . . could you—"

"What?" Singer asks impatiently. "What is it this time?"

"Could you possibly show me your tattoo again?" I ask, grinning.

"My tattoo?"

"That's right," I say. "You know, proof positive that it's the real thing. That it doesn't wash off."

"But this is absurd." He advances towards me, his face now a bright red. I back out of the apartment. "I need show you nothing. Get out of here! Now! You disgusting little worm."

And he slams the door in my face.

"Lucky man," I whisper as I lean my cheek against it. "Lucky man."

I watch the body rise again towards the balcony, flipping back into an upright position, coffee cup in hand, coffee returning in a stream. Outside, the balding man has finished fixing his motorcycle. He mounts it and drives off. I look at my watch. It's now past ten. I've wasted my entire morning on a wild goose chase. What possessed me to imagine that Singer and his friends would be able to provide the answers for me? Glistening, snap-on penises, that's more their style. Women pretending to be men pretending to be women.

180

Berlin

I must hurry if I'm to get to the symposium on time. After all, Dr. Zweck is depending on me. I head for the nearest U-Bahn station. In my rush, I don't really watch where I'm going—and end up at the Friedrichstrasse stop, one of the points of entry into East Berlin. Across the tracks, I can see grim-faced soldiers carrying rifles and semi-automatic weapons. A sign points to the passport and customs control. There's no other way out of the station and warnings to beware and to halt are everywhere.

I get back on the train which is waiting for passengers for the return trip. It's then that I begin to get nervous. What if someone notices that I simply went from one train to the other? And with a suspicious briefcase in my hands? I shut my eyes and lean back against my seat so I can't be easily seen from outside. This is technically enemy territory. If something were to happen now, if war were declared, the soldiers would storm across from the other side of the tracks and I'd be taken prisoner. Or worse. They might just open fire and save themselves the trouble. One less capitalist mouth to feed or rehabilitate.

But no. They would want to interrogate me, no doubt. You mean to tell us you have no idea how you got here? And you expect us to believe that? A displacement in time, indeed. An unexpected shift while you peacefully wended your way to the *Freie Universität,* right? Yes, I see. It often happens to people, one interrogator would offer to the other with a smirk. Doesn't it, Hans? Do you mind if we look through your briefcase, bitte? And what do we have here then? Oh God, Seppanen's paper. I have her paper in the briefcase. I remember Professor Matlab's explanation of its strategic value. If they find me with that, it would mean . . . what would it mean? What does it mean? And what would I do? Swallow it? Tear it to shreds and swallow it piece by piece?

On the other hand, did I really expect common soldiers to understand the importance of the paper? No, they would shoot me on the spot—no doubt about it. Put a rifle to my head and blow me away. Blood and bits of brain splattering. With a jerk, the train begins to move. Come on, come on, I say. Get me out of here. Get me back on safe ground again. Back where the surrounding enemy can be forgotten amid the normalcy of daily events. It seems to take forever but soon I can look back and see the station receding. Soon, I can release my grip on the briefcase. And soon I'm emerging from the Oskar-Helene-Heim station (one stop before Onkel Toms Hutte) onto the familiar landscape of the Dahlem campus.

"Professor Serratura," Matlab says as he greets me at the door to the auditorium. "We have been very worried."

"I'm late, I know," I say, looking around the almost completely empty room. "Seem to have lost my way."

"Well you are here now," Matlab says, taking my arm. "Come. Dr. Zweck has been anxiously awaiting your arrival."

We walk slowly to the front where Zweck and the remaining handful of participants have huddled. I can't help thinking of them as a ragged band of pioneers fearful of the final attack, the one that will wipe them out once and for all. Zweck looks up and comes hurriedly towards us.

"My savior!" he says, taking my hands in his. "Are you ready?"

"A little tired," I say. "But, yes. Let's get on with it."

"Good, good," Zweck says as he leads me to the stage. "As you can see, only the—how do you call them?—the diehards remain." He shakes his head. "A sad business. A sad business indeed. But enough!" He slams his hand on the conference table. "On with the show."

"On with the show!" I say.

"The Cabaret of the Intellect promises stimulation,"

Zweck says. "And the lust for knowledge must be sated."

"Bravo," a voice says behind me. "The only man I know who believes that Kant's *General Introduction to Pure Phenomenology* would make a good Brazilian soap opera."

I turn. It's Celine, wearing sunglasses. And a black dress.

"Celine!" Zweck exclaims. "You have made it."

He hugs and kisses his wife.

"Moral support, *mon cher.* It seems we all need it this day, yes?"

She pulls the sunglasses away for a moment. Her eyes are still red and swollen, the tears not too far away.

"Hello, Professor Serratura. Anthony." She leans forward to kiss me on the cheek. That fragrance again. Snaking through the air towards me. "*Vous avez oublié quelche chose chez nous hier soir, n'est-ce pas?*"

"Did I?"

"A certain poster, I believe," she says, replacing her glasses. "Very provocative, yes? Not to say disturbing."

"Oh God, yes," I say, slapping my forehead. "My Lady of the Berlin Wall."

"It is safe," she says. "Perhaps you wish to pick it up afterwards?"

"Yes, I'll do that. Thank you."

Celine sighs. Then she turns and walks off the stage to one of the front row seats.

"Are you ready, Professor Serratura?" Zweck asks.

"Ready as I'll ever be."

"Good. I will make the announcement then and we will start right away. Before we lose the few who are left."

Zweck walks up to the microphone and begins speaking from a prepared text, first in German, then in English:

"Ladies and gentlemen, in light of yesterday's unfortunate and extremely saddening events of which I am sure we are all aware, Professor Anthony Serratura, our colleague from Canada, has been gracious enough to volunteer his services in the reading of the late Professor Kianta Seppanen's seminal paper. However, because of the technical nature of the material, especially when dealing with Catastrophe Theory and its consequences, Professor Serratura feels that he can act solely as a medium and, unless the spirit of Seppanen inspires him, he will not be able to answer any questions you may have. But the paper will be freely distributed if anyone wishes to study it. Without further ado then, I give you Professor Serratura."

I make my way to the podium. I can see Celine following me from behind her sunglasses. I place the paper down on the lectern and fold open the first page.

"Thank you," I say, clearing my throat. "I hope I can do justice to Professor Seppanen's work—and perhaps inspire others to take up her research where she left off." I look up. "However, I hope you don't expect me to put on one of her patented performances. I'm afraid I don't have her flair for the dramatic." I smile. "Neither for catching knives in my teeth nor for pulling philosophical rabbits out of a hat."

Several in the audience laugh hesitantly. Celine continues to stare, her face expressionless. I begin to read:

"Professor Kianta Seppanen's *Cusp Geometry and Doubly Infinite Series in Deterministic but Random Effects*. Take an event. For our purposes, any event will do. A suicide, perhaps."

I stop. Wait a minute, I say to myself. That's not what the paper said the first time I looked it over. Definitely, not: "A suicide, perhaps." I glance up. Zweck has his head down, chin tucked into his chest; Matlab's eyes are shut; Celine sits impassively. I look at the opening words again, making sure I haven't misread them. No, no mistake. That's what it says. I go back to reading:

BERLIN

"Call this event a catastrophe, in keeping with Professor Thom's definition. There is definitely a major change in the internal system—a ceasing to exist—while only minor changes in the external variables: the slight breakage of skin, the insertion of a long, thin piece of metal with a hole in its centre, the injection of $C_{17}H_{17}(OC_2H_3O)_2ON$ into the bloodstream. If we take a person's life to resemble a marble going down a gradient, then we can call this point the cusp. At this point, there is a slight bump, a second equilibrium, that prevents the marble from falling all the way down into the trough—picturesquely known as the abyss of nothingness or, more prosaically, the cessation of life functions. The injection of that colourless liquid into the bloodstream is equivalent to the smoothing out of that bump, the elimination of the equilibrium point. As you can see, a slight change here leads to catastrophe, an irreversible event causing major havoc within the system. This is all well-known and previously documented by pathologists, morgue attendants, forensic scientists and grieving family members."

I stop again. I'm sweating profusely, can feel the perspiration slide down my forehead and into my eyes. None of this material was there the previous night when Zweck handed me the paper. I'm certain of that. A switch! Perhaps a switch had been made at the Friedrichstrasse station and I hadn't noticed. While my eyes were shut. And the real paper is now on its way to those who can make good use of it, a perfect fit to slot, without any changes, into their war plans. The words swim around before me, making it hard to pin them down. But the others take no notice. Some are nodding their heads sagely; others seem to be examining their fingernails or the tips of their pencils. It's almost as if the paper were reading itself, without any help from me:

"And, so far, this has been considered the most important thing about a catastrophe—that, like time, it is not reversible. Once the marble has emptied itself into the lowest trough, there is no way it can get back up to the second equilibrium point on its own. Nor can it be forced back up. Attempting to suck out the liquid, to pull out the hollowed-out metal, to seal the minute break in the skin will accomplish nothing beyond those three things. At least, that is normally believed to be the case, normally taken as a datum. But perhaps not necessarily so. Perhaps there is a way to restore that equilibrium after all—from within the system. To pull it up by its own bootstraps, as it were. That is precisely what the rest of this paper will attempt to do."

There is a swell of murmuring from the audience, a combination of awe and disbelief. Some lean forward, notepads ready; others shake their heads.

"I have tried to keep the mathematics to a minimum but, without at least this much, nothing can be explained. As a matter of fact, there is really no verbal explanation—just a well-ordered group of formulae that keep breaking down into further formulae, into finer and finer details. A fractal amalgam, in other words, in a world without end. Amen."

Something makes me look up—a command or imperative. Sitting in an aisle seat near the back of the auditorium is the smiling figure of . . . of . . . Professor Seppanen. Her hair has been dyed jet-black with one streak of white hanging across her eyes. She has her legs crossed, revealing a pair of ripped black stockings held together in places with safety pins. Her chin is poised on her hand as if she is listening intently. As she turns her head, one of the auditorium lights glints off her crucifix earring. I look down again. Then back up. Seppanen is gone—to be replaced by Louise.

Louise?

"Ah," I say. "Ah. . . ."

And for a moment it's all clear, it all makes sense. The whole structure becomes transparent: predicates, objects, concepts, scope, quantification, sense, reference, first-order madness, second-order sanity, third-order. . . . Of course, I say. That's it.

And then I collapse with a thud to the floor, the sound of footsteps rushing towards me, hands reaching out to cushion my fall, to soften the blow. Too late. They're all too late. I, too, have succumbed to catastrophe—although, it's hoped, not an irreversible one.

I open my eyes—and find myself with my head on Celine's lap, staring up at her concerned face. Another lap, I think. But no bulge this time. No woman pretending to be a man pretending to be a woman pretending. . . .

"He is coming to life," she says, pressing a wet towel against my forehead. "He is waking up."

"Please, you will relax," Zweck says, coming into my line of vision. "Do not move too quickly. We do not wish for you to faint again for lack of blood."

"I . . . I saw her," I say weakly, trying to keep the objects from swimming before my eyes. "I saw . . . Professor Seppanen . . . It isn't possible but—

"But it is possible, Professor Serratura. Not only possible but necessary. Because here I am."

I sit up. Seppanen stands near the window with one hand on her hip, the other holding a cigarette. Smoke curls from her nose. Other people are crowding into the Zwecks' living room: Fritz and his sister, the Nazi midget, Singer, Matlab. They all smile idiotically as they gather around me.

"I believe we owe you an apology," Zweck says. "In fact, I know we do. It was an experiment, an experiment that went too far. We never meant to cause you physical harm."

"You mean. . . ." I look around again. More and more people are filing in. Annie Oakley, Fritz's mother, the two bird ladies, skeleton demonstrators, the couple from the Wall. As they enter, they start by clapping but soon realize it's not the appropriate reaction.

"I must take the blame," Seppanen says, stubbing out her cigarette but then immediately lighting another. "It was all part of my theory of 'guerrilla philosophy,' a theatre shaped by the framework of 'real life.' I guess I let it go too far."

"No, no," Zweck says. "It was my fault for allowing it in the first place. I should have put a stop to it right away, the moment you got off the plane. No, even before that. I should have sent you a telegram before you even came to Berlin, should have told you not to bother coming."

"I'm the guilty party," Singer says. "I led him to believe our meeting was purely coincidental, that I was interested in his theories, that I wanted my friends to seduce him."

"You are all wrong, *ja*," Fritz says, straightening his base-ball cap. "The actions of Frieda and I went beyond the bounds of morality. Even our coffee was drugged, spiked with powerful hallucinogens."

I look from one to the other as they stand there, some with sheepish grins on their faces, others avoiding eye contact altogether. They resemble wax. Any moment now the flame will come too close and they'll become shape-less, lacking any identity. Until, of course, they re-form into something new.

"You toyed with me," I say, clenching and unclenching my fists. "From the beginning, it was all a game, wasn't it?"

"I am afraid so," Zweck says, hands out in front of him-self, like a priest offering Mass.

"The invitation to the conference? The choice of *pensions*? The so-called suicide? The Nazi midget and his wartime memories? Fritz and Frieda and the switchblade-feather?"

"All a set-up, as you would call it," Zweck says. "An experiment. The night we were supposed to meet for dinner, for example, and you ran into Singer instead. We wanted to see what you would do given a spur-of-the-moment choice."

"We wanted to see what choices were all about," Seppanen says. "What they meant to events. We wanted to see how far we could push you. We wanted to build a web around you that funneled you in one direction and one direction only."

"All a set up," I say blankly. "Every single moment of it. Is that right?" No one says a word. "I would never have been invited here otherwise, am I correct?" Again, no one answers.

"Am I correct?" I say more loudly. "Somebody answer me!"

"Yes," Matlab mumbles at last, head down. "It was felt you were the perfect . . . the perfect. . . ."

"Guinea pig?" I prompt.

"If that is what you wish. Yes, guinea pig."

"I was, wasn't I? The perfect guinea pig. The perfect patsy."

I stand by the window where I can look out at the soccer field. Still the same two boys pushing the same ball back and forth. "What's the old saying: 'A little knowledge is a dangerous thing.' You used my own vanity, my own belief in order and sanity. You used the fact that I was actually a fairly competent philosopher to bait the hook. And you reeled me in with the greatest of ease—for your own amusement and pleasure."

"Not amusement," Seppanen says. "And certainly not pleasure. There was no pleasure in it. No emotion whatsoever, in fact. I repeat. It was an experiment. Pure and simple. And I take full and complete responsibility for it.

I'm ready to accept that responsibility and any punishment you deem necessary."

"Tell me." I reach into my pocket and hold up the little black book. "What about this? Was it your idea then to alter my father's diary?"

"Correct." Seppanen takes what looks like an identical black book from her own pocket. "We had Frieda sneak into your room yesterday morning and remove the original. Then we photocopied it, altered the last page and replaced the real one with our copy. It was necessary, you understand. We wanted to see how you'd react to your father's betrayal. You do understand?"

"Oh yes, I understand. As you've said already, what's there not to understand?" I walk up to Fritz. "So Fritzy, you were in on it, too?" Fritz nods. "And your 'breadfruit' sister—who probably has a Ph.D. in masturbatory techniques?"

"We were all in on it, as you say," Zweck says. "I do not see the need to conduct individual questioning—or to fling insults about."

"Oh, you don't, eh?" I stop in front of Celine. She's crying silently. "*Et vous?* Singing the Sub-Atomic Particle Blues? Getting ready for another half-spin of your quark-y charm?"

I reach up towards her. She flinches and several of the others make a move as if to stop me.

"What?" I pull back my hand. "Afraid? But I won't hurt you. I would never hurt you." I smile. "Not unless it was part of the experiment, of course." I touch her face and brush away her tears. "You knew. You knew . . . and said nothing."

"I knew . . . and said nothing," Celine admits, the tears starting up again.

"But, of course." I hold her hands. "And, I bet there

were many times when you wanted to warn me, to clue me in. Many times. But you couldn't, right?" Celine half-nods. "You just couldn't. After all, you, too, are a scientist. And a scientist can't warn an experiment or even tell it what's happening. That wouldn't be ethical. Besides, it alters the results and introduces a factor, an element not even catastrophe theorists have yet worked out to their satisfaction. Am I not right?" I turn to Seppanen. "So, tell me, Professor. How did I do? I'm curious."

"The data aren't all in yet," she says curtly. "It may take years to analyze it all."

"Come on," I say. "Don't be coy. Surely, you can give me some preliminary results."

"Well, if you really want to know," she says, putting out another cigarette. "Your getting lost this morning is an indication the experiment worked. That was a totally spontaneous action on your part."

"Really? You mean my self-willed actions are those that I can no longer control? Or put it more precisely: if my action is self-willed, that means I can't control it; if what I do is under control, then it is out of my hands."

"As I said, we don't yet have enough information to come to that—or any—conclusion."

"Answered like a true scientist."

"I'm sorry," Seppanen says. "You weren't supposed to find out."

"Naturally." I turn and head for the door. "I'm leaving now. You'll do me the kindness not to follow me. Or to contact me. If your theory is right, I might no longer be responsible for my actions." I stop and laugh. "Come to think of it, have I ever been?" I shrug. "Well, at least, I have an excuse, don't I? Unlike the rest of you."

On my way out, I throw the bogus diary on the sofa. Seppanen tries to hand me the real one but I brush it aside, having no more need for it. She simply shrugs and places it on top of the fake one. Now, they can't be told apart. I walk out the door and onto the street. The others crowd onto the balcony. It's almost as if they're sad it's over, as if they've grown into their roles and are disappointed at having to return to ordinary living, to whatever they were doing before the experiment began.

"Where are you going?" Zweck calls out behind me.

I stop but don't turn around. Rather, I look up directly at the sun which forces me to squint. Everything turns white.

"Surely you're not leaving us now?" Zweck says, almost in a pleading tone. "Why not stay with us, at least for the evening? Give us the chance to explain. Celine has prepared some *boeuf bourguignonne* for everyone. Your favourite, is that not so? Please. You must understand. It is important that you understand. We are not the monsters you think us to be. We have . . . we have grown to love you."

I don't answer or turn. Instead, I shrug and continue walking down the leafy street. After pausing for a moment, as if deep in thought but not really, I descend into the Oskar-Helene-Heim station. The others—all but Seppanen who remains on the balcony smoking and Zweck who retreats into the house—follow a few steps behind.

"Please," Singer says. "We would like to make it up to you. Give us the chance."

"Yes," the others say in chorus. "Give us a chance."

But I'm not about to give them the chance. That might be the same thing as letting them off the hook. I stand whistling on the subway platform and ignore them as they take turns trying to explain to me, trying to convince me I should return with them to the house. Instead, I think back on the events of the previous two days—in particular the encounter with Singer and his friends at the cabaret; Seppanen's "suicide"; the Nazi midget and the brother-sister pervert

192

act; the switching of both my father's diary and Seppanen's paper.

I reflect on the meticulousness and thoroughness of their preparations, on the fact the seams never once showed through. And I imagine they had a whole series of contingency plans to fall back on—if I hadn't gone to the Europa Centre that night, for example. If I hadn't decided on a trip to the wall. Or perhaps these had been the contingency plans. Or it was all one massive contingency plan. Nothing, it appears, had been left to chance. Well, almost nothing. As the train speeds in, I turn and wave at the tightly bunched group a few feet away.

And then throw myself directly in front of the lead car. The last thing I hear is Celine's cry of horror and despair. Serves her right, I think, before exploding into a million pieces.

When all the other possibilities have been cut off, have been reduced to zero, I snap awake. I'm flat on my back, staring up at a pair of large, circular fluorescent lights. One is working properly, I note; the other flickers on and off. I shut my eyes again for a moment, still groggy, still uncertain, convinced that somehow my body has been turned inside out. Has been negativized, its internal structure exposed for all to see.

"Thank God," I hear a voice say. "He is awakening at last."

Zweck leans over me and smiles, a look of relief on his chubby face.

"Hello, there," he says. "You gave us very much of a scare."

"Where . . . where am I?" I struggle to sit up, catching a glimpse of tile-covered surfaces and several cots like those used in hospitals. I'm lying on one. Maybe it's a surgical procedure, after all. First, they had emptied me out and then they filled me with their own material. Now they're testing to make sure the procedure is a success, that I am going to react in a reasonably human way—all the while following their orders.

"You will relax, *ja*," Zweck says, gently easing my back against the wall . "You are in the first-aid room at the university. It is best that you take it easy for a few moments. You have had a bad tumble. A very bad fall. There is a lump on your head where it struck the floor."

"I'm . . . alright. . . . I'm fine now."

I look around the room. There are several other concerned faces staring down at me. I recognize some as fellow speakers and participants in the conference. And then there's Celine, who smiles as our eyes meet.

"I'd like to try to stand up," I say.

"Do not rush it," Zweck says. "There is no longer any need to. We have cancelled the rest of the conference. Please take all the time you wish."

"Cancelled? But—"

"No, no," Zweck says, waving his hands in the air as if precluding any further argument. "I felt it was for the best. The fainting was the last straw, as you Americans say. I cannot risk anything else."

"My husband is right," Celine says, placing a hand on my shoulder. "It is obvious the gods are against you. This conference was ill-fated from the beginning."

"But I'm fine now," I insist, feeling the warmth of her hand where it has touched me, the outline of her long, thin fingers. "Perfectly fine. It was nothing but a dizzy spell caused by lack of sleep. I was tired and I thought I saw . . . I thought I saw—"

I stop, not sure exactly what I can say that won't make me sound unstable and on the verge of a breakdown. Where would I start—with the vision of Seppanen or the outlandish scenario I imagined? The one ending with me hurling myself in front of a U-Bahn train?

"What, Professor Serratura?" Celine asks, squeezing my shoulder. "What did you think you saw?"

"Nothing. It was nothing." I shake my head, visions of Seppanen dancing before me. And Louise. Where had she come from? "Certainly no reason to cancel."

"Too late," Zweck says. "The dirty deed is already done. All that is left now is to clean up after ourselves, to leave no traces behind. So, if you are feeling well enough to move, why don't you and Celine go up to our house? You will be able to rest up all the better there. I will be along in an hour or so. Perhaps we can have some lunch, *ja?*"

Go up to Zweck's house? Is he crazy or something? I recall all too vividly what happened at Zweck's house—not, it seems, but a few moments before. Had it been a premonition? A vision of things to come? If so, I'm not anxious to find out what else is in store for me. Or to repeat any of the patterns that might lead me to a similar fate.

"I'd like to stay and help—if you don't mind," I say, managing with some effort to stand up.

"Even if my husband does not mind," Celine says, "I do. You are coming with me. I will not take no for an answer. Come along. Lean against me if you must."

"Yes, yes! Go!" Zweck says, giving me a gentle push. "We have cleaning people here for the job."

Celine takes me by the arm and leads me away. I can feel my thigh brushing against hers as we walk out the door of the first-aid room and up the stairs of the auditorium. At one point, we pass right in front of the spot where I thought I'd seen first Seppanen, then Louise seated. There's nothing there, of course—no matter how hard I stare. But that doesn't really mean a thing, does it? There may well have been something a few moments before, something that had retreated, gone into strategic hiding. And I could be heading right for that hiding place, right into its lair.

Several times, as we walk along the quiet street, arched overhead with branches through which the sun glitters, I almost bolt, almost shove Celine violently aside and dash off into the nearby woods. She holds me tight, however, and, in her grasp, I feel like a chronic hospital patient who yearns for nothing save the warmth of his nurse, the solid motion of healthy, perfumed flesh beside him. It's as if she has managed to reach into some secret place and has fished out my will, pulled it out to yoke to her own. Escape is thus impossible, as impossible as not waking up had been a few moments earlier.

"*Et voilà,*" Celine says with a flourish, throwing open the door to the cottage. "*Nous sommes arrivées.* The house of calm and respite. I hope."

I hesitate, expecting any moment the army of malicious, misbehaving characters to come popping out, led by a resurrected Seppanen with a deadly smirk on her pale, blood-drained face. Or the syringe still stuck defiantly in her arm, twanging in the air as she walks. But nothing of the sort happens. All I can hear is what sounds like a bird in the kitchen, whistling in response to Celine's call. Perhaps they're all hiding on the basement stairs, at the edge between light and dark, ready to burst upon me the moment my guard is down, the moment I shut my eyes. Surprise!

"Is something the matter?" Celine says when she notices I've stopped in the doorway. "You are not feeling dizzy again, I hope? Come, sit on the sofa. I will get you a glass of something to drink. Come."

I move cautiously towards the sofa, making sure there's no way they can sneak up behind me—or come rushing down from the second floor. When Celine is out of the room, I fling open the basement door and jump back. Nothing. I sigh. I've obviously imagined the whole episode, starting with my vision of Seppanen and ending at the subway station. Obviously experienced it while I was still unconscious following my collapse. But it had been so vivid, so crystal clear in its sharpness. On the other hand, they could be in the very woods I thought were safe, where I had felt I could make good my escape.

I look out the window—only shadows of tree limbs in the sunlight, waving gently. I check my coat pocket. Still there. My father's diary is still there. At least that's real, something that can't be denied. And Singer's business card. And Seppanen's I.D. pin with its sharp prick. That's what lack of sleep will do to you, I say to myself, and once again feel the tiredness, the sledgehammer weight. I fall back on to the sofa. Beside me is the rolled-up poster I'd forgotten at the Zwecks' the previous night.

I remove the rubber band and it unfolds by itself. This time the effect of the cement growing out from between the prone woman's legs and belly button translates not simply into a sense of injustice or indignation for the human condition but one mixed with erotic pleasures amid the inflicting of pain. It is, in other words, that of the torturer for his victim, each trapped in a set of circumstances carefully chosen to define them, each unable to shake off what is required of them. I remember clearly Fritz and Frieda, going over the same set of motions time and again. Another vision? It would seem that way.

"Here we are," Celine says, carrying in a silver tray with several snifters and a crystal decanter of cognac. "Spirits to revive the spirit. A shot of this and you will be as good as brand new. You will be up and dancing a tarantella in no time. That is my guarantee."

I see her approach in slow motion, her long black skirt swirling, her beige bra straps visible beneath a shimmery blouse. I reach up for my glass—as if from a great depth, as if I were underwater. I'm trembling so much I need both hands to hold the snifter steady. Even then I spill some on myself before managing to gulp down the rest. Celine places the tray on the floor and sits down beside me. She takes a sip.

"Umm," she says, rubbing her stomach. I follow the motion of her hand as it goes round and round. "That is better, n'est-ce pas? Makes one feel warm all over." She leans her head back, exposing her long smooth neck. Her swan throat. "Whenever I have a glass of cognac, I think of autumn in Normandie. The cold ocean; the warm fireplace; the sharp stones on the beach. I miss that very much. And you, what do you miss?"

"I think I'd best be going," I say, realizing it's now or never, that in a few moments it will be too late, that the whole complex edifice I've built brick by brick around myself is about to come tumbling down. And no one or nothing will be able to prevent it. Not even Berlin's massive solidity. Or the overgrown scar down its middle.

"No, no," Celine says, gripping on my arm. "You are in no condition to go anywhere. *Pas de question. Point du tout. Du tout.* I will not allow it."

"But you don't understand," I say weakly, the odour of her perfume causing me to sink even deeper, caressing me into a chill-like stupor.

"I understand to perfection," she says. "You wish to play the Joan of Arc—the martyr. But I will not let you. You will just stay here until my husband and Professor Matlab return. Then we will decide how to get you home. Is that understood? *Comprenez-vous?* The U-Bahn is much too dangerous for one in your condition. You might fall in front of it. *Kaputt, ja,* as *les allemands* would say. Molecules spread throughout the universe."

No, no. This isn't happening, I say to myself. This can't be happening to me. I search for some way to pull myself out of it. I look first at Celine, at her kind, open, inviting face, at the warmth exuding literally from her every pore. Then at the poster. I'm having difficulty breathing. The first words start to appear, the words I can no longer control: ontology, compactness, sense, meaning, reference, logic, meta-logic, language, meta-language, meta-meta, meta-meta-meta. . . . They circle and circle—like swirls in a whirlpool, like birds of prey, like turds being flushed down a toilet.

"If I stay here any longer . . . if I. . . ." I slump back, the images of Celine and the cement woman melting into one another, no longer discordant or mismatched but dangerously appropriate.

"Good, Anthony," Celine says, placing her hands on my temples and rubbing them gently in a counterclockwise direction. "Relax. Close your eyes and think good thoughts. That is good. Relax. You will soon feel better. Much better."

I shut my eyes. Out of the dark come more of the words, the words I can't control, now strung along by some sequence I also can't control. Words that make perfect sense, make perfect sentences—and yet don't: "There is no second-order logical calculus." That's it. That's it? Doesn't that make sense? Of course, it does. "The set of second-order logical truths is too rich to be rationally subjugated." Of course, that's obvious. I suddenly blurt out: "The predication of relations. The predation of relation ships. In the night. Russell's paradox. The moxie of orthodoxy."

"What?" Celine says. "What did you say? I am sorry. I did not hear exactly what it was you said."

"I love you," I say. "I want to kill you."

Before she has a chance to move back, I reach for her throat with both hands while at the same time sprawling across her and pinning her against the sofa with my body. Celine lets out a muffled scream and uses one of her fists to pummel my face until I have to release her throat to defend myself.

"You are hurting me," she shouts, struggling all the harder beneath me. "Stop it! *Cochon! Maudit salaud!* You are hurting me! Stop it!"

I push my face down into her chest so she can't get enough leverage to poke my eyes out with her fingers. From there, above my own laboured breathing, I can hear her heart-beat, like that of a bird, a small huddled bird. My cheek is against her nipple, against the thin cloth outlining her nipple. I want to suck at that nipple through the cloth, to strain it through the cloth, to have the flesh ooze out and re-form itself, purified at last and fit for my consumption alone.

"Let me go now!" Celine says, heaving her body in an effort to throw me off, but not strong enough to do so. "Let me go and I will not tell anyone about this. *Je te jure.*"

"I can't," I say, reaching into my pocket for Seppanen's I.D. badge. "It's either this or . . . or. . . ."

"Please," Celine pleads, this time letting herself go slack. "Do not hurt me. I do not wish to be hurt. I will do what you want."

"This . . . or madness." I press the fist with the badge in it against her stomach and push, sliding down into her crotch. I'm a surgeon making an incision; a butcher gutting a lamb. She lets out a gasp of pain, the pin tip slightly scratching her skin. "Pure madness." I push harder, feeling the flesh separate beneath the black cloth. She's crying uncontrollably now, blubbering, her mouth twisted. "At the height of sanity lies logic." I pull the pin away, bring it back up to her chest, as if stitching her up. "At the height of logic lies madness. I love you madly."

"I love you, too," Celine says in a pathetically thin voice, her breathing becoming more and more shallow. "Please, do not hurt me again. Please. I will make love to you. I will make you happy."

"Make me happy?"

"Yes."

"Like you did with Seppanen?"

"Yes. I will show you."

Is that what I want? She lifts my face from where it lies on her chest and brings it up towards hers. Her mouth is quivering. Her mouth is slightly open. Her lips are white, drained of blood. She allows me to kiss her. Her lips taste of salt. I feel damp, clammy. The sweat has soaked through my clothing. I'm bathed in sweat. I pull away, feeling my clothing separate from hers.

"You've always loved me, right?" I say. She bites her lip and nods. "Forever and ever."

"Forever and ever," she says, sniffling.

"More than you ever loved Seppanen?"

"Yes," she says, the tears coming down her face, spilling down the sides of her face.

"I love you, too," I say. "It doesn't make any sense. There's no logic to it, you understand? I'm a happily married man. With a wife and child waiting for me back home."

As I speak, I grope around with my hand on the floor beside the sofa till I find the cognac decanter. It tips over, spilling the liquid and releasing its rich aroma into the air.

"But it's you I love," I say, holding the decanter. "Not my wife. She vanishes from my sight in your presence. Does Seppanen vanish from your sight?"

"Yes," she says, now shuddering and crying uncontrollably. "Come. Upstairs. There is a bed there. It is comfortable.

I will show you . . . show you what true love is . . . forever."

"Ah," I say. "But there's nothing like the wonderful completeness of first-order logic. It always comes full circle when you least expect it. It must always come full circle—to complete the circle."

And I smash the cognac decanter against the side of her head—once, twice, as long as it takes for her body to stop twitching and jerking in spasms beneath me. All the while, I'm surging back up to the surface. All the while, I see myself hoist Celine's skirt above her head—to cover the wound, to hide what I'm doing from her prying, still open eyes, to distract her, dead as she is, from the intended violation. It's the horror of the act that fascinates this person I'm watching, that makes me tear at her pink panties, that makes me lower my own trousers, that makes me poise myself above her still body.

And then it's gone, vanished from whence it has come. The person I've been watching goes limp, sees himself as a pathetic little creature wiggling, wriggling high above an unfathomable chasm. I watch that pathetic little creature fall off the sofa, pull up his trousers, stare unperceiving at the bloodstain beneath the hoisted skirt, the bloodstain that grows larger by the second. We both start crying at the same time—one out of pity, one out of frustration. In an effort to hide that frightening gap, that yawning fissure in my world, I place the unfurled poster over Celine's mid-section and tuck it in beneath her, leaving the perfectly tiny pink panties gnarled around her knees.

There is, as yet, no registering of what I've done, no rundown from premise to conclusion, inescapable and final as it seems. Perhaps, there will never be such a registering, a proof by disproof, a reductio ad absurdum. Some have been lucky enough before, to become disjointed at the moment when things were at their clearest. I go through the motions of washing my hands and face, of using the toilet, of feeding the bird, of urinating on the painting that dominates the dining room, of smashing the deer, the angel and the unicorn.

And then, without even bothering to close the door behind me, I stumble out of the house. Stagger out into the brilliant sunshine. The streets seem more quiet than usual. But it is Sunday, after all. A day of rest—at least in Christian countries. Only mothers out strolling with their infants; only fathers out cycling with their sons and daughters; only grandparents holding each other up. As I walk along, I begin to think of reasons why I killed her, why I brutalized her—a woman I hardly knew who'd treated me only with kindness and respect. And, perhaps, even with a touch of love.

She must have been dangerous. That's it. She'd betrayed me. Of course she had. She'd admitted it herself—at least in the vision. She was in on it along with the others, in on the humiliation. In on it for sure. No, she was the mastermind behind it all. She'd laughed at me behind my back, at my confusion, at my status as a guinea pig, a part of a scientific experiment on the nature of randomness. I'd had to pay her back for that. It was either her or me. They had played a game with me and must now suffer the consequences. Catastrophe Theory claims another victim. Now, that makes sense. At last, something that makes sense.

There's a loud cheer behind me. At first, I assume it's for me, for having analyzed the situation so swiftly and cleanly, for having come to the crux of the matter in my customarily fearless way. But no. A goal has just been scored in the nearby soccer game, a soccer game that hadn't existed a moment before. The fans are yelling in their seats, waving their arms. The jubilant scorer, knees scraped with mud and blood, is running up the sideline with his teammates in hot pursuit, ready to celebrate by pouncing on him, by forming a huge mound on top of him. I would love dearly to join that mound, to lose myself in that pile of flesh.

Instead, I find myself—without remembering exactly how I'd made my way there—in the central lobby of the Europa Centre. It's crowded with shoppers and diners, with people just out for a stroll. The stores and restaurants are packed; the slot machines are going full blast. Celine herself admitted to a passion for gambling, to taking chances and bucking the odds. But she'd lost, hadn't she? Someone taps me on the shoulder. I freeze. The police? No, it can't be the police already. Even if they'd found the body. . . . Slowly, I turn around, ready to plead my innocence. It's no policeman. It's a young man in a bowler hat and army boots, bow-tie askew and tight black pants riding up past his ankles.

"*Bitte,*" the young man says, smiling, the glint of a gold tooth. "*Wie spat ist es?*"

"*Ich verstehe nicht,*" I say, almost automatically, and make to turn away. To move off before he points an accusing finger at me.

"*Die Zeit, bitte?*" the young man persists, pointing at my wrist. "Time."

"The time? Oh, the time! It's. . . ."

I have no idea how to say the time so I pull back my shirt sleeve instead to show the young man. But the watch isn't there. I'm not at all surprised.

"I'm sorry," I say, shrugging. "I don't have it."

The man walks away, his boots clicking on the marble floor. And then it strikes me: Why on earth did he ask me for the time in the first place? There's a perfectly good timepiece. . . . I look up. The Clock of Flowing Time has stopped. Or rather, someone has cut off the water supply, leaving the clock itself high and dry, its two arms stuck at an impossible confluence. Does this mean I'll finally be able to step into the same river twice? Does this mean I'll be able to undo what I've done?

I don't know. All I know right now is that I can't just wait around to find out. I can't just sit here staring at a stopped clock—even if it is one of the scientific wonders of the world. Someone is bound to discover Celine's body. Probably sooner than later. Oh God! I cover my eyes. I should've at least pulled up her panties, wiped some of the blood from her face, cleaned up the spillage. That would have been the civilized thing to do. Everyone at the university had seen me walk out with her. Under her arm, in fact. The connection between that walking out and the body on the sofa is practically automatic. And who'll be the first to discover it? Why, Zweck, of course.

Try as I might, I just can't imagine the look on Zweck's face when he walks into his home and is confronted with his wife's body on that sofa. It'll reduce him to a blubbering bug-eyed idiot, useless forever more at conference organizing. Perhaps he'll have to spend the rest of his miserable days on earth teaching Philosophy 101 classes: On God, Existence, Free Will and The Essence of Being—Part Two. I smile at the sadness of it all, at the intolerable and yet so appropriate sadness. Despite the indeterminacy principle, what exactly are the chances of Celine ever again sitting on Zweck's knee? Ever again tossing double-edged banter, like hot coals, back at him? Ever again delving into the mysteries of subatomic particles? Ever again attending Dead Kennedy concerts with Seppanen? Ever again being bashed across the head with a cognac decanter?

If there is even the least possibility of those things happening again, then maybe I should just sit there beneath the Clock and wait for my murdering self to catch up with me. Or I might intercept my murdering self before it actually does any of those things. Intercept it even before it takes that fateful plane to Berlin. Send a note of apology instead: "I'm terribly sorry, Dr. Zweck. But it seems you have the wrong fellow here. A case of mistaken identity. I never should have been invited to your conference. And, if I did accept, it would be under false pretenses."

False pretenses? What am I talking about? I have every right to be here—as much right as Matlab and Seppanen and all the rest of them. There's a sound like rumbling above me, as if an angry god has spoken. I look up. It's only the water roaring down to fill the Clock once again, to set the hands in motion one more time. To free us all from stasis—and the possibility that the past might catch up with us. Now, everything is moving forward again.

I make my way out of the Europa Centre and begin to walk. Where am I headed? I'm not exactly sure—only that it's in a direction opposite to the *pension*. The *pension* is definitely not a safe place. The police net is probably closing in on that very spot right this moment. They've spoken to Fritz by now and he'll be more than happy to help spring the trap. More than happy to fill in the gaps in my pathological behaviour patterns with tales of what had taken place that morning:

"Just like that, officer. Just like that. He exploded and went bananas. In front of respectable guests. Nazi midgets and accusations of the senseless variety. Screams, *ja*. Lots and lots of screams. Nutty as a fruitbread, I tell you."

There's only one thing I can do—and that's to lose myself, to disappear without a trace. But is that possible? Is that a viable option? I don't believe so. No matter what road I take, I fear it will eventually end up back at the *pension*. It's as if my life has been poured into a funnel, tumbling down the slanted slopes at an ever-increasing rate. If there are any stops along the way, any footholds, they're merely temporary. Merely indent marks to divert the flow for a moment or so.

The only real way to avoid discovery is madness, that true loss of self, that true and utter shattering of personality. But there's one little problem with that, one teeny-weeny problem with that. No map with which to find myself again if I ever change my mind. ("Change my mind"—now isn't that a most strange, most wonderful expression?) No well-ordered formulae to bring all the pieces back together once the trip is deemed over and the coast is clear. Besides, madness can't be willed upon someone, can it? I don't think so. It must come on its own. Or I must allow it to find me, to leap upon me from some dark corner.

Soon, I'm walking through a familiar area, dark and grey. Where the houses creep up right against the curb and the sun shines for some other planet. Kreuzberg. If madness is anywhere, it'll be here. Some people hold handkerchiefs to their mouths, trying to keep out the soot; others scurry by, eyes averted. I sit on a scarred bench in a treeless, dusty park and watch entire families fly kites. They're wrapped in loose robes that swirl about, that threaten to lift them to the sky as well. Just as the kites are about to take flight, a band of black-masked marauders swoops through, scattering the families, stealing their picnic baskets, forcing the women and children to beg for food.

It's too much for me and I leave. I climb a hill with a monument at its summit (similar to one left back in Montreal not three days before). I sit cross-legged before it and concentrate all my energy. I want to levitate the monument. To lift it off the ground and send it flying to the moon. It budges—I swear—but that's all. No more to be done here. I stand and brush myself off. Below me is a canal that meanders through the district. It's covered in green and violet scum, radiant in the setting sun. I follow it, curious to see where it goes.

When I look up again, I see before me in the dark a giant tent, a giant multicoloured tent of the kind used by circuses. But this one's filled with musicians and dancers stamping their feet to a concussive beat. Most are naked to the waist. Their bodies glisten in the spotlights. "Africa!" a singer shouts, looking directly at me. And then, without warning, as silent as the future, the black-masked marauders return. They slash the tent with straight-edged razors, set fire to the food concessions, trample the fleeing revellers. I'm standing beneath the Victory Column, watching the traffic head towards me from five directions at once. The lights are mesmerizing as they flick past. They want me to jump out, to take my chances. They're whispering for me to come right out there in the open where they can see me better.

It's the end of the line, I know that. I've been funnelled back. But still I refuse. I'm directly across the street from the *Pension Aryana*. I'm hiding behind a rusted tree that needs a metal plate to hold it up, a plate that has insinuated itself into the living bark. Not concrete and flesh exactly but close enough. I feel the rain start to come down, the fine thin almost therapeutic rain of Berlin. Somehow that helps a bit. As far as I can tell, there don't seem to be any signs of the police surrounding the house. But, of course, that's the nature of a good police operation. The trap is practically invisible.

Still, I might be able to return to my room without anyone noticing. And then what? I'll decide once I get there. One thing at a time. That's my newly adopted motto. Why, I might even manage to slip out of Berlin, might even make it to my home, to my comfortable, book-lined study, might even get to see my wife and daughter one last time. Before the rubber band, stretched to its limit, yanks me back to justice. Or snaps, leaving me stranded forever in some limbo of my own making.

BERLIN

I dash across the road to the shelter of the doorway. Not only is it dark but the shops are closed this evening. I don't have to worry about some computer programmer or milliner inadvertently looking up and identifying me. Only the endless line of figures and letters across the computer monitors, patterns repeated every few minutes. The door creaks as I slide it open just enough to let myself in. I hold my breath, waiting for a head to peer out of the darkness, or a challenge to sound. Halt! Who goes there? If it's the murderer, stand and name yourself. But none comes—neither head nor challenge.

I ease the key into the door of the *pension*, keeping the others separate so they don't clink. I can hear faint music inside but no voices. If my luck holds, I can be in my room within seconds—and no one will be the wiser. The hallway is empty. I slowly push the door shut behind me. There's the sound of water in the corridor, the splashing of a mop. Any moment Frieda will come bouncing around the corner, straightening her kerchief. Or balancing herself on the broom handle. Any moment.

I fumble with the key. One click; two clicks. I'm in! I lean against the door trying to catch my breath, at the same time listening for the slap of water on the floor. The sound slowly recedes, as if it has lost interest. The air is filled once again with the strains of delicate music—a waltz of some kind. I sit on my bed. I sink into its softness. The warmth reaches out for me, drains me of whatever energy I have left. I don't care who comes for me now—as long as I can sleep. Perhaps my luck will hold. Perhaps they'll scour the whole city for me while I sleep peacefully beneath a thick, white comforter. Perhaps they'll be showing my photo to young men in bowler hats, to men-women-whatever dressed like Annie Oakley, to restaurant supply salesmen with Valhalla on their minds, to kite fliers and black-masked marauders and African dancers and balding men on motorcycles.

Photo? What photo? The only photos of me are back in Montreal: one a portrait of the dedicated scholar in cap and gown; another wild-eyed and bearded with flower-child Louise seated on my knee. Not true. There *is* a photo—passport size. I sent one with my original application to read at the conference. But that really doesn't matter, does it? The police know exactly where I live. If they're spending time questioning the others at this very moment, it's only because they have to make their case water-tight. Air-tight? Iron-clad? They can come for me at any time, complete the circle at their leisure. Perhaps that's the reason I haven't seen anyone at the *pension*. Perhaps they've all been re-placed by police agents—both employees and guests. One more masquerade.

I wonder if the police know the people they've replaced aren't who they pretend to be, are in fact themselves play-acting. And what about the police agents? Who are they really? Infinite regress, ha ha. Vicious infinite regress. I feel myself falling asleep, face buried in the pillows. There's no reason for it but I expect things to start happening while I sleep, for events to take on a new menace, to rage totally out of control. For one thing, the police will barge in at last, bursting through the door and window at the same time. Dozens of teenagers in full riot gear filling the room, ransacking my closet, smashing mirrors and lamps. Then, once the position is secured, the secret service will follow close behind, men in dark sunglasses and trench coats.

They will read out charges against me, political crimes against the common sense man. Two of them will haul me out of the bed where I lie naked and shivering, back to the wall. They'll force me kneeling to the ground and then handcuff me face first to the bedpost. There I'll remain, completely helpless, while a long line of people with animal heads from the zoo (prison camp escapees, perhaps?) take turns sodomizing me with every implement at their disposal. Till my guts feel as if they're falling out. Till they do fall out in a bloody heap. And the last thing before oblivion will be my own orgasm, the flashing of murky liquid against the bedpost. Corrosive and useless. That's what I expect. Instead, I sleep peacefully, with a smile on my face and seemingly without a care in the world. Right up to the knock on the door.

I sit up, almost as if I've been folded in two by a blow. Still half-asleep, I'm about to answer when I remember where I am and what has happened. I concentrate on holding my breath instead. The room is completely dark. Maybe whoever knocked doesn't know I'm in here and will go away in time. I look at my watch, my newly returned watch. No, that can't be! I push a red button. The digital read-out flashes: "One a.m. Mon." That's not possible. I can't have slept for almost four hours.

Slowly, I get out of bed and lower my feet to the floor. I try to be as quiet as possible. I don't want to give myself away—just in case someone *is* still out there. But I haven't taken more than three steps when I stumble against something and nearly fall on my face. I crawl over to the desk, switch on the desk lamp. Right in the middle of the floor and leaning on its side is my briefcase—with a rolled-up poster next to it. My briefcase! I'd forgotten all about it. But how. . . ? Didn't I leave it. . . ? Back at. . . ? Stuck to its handle is one of those little yellow personalized adhesive notes that are all the rage these days. With cute little drawings across the top and announcing they're "From the desk of so-and-so."

I rip it off and hold it up to the light. This one has a saying on it: "Undergoing change as I do, how can I be said to continue to be myself?—W.V.O. Quine." Then a note scribbled beneath: "My dear Prof. Serratura—You left these at the university after you fainted this morning. Thought you might like them back so I had them sent by taxi. A copy of Seppanen's paper is inside your briefcase. Look on it as a memento if nothing else. Good-bye if I do not see you again—and better luck at your next conference. Zweck. P.S.: Celine sends her love and she looks forward to discussing sub-atomic philosophy the next time she's hitchhiking through Montreal."

I shake my head. No, no. There's a mistake here. A category mistake? I smile. This note has been sent to the wrong person. Really. It's addressed to the Serratura who hadn't killed Celine, the Serratura who . . . who had jumped in front of the U-Bahn train, perhaps. Or the one still sleeping, the one held tenderly in Annie's arms, true love in his grasp at last as he fingers the lubricated condom 20 stories above the ground. Something has slipped, no question about it. After countless eons of infallibility and impossibly smooth running, the universal sorting machinery has missed a slot. And now it scrambles to set things right but only succeeds in making them worse, in missing more slots, in grinding away the gears like a motorist who has lost control on a very busy stretch of highway.

It would be great to watch this, I say to myself, from an objective platform, to examine and probe it, to break the images down into their constituent parts and then reassemble them, leaving out the pointless premises and useless, dead-end arguments. But I can't—for the simple reason it's happening to me. All happening to me. That's the irony, isn't it? I'm inside the images, in touch with the structure itself, and therefore can quickly tell if something has gone wrong. But I'm helpless to change that structure, to alter its ongoing shape, to repair that damage. Like a prisoner inside his cage.

BERLIN

On the other hand, those on the outside, those capable of doing something about it, won't because in their eyes nothing is amiss. If I'm a prisoner inside a cage, then that's the way it should be. The shape is unfolding in the only way it can. If there are cracks, if it looks as if things aren't going right, that's simply the nature of the structure. It's the only explanation. Well, isn't it? That—and madness, of course. Which itself is a structure. . . . Oh no, not that again. I clutch the sides of my head and sit back on the bed.

There's another knock at the door—a solid rap. This time I rush to throw it open. I don't care who's there, don't care if I'm discovered in the room. I just want to get it over with. The hallway, lit only by the twin night-lights, is empty. Someone's definitely playing games, definitely playing with my mind. I pretend to shut the door, then pull it open again—like in one of those silent film comedies. No one. Of course, there's no one. Only logical. If my theory's correct, then even the knocks are meant for someone else. Aren't they?

I slip down the hallway, barely visible, gliding as close to the wall as possible. I stop for a moment at the corner, then take a quick glance down the length of the corridor. That, too, is empty—except for a mop in a bucket of very soapy water which has been placed in front of the first door. I take the mop out and splash it on the floor. I begin to push it back and forth in a semi-circular motion, slowly making my way towards the other end of the corridor. Each door I pass beckons to me, invites me to enter, to make myself at home. But I use all my strength to ignore their siren call.

Behind those doors are lies and half-truths, a veiled pretense: Fritz and his sister, perhaps, in switchblade love, knifing and being knifed in turn—or tickling one another to orgasm upon orgasm. Fritz's mother astride a dead man, her turban askew, her dress above her head, mistaking his

frozen stiffness for the possibility of new life. The bird ladies waiting patiently for their eggs to hatch, refusing to believe what the X-rays show—ravenous monocled monsters
in double-breasted suits and upper-class accents eager to
snap up the world. Zweck and Celine, oblivious to everything but one another as they go from flesh to bone and
back to flesh, fingers in constant touch. Seppanen, lying
beside them in bed, fake needle stuck in a fake arm, strok-
ing Celine softly. And Singer, his entire existence spent
crawling away from that open grave, the yawning crevice
into which he tosses back his love.

They've all stopped short—and now they plead for me to
do the same. I can hear their voices through the doors—su-
surrations, icy murmurings, mutterings that leave patterns
like frost: Halt! Go no further. Come with us while you still
can. Don't push this to the end. We offer you love, a chance
to belong, your own niche deep in the heart of the honeycomb. Don't pass it up now. Or else. Or else what? There's
no answer—at least none that I can make out. Instead, the
voices fade, replaced by a silence that's meant to stop me
in my tracks, the rattle of a wind rippling the length of the
corridor, a chill that doesn't know and will never know
warmth.

But what they don't understand is that I've discovered
their little secret—and all by myself, too. By now, I'm used
to their feints and ill-disguised attempts at misdirection.
Their masks are token, language-heavy and badly translat-
ed. But it's their half-measures that really give them away,
that label them without fail as failures. There's no road that
doesn't have a trap across it—too wide to skirt, too broad
to jump, too deep to climb through and over. And, if not,
then the road itself becomes a trap. So, why not just choose
my own?

Why not indeed? I realize now that the choice was made

from the moment I'd landed in Berlin—and from all the moments before that. I lean the mop against the wall and throw open the familiar second-to-last door. Aha! Just like I thought. Fritz's intervention that morning had been but temporary. The gramophone, the film projector, the elaborate trunk have returned, icons standing out clearly in the dimly lit room. And there—lying on the bed with the blankets tucked up to his neck and his back to me—is the midget. A lumpen proletariat despite himself.

The regular rising and falling of the sheets indicates he's either asleep or pretending to be. An IV bottle has been suspended upside-down from one of the bedposts. Clear liquid flows from the bottle through a thin plastic tube into the midget. Boy oh boy. They're certainly going all the way this time. Whole hog. As I take another step forward, the floor creaks. The midget stirs and turns slowly to face me. I stop in my tracks, on one foot, much like a character out of melodrama. Or cartoon strip.

The room spins on its axis, tilting first one way and then the other, in gyroscopic fashion, making it hard for me to maintain my balance. Its walls grow immensely white, so white and cold they seem blue. Row on row of fluorescent lights pop into the ceiling. Machinery springs up along the headboard, monitoring equipment, the beep of a pulse, the gurgle of blood, the forced air of the respirator. And, in the bed, it's not the midget . . . no, not the midget . . . definitely not the midget lying there . . . it's . . . it's. . . .

"Fa . . . father," I say at last, feeling my legs buckling beneath me. "What. . . ? You're supposed to be . . . you're dead. Aren't you dead?"

The figure in the bed smiles weakly, his face cracking as if made of old paper. Or tree bark. Then, laboriously, ever so slowly, he crooks a finger and motions me forward. I hesitate for a moment, as if expecting Fritz or another of his nemeses to come bursting through my father's shell, to come rippling out of his distended stomach—alien-style. Only this time a human palimpsest. Nothing of the sort happens. The old man just waits there, occasionally half-shutting his liquidy colourless eyes. Then, the eyelids flutter—as if on the verge of flying off.

"What is it, father?" I ask, not so much out of an urge to know but for fear of the quiet, to drown the sound of the bellows, the drip-drip of the intravenous. "You have something to tell me, is that it?"

I stumble forward, kneel by the side of the bed. Like a servant. A faithful, humble servant. The old man struggles to talk. But there's a roar between us that prevents me from understanding. A gulf.

"No, no," I say. "You'll have to speak a little louder if you want me to understand. I can't hear you."

I move closer, bring my ear right up against the old man's lips. So close I can feel his hot, acidic breath, can smell the curdled hatred that has incubated for decades. That has finally eaten him away and left him crackling with futility.

"It's about the diary, isn't it? You want to explain to me about the diary. You want to get it off your chest."

The old man's lips continue to move, to vibrate—but the words fail him, dribble down his chin and lose whatever power they once had.

"Yes, yes," I say. "Speak up. I know all about it. There's no need to hide any longer."

I take the diary out of my pocket and place it on the bed. The old man covers it with a gnarled, oversized hand, his fingers running over the pebbly surface. He shuts his eyes and smiles again.

"Ah, so you do remember," I say, standing up. "And you're the only one who can explain what happened. I want you to tell me what the meaning of all this is. That's the key to it, isn't it? I want you to bring my selves together, to gather all the momentary slices into a whole. Nothing else will do. Do you understand what I'm saying? Quantify me, father, and I'll leave you to sleep in peace. I promise. You have my word on it. Do you understand? I need to know. I won't let you go otherwise. I won't let you rest."

I suddenly reach down and shake the old man. But he just keeps on smiling. And, as I shake him, the room begins to shimmer as well, to lose its shape. I let go but it's too late. Already, the lights have gone, replaced by naked bulbs dangling from frayed, sparking cords. Now, the trunk flies off, spilling its contents—the passport with the photo excised, the honourable discharge papers, the transatlantic steamship ticket. The walls and floor warp into raw planks painted a metallic grey.

I find myself in the doorway of a long, low, narrow, windowless room with bunks against either wall. Each bunk is barely wide enough for someone to sleep on his side without falling off. In the dim light, I can see the thin, luminous faces of those occupying them. They're somehow trusting—even if they ought to know better by now. An acrid, nauseating odour fills the room. I recognize it as the same odour described in my father's diary, that of burning flesh, the tractor-piled bodies doused with gasoline and reduced to ashes. I walk slowly down the centre aisle. I'm feeling lightheaded. I know precisely why I'm here. My father hasn't answered me with words—but he's answered nonetheless.

Now, I can see for myself, can find out for myself what has happened. All the barriers have come down; all the subterfuges are out in the open. There's no place to hide now, I say. I've got you cornered at last, you slippery old goat. No murders, suicides, tortures or other declarations of love can sidetrack me. I stop in front of an empty bunk, lit only by the greasy flames from the surrounding countryside. The shadows of flames that seem to come through the walls themselves, that turn the walls into inconsequential barriers. I curl up on the bunk, pulling a ragged, filthy blanket across my shoulders. And then I wait.

On the other side of the wall, though they're miles and miles away, I can hear the screams of those who are being operated upon without anesthetics; I can see their bodies spasming to the shock of the cold blade as it cuts across the layers of flesh and works its way to the vital organs; I can feel what they feel as they're tossed, still alive, onto the funeral pyres and set alight. Some are professors of logic, just like me; some are unskilled labourers and winemakers; some are restaurant supply salesmen; some are housewives and nuclear physicists.

The lights flicker. A shadow crosses before me. Someone with his back to me is kneeling on the floor beside the bunk. I watch as he carefully pulls away a plank and reaches in. At first, he's very casual about it, as if he does this sort of thing all the time. But, when he can't find what he's looking for, he becomes more and more frantic, finally inserting his arm all the way to the shoulder socket.

"Is this what you want?" I say, holding up the diary and certain at last of having the upper hand. "Is this what you're looking for?"

The shadow spins to face me. It's me, of course, caught in the act. It's me with a scowl on my face. The scowl of justice.

"How could you?" the other me says. "After all she's done for you. After all the sacrifices and self-denial. How could you bring yourself to do such a thing?" I shrug. He brings his face right up against mine—and spits at me. "Murderer!"

BERLIN

The accusing words echo—as if down an endless corridor. I let out a scream that's all the more frightening for being soundless. The room rushes back around me, back through the old man dying in the hospital bed, back into the *Pension Aryana* where I collapse into the arms of Fritz and Frieda. They manage to drag me along, one on either side of me, until they get me back to my own room and ease me onto the bed.

"Time for you to depart from us now, *ja?*" Fritz says. "Can you stand alone?"

I nod, even though I feel as if I've been awake the entire three days. Perhaps that's the way I'll always feel from this moment on, with the possibility of sleep something strictly reserved for others.

"*Güt, güt,*" Fritz says. "You will try then. *We* will try then."

I stand up half way, wobble. Fritz and Frieda reach out to hold me. I wave them away—and continue rising until I'm on my own two feet.

"Bravo."

Both Fritz and Frieda clap.

"I hope it is not a problem for you," Fritz says. "My sister washed some of your clothing."

He points to a garbage bag on the floor beside my suitcase.

"No problem," I say. "Thank you."

Frieda grins and flips my suitcase up in the air. It lands flat on her head, balancing there. She tilts her head forward to let it fall onto the bed. Then, with a flourish, she opens it and stuffs the garbage bag into it.

"There!" Fritz says. "All set."

He places the earphones on my head, the suitcase in my right hand and the briefcase in my left. Frieda holds up the poster. Waves it in front of his face.

"Oh yes," Fritz says.

He takes the poster and slips it under my arm.

"Off you go now," he says. "*Auf Wiedersehen.* Come again. Berlin awaits you. Always, with open arms."

He gives me a slight push and I start walking. The young couple are seated in front of the TV, squabbling playfully over what program to watch—quiz show or political telecast. Fritz's mother, both dogs in her arms, is having breakfast. Her turban is beside her. She's bald beneath it. Pinkishly bald—but somehow I don't find it funny. She spoons a bit of cereal for herself and a bit for the dogs. And there are the two bird ladies, too, making faces each time one of the dogs licks the spoon.

I walk out of the front door of the *pension* and down the cool, dark passageway. Someone, either Fritz or Frieda, pulls open the main portal for me. It squeaks, grating. Outside, it's bright, almost dazzling. Stores, shops, restaurants, boutiques, road-side stands are opening for business. Morning traffic funnels its way towards the Ku'Damm.

"Good-bye again," Fritz says, reaching down to press the "Play" button on my portable tape cassette.

I hesitate, unsure for a moment where to go. Fritz points me in the right direction and I head down the street. The mellifluous voice starts up: "Isn't it a shame about poor, old Berlin. . . ." I turn and wave to Fritz and Frieda who are still standing at the doorway. They wave back. Fritz pulls up his pants and adjusts the peak of his baseball cap; Frieda leans on his shoulder. Together, they disappear into the building.

I have a sudden urge to rush back to them, to throw myself at their feet and beg to be let in. But I know that's not part of any possible scenario. At least none that makes any sense at this moment. I continue down the road, the voice droning in my ears. At the corner of Kurfurstendamm Strasse I stop for a moment to rest, lowering my suitcase to the ground. For no reason, I spin on my heel, trying to capture one last time the sensation of the city all around me: the Adenauerplatz U-Bahn station. The Kaiser-Wilhelm Memorial Church. The Europa Centre. A slow-motion merry-go-round that mixes it all together. That makes it seem so brilliant and never-ending.

But I know it can't last. I know that I'll soon come back to my original position. And, when I do, I pick up my suitcase again and walk down the steps of the U-Bahn station, marble clicking beneath my feet. There's a moment when the outside brightness clashes with the dark tunnel—and I'm forced to adjust my vision. To blink. To dilate my pupils.

• • • • •

On the other side of the tunnel, you come out at an underground train station. Above a booth where a bored man waits tapping his fingers on the counter, a sign indicates: "Lockers For Rent. By The Day. By The Month. By The Year. By The Lifetime!" You tell him you're interested in a long-term rental—and pay for five years. After you sign a waiver, he hands you a key and indicates the direction of the lockers. You find the one matching your key number.

You open your suitcase and pull out the garbage bag. You dump the clothes out of it and replace them with one of your suits and a good pair of shoes. Then you search your pockets. To your surprise, you discover you still have the set of keys from the *Pension Aryana*—and Seppanen's name tag. You place those, as well as your wallet and passport, inside the garbage bag. And stuff it into the locker. You do the same with your briefcase, the briefcase your parents bought you when you graduated from high school. You're about to put the poster in there as well but change your mind at the last moment.

When you emerge from the railroad station, you're not at all surprised to find yourself in downtown Montreal rather than Berlin. And, half an hour later, you're walking down a tree-lined boulevard which you quickly recognize as the street on which you live. The trees form a canopy that touch above the centre of the street, keeping out most of the sunlight in the summer. There are people mowing their lawns, people sitting on their front balconies, people talking across their fences.

You're glad no one waves at you. Or calls out your name. None of your neighbours really know you and that's the way you want to keep it. No backyard barbecues or block parties for you. You climb the few steps to your cottage. Home at last, you think. It's so peaceful here with the birds singing and the soft breeze carrying the scent of roses. You put down the suitcase, click off the portable tape deck, and then fumble in your pocket for the key. The first one you pull out turns out to be the key to the locker.

"Not that one, you silly twit," you say. "That's for some other time."

You find your own key and insert it into the door. Zeno the cat comes rushing at you, rubbing herself against your legs.

"Hello, Zeno, my old friend," you say, bending down to stroke her. "I'm home. Are you glad to see me? I'm certainly glad to see you."

You step inside. There's a strong odor in the place—like something gone bad. And the faint sound of buzzing. Like flies trapped between the windows. Time to fix those windows, that's for sure. Time to put in Thermopanes. Better for the heating bills as well.

"Hello," you call out. "Anyone here?"

Doesn't seem like it. You check your watch. Four in the afternoon. Berlin time? No, the watch has been adjusted.

BERLIN

Or has adjusted itself. Louise must have gone to pick up Cathy at school. Although she's normally back by this time. You put your suitcase down at the base of the stairs leading to the second floor. The telephone answering machine is flashing. Messages. You press the "Playback" button. It's your own voice: "Louise. It's me again. Not much to say really. I can't wait to get home. Hope you've missed me as much as I've missed you guys. Some crazy things have happened here. Some things I still find hard to believe. But I'm alright. And I'll tell you all about it when I get there. Okay? We'll have a good laugh over the whole thing. Bye, now. All my love to Cathy."

As you listen to the series of messages—all your messages, you walk towards the kitchen. The fridge door is open. That explains the smell. You're always telling Cathy to make sure she shuts the door. A package of hamburger meat has fallen to the floor—or has been dragged out of the fridge by Zeno. It's swarming with larvae. You back away and start to cry. Why are you crying? Since when does a package of rotting meat bring out the tears in you?

You wipe your eyes. Louise and Cathy must have spent the entire weekend at your mother's house. The answering machine repeats your first message and then clicks off. Carrying the poster under your arm, you climb up the stairs to your study. With the blinds drawn, it's dark and cool in here. You pass your hands tenderly along the cracked spines of the books that line all four walls. Did you miss me, my friends? you ask. Of course, you did. You slip the rubber band from the poster and it unfolds stiffly. You stare at it for a moment, at the flesh made concrete. Then, letting it drop to the floor, you sit at your desk, sit before the amber glow of your computer screen.

There's a note stuck to it. It's from Louise: "Dear Anthony—I couldn't think of a better way to do this. I'm leaving you. I know you'll think it's another man but that's not true. I just think this will be best for the three of us. Good-bye—and good luck. When things are straightened out a bit, I'll make arrangements for Cathy to visit you."

That note should make you angry and disappointed. It should make you scream with rage. But it doesn't. It doesn't because it's an old note, a note you read before you left for Berlin. And it's no longer relevant. No longer has anything to do with the situation. You tear it up and drop it in the waste paper bin. Louise came back to you. She changed her mind about leaving. And now you're going to live happily ever after—the three of you one big happy family.

You lean back in your comfortable leather chair and smile. In the silence of the afternoon, the buzzing returns. You're frowning now. This won't do, you say to yourself. You push your chair back and stand up. It won't do at all. You follow the sound of the buzzing. You must get rid of them before Louise and Cathy come home. Where are they? Where are they stuck? You check Cathy's bedroom. Nothing. The guest bedroom? Nothing there either. The bathroom? Clean as a whistle. There's only one room left, only one place they can be hiding. You throw open the door to the master bedroom. The smell clogs your nose. Louise lies on the bed with Cathy in her arms.

"Shoo!" you say, making a sweeping motion with your arm. "Can't you see they're sleeping?"

The flies rise in a cloud from the bed. Then settle again.

Postscript IV

At the hospital, Wilhelm ("Billy") Ryle rubbed his eyes in a vain attempt to erase the tiredness. He couldn't understand what was happening. Perhaps for the first time in his life, there was something here that he couldn't quite put his finger on. He realized the problem wasn't the usual psychological give-and-take that hard-core scientists liked to use as an example of failure in this area. As a way of putting down the psychoanalytic "mumbo-jumbo."

It had nothing to do with slackness or incoherence or inability to define the terms properly. That would have been easy. All he needed to say at that point was: "Pull up your slackness." Or: "You're being incoherent." Or: "You've failed to come to terms with your terms." No, it wasn't that at all. He knew that, vaguely, it had something to do with the words themselves, the way they could be stretched beyond the axiomatics, beyond any ability to break them down into their simple components, and thus to build them up into the complex entities that allowed people to talk to one another in any meaningful way. That allowed the lover to communicate her intentions and der Kommandant to "suggest" to his underlings they could commit whatever atrocities they felt like committing—without fear of reprisal.

So, if that wasn't the case, then what was really being said here? What was really at stake? The Sunday.doc file had been the most enigmatic of them all. After rereading it a second and even a third time, Ryle realized only one thing: it made a joke, a travesty, a mockery of objective reality. Was the character called G. Antonio ("Anthony") Serratura merely making sure to cover his tracks by the creation of multiple possibilities into which he could have fled—avoiding both punishment and logic? Or had Giulio A. Chiavetta never even. . . ? After all, what was the best way of covering up tracks? To send out a decoy. Of course! To send someone off in the opposite direction. Or to send someone else in your place.

Ryle stood up suddenly, so quickly his chair fell over and bounced several times on the floor (in an unintended imitation of Chiavetta's reaction several days before). Shit! He slapped his forehead. Of course. . . . It finally came to him why the police hadn't been able to collar Giulio A. Chiavetta—and why they'd never be able to find him: they'd been searching for the wrong man the whole time. And now that he knew who he was looking for, Ryle had no trouble deducing where he was. After all, where would a stationary engineer be found?

Ryle switched on the basement lights. He walked slowly down the wooden stairs. Dust flew into the air with each step he took, coal-black dust. The dust became deeper and more insistent as Ryle made his way to the far corner where the old furnace was kept—it not being worth anyone's while to dismantle it. There, by the light of a naked bulb, he found his Giulio A. Chiavetta, twirling slowly a foot or so off the ground from the beam where he'd looped the rope.

Ryle straightened out the chair Chiavetta must have used to position himself. Then he lowered the body onto it. Ryle knelt before Chiavetta. He couldn't help notice a fixed smile on his face. Or it might have been nothing more than the rictus of death. We could've helped you, Ryle said out loud and in an admonishing tone, as if Chiavetta could still hear him. We could have pulled you back and redeposited you into the real world. But now you've escaped us for good, haven't you? You've escaped us for good.

• • • • •

Yes, says the man called G. Antonio ("Anthony") Serratura. Yes. He stands once more at the door of the building that houses the *Pension Aryana* just off the Ku'Damm, the one and only tourist-trap Ku'Damm, still in the heart of a newly reconfigured Berlin. Perhaps even closer to the heart now. He looks around, then slowly shakes his head: partly out of disbelief and partly out of wonder. The streets are thick with people selling all sorts of objects: from homemade jewelry to pieces of metal imbedded in concrete, from brightly coloured scarves to East German passports ("Be the first on your block to own a genuine *Sozialistische Einheitpartei Deutschlands* membership book.")

Others are standing on homemade platforms, shouting out either welcomes or denunciations. Still others huddle in the corners, clothes-bundles held tight with ropes or belts. Where have all these people come from? Serratura finds himself asking. Where are they all going? But those are the easy questions to answer. They had swarmed over when the Wall came down, cutting through the line that divided grey East Berlin from multi-coloured West. No more Checkpoint Charlie to act as frontier. Or goal. More importantly, no more Checkpoint Charlie Museum to record their ingenious—if sometimes fatal—attempts at escape.

There is nothing from which to escape—and, as corollary, nothing to which they could run. Overnight, the border has become nonexistent. This will take some getting used to, Serratura says to himself. But, hey, if you can't be adaptable, better pack it in. Besides, there's always the Kabarett Chez Elles where he'd been promised free drinks—and he can assume the offer still stands. Sure. No hard feelings, eh?

He hesitates a moment, then inserts one of his keys into the outside door. At least, the lock hasn't been changed. Inside the passageway, he feels the breeze from the court-yard. It's fairly warm and comfortable and gives him a strong sense of security. The computer screens are still flashing their insistent data. Only they've been recently updated to read: "Welcome to all our new friends! Be the first one from the Eastern Bloc to own a personal computer! Low-est prices in town! Nothing down and nothing to pay until the spring! And we don't mean The Prague Spring either!" And then the same thing in a myriad of other languages. Dozens of other languages. Among them, he recognizes German, Russian, Arabic and Japanese. Japanese?

Using his second key, he opens the thick door to the *Pension Aryana* itself, the one with the lion's head knocker. His heart is thumping now with excitement and apprehension—and the rush of recognition, a type of inverse homesickness. He has hundreds of questions that need to be answered:

Will Celine and Zweck still be waiting to welcome him with their hot *boeuf,* their expensive cognac and their in-timate slam dancing? Or will a shrivelled Zweck leap for his throat the moment he sees him? Are Annie and the fez man still an item? Has Annie finally lowered her penis—or has it become a permanent defence against intruders? Has Singer rediscovered his lost Valhalla—or is the last oven being reserved for his own use? And Seppanen? Is her body back in Finland, just above the perma-frost? Or is she still roaming the back stalls of the philosophical freak show, looking for more companions?

There's only one way to find out. Only one way to know for sure.

BERLIN

"Fritz! You old *Schweinehund,* you!" Serratura shouts out into the accustomed and by now untroubling gloom. "I'm back!"

And the heavy door flies open.

And he holds out his arms in anticipated greeting.

THE AUTHOR

DRAWING BY WURGE

Michael Mirolla is a fortuitous amalgam of Italian and Canadian. Born in Italy, he spent formative years in Montreal and now lives in Toronto where he has pursued a long and exceptionally productive career. His work is known for its exploration of the surreal and twisted shrapnel of the human soul. He is versatile in almost every form of the written word in two languages, and has won major national awards in all forms of expression. In addition to his dark and intense novels, he writes short stories, poetry, plays, and movie scripts.

ABOUT THE TYPE

This book was set in ITC New Baskerville, a typeface based on the types of John Baskerville (1706-1775), an accomplished writing master and printer from Birmingham, England. The excellent quality of his printing influenced such famous printers as Didot in France and Bodoni in Italy. Baskerville produced a master-piece folio Bible for Cambridge University, and today, his types are considered to be fine representations of eighteenth century rationalism and neoclassicism. This ITC New Baskerville was designed by Matthew Carter and John Quaranda in 1978.

Designed by John Taylor-Convery
Composed at JTC Imagineering, Santa Maria, CA